HONOR ABOVE ALL

HONOR ABOVE ALL

MACLACHLAN
BOOK 1

G. WAYNE TILMAN

WOLFPACK
PUBLISHING
EST 2013

Honor Above All
Paperback Edition
Copyright © 2025 (As Revised) by G. Wayne Tilman

Wolfpack Publishing
1707 E. Diana Street
Tampa, Florida 33610

www.wolfpackpublishing.com

Paperback ISBN 979-8-89567-306-5
Ebook ISBN 979-8-89567-305-8

ACKNOWLEDGMENTS

My sincerest appreciation goes to my daughter, Dr. Ann Lee Tilman for the title and to Denise Kearns, Rebecca Thomas Payne, and Susan Stecker for their careful scrutiny of the manuscript as Beta readers.

HONOR ABOVE ALL

1

Beirut/Beqaa Valley, Lebanon, Washington DC

23 October 1983

Towards midnight, the battered old Toyota pickup circled slowly, then drew to a stop outside a bar forty-eight kilometers from Beirut. The man inside was tall, fit and in his twenties. He wore a shemagh tied around his head and a dishdashi robe. Shiny black leather footwear, not unusual for the area showed beneath its hem. His eyes were accustomed to the dark, so he did not bring the torch from the truck as he went into the front door. He diverted his eyes behind heavy framed clear glasses as he approached the light. At the bar, he said "Al-Maza," and was given a pale lager. It was not frosty, but colder than he would have suspected in a dive like this one. He dropped fifteen hundred Lebanese pounds on the dirty surface of the bar and sauntered to an empty corner table. Back to the wall, he sipped the beer and assessed the four customers. All were tough looking and probably armed.

Twenty minutes later, a small man with a beak nose entered and scanned the room. He spied the man in the corner and stopped at the bar for a bottle of Al-Rayess before sitting beside the man in the corner table, both facing outwards.

The younger man's face was tanned. Sunglasses during daylight did a better job of hiding his green eyes. The non-prescription glasses were less effective but at night he generally passed for a Middle Easterner without serious scrutiny.

The beak-nosed man said "marHaba" in greeting and took a long drag on the bottled beer. The tall man nodded to his source and said, "In English," knowing full well his contact spoke English and French as well as Lebanese dialect Arabic.

It took him several minutes to get to the part for which the younger man had come to hear. Following up on a credible rumor the tall man had heard, the Lebanese confirmed that a Hezbollah cell was planning to attack a US target in the region very soon. "Maybe is too soon to stop it," he said.

"What is the target?"

"I do not know," the man responded.

"Do you know exactly when?"

Before he could answer, a black dot appeared in his forehead. The back of his head exploded as the shot was heard.

The younger man dumped the heavy wood table over as cover from the direction he estimated the shot had come. Behind it, he pulled up the dishdashi robe and drew both a .45 Colt automatic and a large Bowie

knife made in Orlando, Florida. He had already identified the threat. And, the threat was aiming at him with a
Kalashnikov with its wire butt stock folded. The tall
man's first two hundred thirty grain bullet hit the man
with the AK in the stomach. Upright, he sucked in
inadvertently. He fell forward as the next round hit him
in the mouth. A man next to him, his shemagh tied
Bedouin-style was aiming a Browning 9mm. The .45
and the 9mm spoke simultaneously. The larger bullet
hit its target, the smaller 9mm round sailed past the ear
of the man in the corner. The second shooter was dead
before he hit the floor.

The tall man slowly stood, still scanning for threats.
Seeing none, he headed out the back door and eased
around the front corner. Several men were sitting in an
old Mercedes sedan. Not good.

He sheathed the Randall-made Bowie and moved
low, zigzagging towards the Toyota. He heard Arabic
yells in the Benz and saw the flash of several pistol shots
in his direction. He returned them, but the steel door
stopped his pistol rounds. A .45 was a great manstop-
per, but the big, slow-moving bullets did not do a very
good job on barriers such as steel Mercedes's doors. He
was sure the thudding against the door inches away
from the driver got his attention because he pushed the
passenger over and both rolled onto the ground through
the passenger door.

The Toyota started slowly with its diet of low
octane fuel. The tall man gunned it and dumped the
clutch. He clipped the rear side of the sedan and spun it
into the two shooters hiding on its far side. He heard
screams of either pain or anger or both. He was not sure
but knew he did not have time to consider it. The old

Toyota was moving with more inertia than power. The tall man spun it in a circle and drove out onto the road from whence it had originally. The two under the Mercedes crawled out, bruised, but primarily furious. They got back in and the passenger picked up an AK-47 from the rear floor. The German car started and sped off in pursuit of the truck.

The man in the Toyota pickup was an American military intelligence officer. He was torn between getting back to his base to report the collateral intelligence he received before his contact was shot or stopping and trying to find a phone to call it in. The latter bordered on the impossible in this part of Lebanon in the early hours of morning. He saw lights coming up fast in his rear view. Whether Lebanese internal security police or the guys from the bar, it spelled real trouble, and more violence.

The lights behind him grew larger in the tiny rearview dangling from the interior roof edge of the truck.

He was jarred at the vehicle behind rammed the rear bumper of the Toyota Hilux pickup. He wrestled to keep the small truck in the road. The American took every turn at the highest speeds as possible in an effort to lose or spin-out the Mercedes. Any lack of driving prowess in the Mercedes was made up by the car's handling and horsepower. They drove in circles for an hour with the big sedan on the rear bumper of the small truck.

The American knew he was unable to lose them. He was surprised they had not pulled up and shot out the rear window of his truck with the AK-47, along with his head and shoulders. He knew he was going to have to stop at his choice of place and kill them.

The two vehicles were racing through the Beqaa Valley on small roads through agrarian area. At a curve, the intelligence officer swerved off the road and plowed into a cotton field. He jerked the wheel to the left and the bed of the small truck spun around perpendicular to the original direction of travel. As the Mercedes made the turn, it slid, and the passenger side wheels caught in a rut and it rolled. The American was out of the truck in a moment. He ran over to the upside-down sedan as the two men were crawling out bruised and bloody.

He kicked the closest in the face and he went down. He jumped over the hood and elbowed the other one on the other side. He went down. He kicked the fallen guns away and drew the .45. He hit each man in the head with the butt. Struggling, he pushed both back into the inverted car. Gasoline was leaking from the tank filler. The American took off his shemagh and let it soak in the fuel. He laid it in a line from the growing puddle to the inside of the car. Eschewing fingerprints, he kicked the AK and one pistol closer to the car making it look like they had flown out during the roll. He flicked a brass Zippo lighter with the emblem of the US Marine Corps on it and lit the end of the shemagh. As he walked back to his truck, he heard the "whoosh" as the Mercedes caught fire. A quarter of a mile down the road towards Beirut, he heard the dull explosion as the Mercedes blew. Even if witnesses in the bar stated that a tall Middle Eastern man had exchanged shots and left in a ubiquitous Toyota with pre-mudded plates. And, it was followed by the Mercedes. There would be nothing to tie him to the incident. The Mercedes had rolled and caught fire in the chase. And, two probable Hezbollah fighters who killed someone in the bar had died. Hopefully, end of story.

AROUND SIX-THIRTY IN THE MORNING, an Iranian named Ismail Ascari drove a stake bodied truck through a five-foot concertina wire fence and a guard shack, then crashed it into the US Marine Barracks building in Beirut, Lebanon. The truck, which would now be called a VBIED, or vehicle-borne improvised explosive device, was laden with twenty-one thousand pounds of TNT. The building collapsed after literally being picked up and dropped it upon itself.

Two hundred forty-one Americans died. Only seventy-five survived the blast. It was the largest loss of Marines in one day since Iwo Jima.

Ten minutes later, another truck bomb, this one smaller, delivered in a pickup truck, struck the French Parachute Regiment barracks six kilometers away. Fifty-eight French paratroopers died.

At the Marine Barracks, Marine Intelligence Captain, James Edward MacLachlan, was returning to base with collateral intelligence about what was, in fact happening, as the flatbed powered past him. He swerved his battered undercover Toyota pickup to the side and stopped it. Marine guards with unclear rules of engagement were stunned at the security breach and had not fired their weapons.

MacLachlan's truck was overturned by the concussion of the blast as the flatbed hit the barracks building.

He crawled out, cut and deafened. He was still under-cover in a long dishdashi robe, now afire. He ripped it off and cast it aside. Below, he had on a tee-shirt and utility trousers. Shaking his head in an unsuccessful effort to restore some vestige of hearing, MacLachlan rolled behind his truck, cocked .45 moving with his eyes as he scanned for additional threats. He did not see any. He saw only destruction.

He arose and motioned for a Marine guard to follow and one to remain at what was left of a gate, rifle at the ready.

"If another vehicle without our guys in it fails to stop, open fire and shoot until they do stop," he ordered the corporal in a voice he still could not hear.

MacLachlan ran towards the building. He saw the Marine behind him stagger and fall. Shock from the concussion, he thought. MacLachlan kept going and found a way in. He saw a badly wounded Marine on the floor to his right and picked him up in a fireman's carry. The man moaned in pain as he was lifted off the deck.

As he laid men on the ground in an improvised triage, he saw more trucks responding, Lebanese fire crews, ambulances and who knew what else. The firemen laid a stream of water uselessly on the rubble but did not enter or help. A few officers and non-comms would arrive from outside and assist towards the end of his grueling task.

But for what seemed to be forever, it was he who entered and re-entered hell. The burning, destroyed building was just that. He carried out many of the survivors and many of the dead. With each trip, he became more cut and bloody. His face, arms and clothes were blackened by soot. The captain knew as he went farther into the structure, becoming entombed by a cave-in became more and more probable. But, as long as he could stand and carry a Marine out, he had to continue. Marines never left a fellow Marine behind. Oooh-rah. He pushed on and found another dead Marine. He scooped him up and took him out. He laid him in group three of his loose triage. And, stumbling with exhaustion and blood loss, began to jog back into the rubble that was once a building.

MacLachlan considered virtually everyone who was not in a Marine uniform to be a potential threat, especially a group of nationals clustered together and doing nothing. As he staggered out of the crumbled concrete, he saw them and drew his .45. He had a grievously wounded Corpsman over his shoulder.

A news photographer had arrived and captured a shot of the bloody young Marine, handsome through the blood and grim, carrying a casualty over his shoulder, pistol at ready.

The photo made the cover of the US's most famous news magazine. The look on MacLachlan's face was said to be the purest look of menace and hatred ever captured on film. It became iconic. The Corps and America had a new hero. The President and Congress moved quickly to award him the highest medal an American service member can receive. MacLachlan eschewed the medal, protesting he was doing what any Marine would do. Or any soldier, sailor or airman. He theorized if had he gotten back sooner, perhaps they could have correlated the intelligence to the barracks and heightened security. He felt he had let the Corps down.

MacLachlan was debriefed the following day at the embassy by a senior State Department official and intelligence officers from two civilian agencies and several military ones. The thrust of the questions was source and how sure he was that Hezbollah was behind the Marine and French attacks. As he began to speak about the firefight at the bar and subsequent elimination of the two gunmen, he was stopped by the State Department official.

"We have Lebanese Internal Security reports that two Hezbollah operatives conducted an operation whereby one individual was killed. His companion, a tall Middle Eastern male with regional clothing returned fire, killing the two shooters. He left the premises and escaped in a rusty blue Toyota pickup truck. Two individuals, also thought to be Hezbollah, pursued him and died in a fiery crash sometime later."

"Captain MacLachlan," the man from State continued, "could you imagine that any remaining fingerprints or evidence that would identify the tall Middle Eastern man could be found by Lebanese police? Hypothetically, of course," he said.

"Hypothetically," MacLachlan began, "there could be fingerprints on the door going into the bar, on the corner table and on the beer bottle. The bottle hypothetically broke during the firefight, but pieces may have prints. Also, the empty casings from the man's pistol may have latents from when he loaded it. The cases themselves and the caliber would be too generic to point suspicion. There is no way the Lebanese would have a name to associate with any prints they lift. It may hamper the man should he return to Lebanon in the future, but if not, I would assume the prints to be worthless to them. If a rusted blue Toyota Hi-lux were to turn up, say, behind the barrack's damage, it should be disposed of in such a way as to not leave the identity of its driver during a Lebanese forensic search."

"Captain, what do you think we should do with you?" asked the State Department official.

"I am afraid I need to be moved out of Lebanon *today*, as expeditiously and covertly as possible." The various intelligence officers around the table nodded.

The Defense Intelligence Agency agent spoke. "We will take care of that. I assume your possessions were all destroyed in the barracks?" he asked MacLachlan.

"I have my pistol, a personal knife and the torn, bloody clothes I am wearing right now. That's it," MacLachlan said. He did not need to mention the various gauze wraps around his head and both arms, band aids and large sling. They were obvious. The meeting adjourned and the captain followed the DIA man down a hall towards a ready room.

"We've got some socks, jeans and a sweatshirt. Are your boots still serviceable?" the black operative asked.

"They have a lot of dried blood. I'd like to hose them off somewhere. But they are okay."

"Nah, toss them. Too much HAZ-MAT. We'll scare up some athletic shoes, or something.

"Here's paperwork to turn in your .45. We can send the knife in a diplomatic pouch. We will have a new maroon cover passport made for your arrival in DC, as well as military ID and some DIA ID. For a while, even after you report to a new duty station, you will belong to us. We will continue to pick your brain in DC and may call on you periodically."

"Got it and thanks. What's your name?" MacLachlan asked.

"Supervisory Special Agent Will Grafton," the man responded, adding "No need to worry about my exact rank. It's irrelevant."

"Will, I spent months developing contacts willing to talk—for a price or a favor—about Hezbollah. Though the main one was killed in that bar, there are others you can use. I will prepare a contact list for you before I get on whatever plane out of here you are able to arrange, okay?" MacLachlan said.

"You're a Slickmeister, man. I will gladly take it and put it to good use. What's the real story behind the two guys in the burnt out Mercedes? Unlike the local gendarmerie, I find it hard to buy that they rolled, were not thrown clear without seatbelts on and managed to be conveniently burned to death."

The Marine looked at the DIA agent for a long time, deciding whether this was a trick that could lead to an inquiry about murdering two men. He let out a long breath which he did not realize he was holding. And, decided to trust SSA Will Grafton.

"It wasn't really like that," MacLachlan began. "They crawled out of the Mercedes with minor injuries. The died without gunshots and were placed back into the car. It was leaking gas. Unfortunately, a gas-soaked shemagh bridged the distance between a puddle of gas and the car. Mysteriously, a lighter ignited it and the car was quickly enveloped in flames. Both men were unconscious or maybe dead from blunt force trauma, so I don't believe they suffered. The seats and carpets caught quickly, and I left as the fire built. I heard the tank explode from maybe a quarter mile away."

Grafton solemnly nodded and took out a pack of Kool's. He patted himself unsuccessfully for matches, so MacLachlan lit it with a polished brass Marine Corps Zippo. He pushed the lighter over to Grafton and said, "I don't need this anymore, my friend." Grafton nodded again, then his face was split with an infectious grin. He took out a switchblade and carved two small notches in it and dropped it into his pocket.

MacLachlan stuck out his hand and shook with the agent. While Grafton worked out a military flight out that day and transportation to it, MacLachlan showered carefully, still getting some of the gauze wet. He put on the clean clothes and some socks and running shoes. He was sore as hell, but at least he smelled better. He looked in the mirror at a man who looked like he had taken on a couple of heavyweight contenders...and lost.

The Corps did not feel he had let them down. There was no way to make a call where he was. Further, his intel did not specify target or time. But he had identified the perpetrators, and, killed four. He boarded a large USAF cargo plane that afternoon. MacLachlan did not have any luggage. His only possession outside of a few things left with his great uncle in Florida, was the Randall Bowie knife. The official reason for his departure was to receive an award and participate in Marine Corps public relations. While that was true, the overriding reason was to get MacLachlan out of Dodge as quickly as possible. The flights on cargo planes were miserable on seats designed without much thought to comfort. By the time he reached DC, he was so stiff he had to be helped off the plane and into a waiting plain vanilla government sedan.

He was taken to and admitted at Bethesda Naval Hospital, also known as Walter Reed. MacLachlan got a full check-up and had all of his wounds examined and redressed. He received a full complement of injections. At the base exchange nearby, he replenished his military clothing and ribbons.

Once released, MacLachlan was sent to Eight and I Marine Barracks in DC and housing was provided.

Mack MacLachlan was promoted to major just before being awarded the Congressional Medal of Honor in the White House. Not fully recovered from the many wounds he had gotten from crawling through broken concrete, glass, and rebar, he wore an arm sling over his newly provided dress blues during the televised award.

MacLachlan was an 0204 Human Source Intelligence Officer and was anxious to get back to what he thought was his calling—intelligence work. The Marine Corps got six months public relations out of its hero, scheduling MacLachlan for parades and on television and magazine interviews and talk shows.

He was issued orders to report to the Pentagon. He was going to be a counter-terrorism officer, something the US military and public did not know very much about in the '80's. It was something in which MacLachlan was already invested. And, he suspected the job had enough of an intelligence element to fulfill his true interest.

2

The Pentagon, Shenandoah Valley, Virginia, East &
West Berlin, Český Krumlov, Czechoslovakia, Melk,
Austria

May 1985

MAJOR MACK MACLACHLAN reached his one-year
anniversary at the Pentagon, wearing his Class A
uniform of olive garrison cap, tan shirt and tie, olive
trousers and spit-shined black oxfords to work. He only
wore more comfortable utilities to requalification's at
the pistol and rifle ranges and gym clothes for his physical training or PT requals. He lived at the closest BOQ
or bachelor officer's quarters.

He directly supervised eight 0-3's. They were
Army and Marine captains, two Navy intelligence lieu-
tenants, and an Air Force captain. They, in turn, supervised 24/7shifts of non-commissioned officers who
collected and screened field intelligence reports from

each branch of the Department of Defense. The object was to identify terrorist trends, threats and names. The particular emphasis of the small, but elite, Pentagon office was threats against the US mainland.

The non-comms reported high priority collateral intelligence immediately and a consensus of all their findings each shift. The O-3 shift supervisors collated and summarized the day's reports for submission to MacLachlan, who did the same in his verbal report to the one-star admiral who headed the function. After hours emergencies were reported to MacLachlan who passed them upwards to the admiral no matter where either were at the time. All of the officers wore the latest technology pagers and were on call all the time.

They worked within an inner ring of the Pentagon. The flag officer, Admiral Chester Howard, held both MacLachlan's actions at Beirut and his intelligence in high regard and was glad to have a man wearing a CMH ribbon as his number two. He saw MacLachlan as being on a fast track to become Lieutenant Colonel, despite his youth.

MacLachlan settled in and was beginning to think about a more permanent home. His work was both interesting and important, but devoid of the action the young Marine wanted. A place of his own, far enough away from the National Capital Region to allow for forests and streams would help allay that need.

His late grandfather left him a now run-down cracker house on Casey Key, south of Sarasota, Florida. Its land was cut by the north-south road on the Key and had dockage on the bay and beach on the Gulf. The trust had a provision allowing MacLachlan's aged great-uncle live there until he passed or could no longer live alone.

The set-up on Casey Key was a perfect base or home. The house was sound and only needed some basic repairs and updates. The dock was usable and there was a chickee hut on the beach where MacLachlan played his bagpipes at dusk during visits, much as he had years before to his non-Scottish grandfather's occasional dismay.

The cracker house survived over fifty tropical years, with its cedar stilts and siding, aluminum "tin" roof and yellow pine flooring and frame.

For now, that gave MacLachlan a cherished childhood home to visit at will but did not answer the immediate need for a real home more stable than bachelor officer's housing.

He had a cabin in the woods in mind. Ideally, it would have a fresh stream that was canoeable and had trout for the catching. From pre-Marine Corps trips, he liked the area in the Shenandoah Valley of Virginia around Front Royal. MacLachlan subscribed to the local Royal Examiner and watched for land offerings. MacLachlan needed transportation. He had saved most of the money paid him by the Marine Corps and shortly after being assigned to the Pentagon wrote a check for a used 1977 Ford F-250 pickup 4x4 at a local dealer.

A month later, he saw an ad for acreage on a fast-flowing stream near Front Royal. He had the upcoming weekend off and arranged to meet a realtor on Saturday afternoon. In the phone call, the realtor asked if he had a tall four-wheel drive since she did not.

"I do, but I'm curious. You emphasized tall. Why?" he asked.

"There is no bridge across Cedar Creek to the small track that leads to the property," realtor Evelina Bilirakis said.

"How deep is it?"

"I'm not really sure. We've had some rain and it was flowing pretty fast last week."

MacLachlan grinned to himself. "Perfect." he thought. "Think we could wade it if my 4x4 won't get us across?" he asked.

"It will be cold water, even in early summer. And, we won't have swimsuits..."

MacLachlan fantasized a moment, hoping Miss Bilirakis was as cute as she sounded on the phone.

"Let's chance it. I'll bring some towels and pick you up in my 4x4 pickup on Saturday at noon. Your office. Okay?" he asked.

"See you then," Evelina Bilirakis said.

MacLachlan told the Admiral of his plans to drive southwest of the Pentagon on Saturday. That he would carry and monitor the high-tech pager was a given. He recognized his F-250 was not a great highway vehicle. It got lousy mileage and a harsh ride with its lift package and tall off-road tires. But, pull it off the road and drive across a creek? It was in its element. And, MacLachlan was in his.

He left Arlington early on Saturday. He would always rather be early than late to any appointment. It gave him sufficient time to conduct surveillance detection practices that had become routine. He also wanted to leave time for breakfast which he considered his favorite and most important meal. Along with running almost daily, a habit he had developed in college, he ate a medium breakfast, larger lunch, and small dinner whenever possible. Those things and good genes kept him at a lean, but muscular hundred seventy-five pounds.

MacLachlan took I-495 to I-66 west, then left the Eisenhower Interstate System and headed south on Rt. 522 to Front Royal. He parked the big Ford in two spaces near the real estate office and went in. Evelina lived up to his hopes. Those hopes were soon drowned by a plethora of photos of a husband and three small kids everywhere in her cubicle. They left on a paved street and soon turned on a dirt track. It seemed to end at a fast-flowing stream about forty feet across. MacLachlan's first thought was "trout," followed immediately by "depth."

Evie, as she preferred to be called, reiterated that she had no clue to the depth. MacLachlan got out, found a six-foot branch and took his boots and socks off. He waded in around five feet from the end of the road and began probing with the branch. Despite the appearance, he walked halfway across and it never rose above his mid-thighs. Cedar Creek did its best, however, to topple him and float him downstream. He managed to stay upright and knew the big Ford, at three tons, would be pretty difficult to push over.

MacLachlan turned both front hubs to lock them. He got back in the cab, pants dripping with creek water, grinned at Evie, put the truck in 4 low and crossed effortlessly. The bank on the opposite side was steeper than the entry, so the wheels slipped briefly before digging in and powering them over the hump and onto an almost invisible track. Evie said, "go to the left." He shifted into 4 high, then after a while, back into two-wheel drive.

The track paralleled the creek for about ten minutes. She said, "Stop here," at a bend where there was a pool. Shortly after, the creek narrowed again and flowed on, picking up speed. A rise, perfect for a cabin, was across the track from the "swimming hole" as MacLachlan had already named it.

"What do you think?" Evie asked after they had gotten down from the tall Ford.

"Pretty much what I have had in mind. Tell me about the land."

"It borders parkland that will never be developed. It has six acres with options on several adjoining ten-acre parcels. The options are, pardon the expression, dirt cheap. I'd say buy them for ten years, then decide," she said.

"I guess electricity and sewage is an impossibility?" he asked.

"Pretty much, Mack. You will have to haul in materials for a cabin, as well as have a well and septic system put in. Electricity will have to be by generator. You will have to bring in fuel for it."

"Any other neighbors, Evie?" he asked.

"Not for several miles. May see a deer or bear hunter periodically. Could put up No Trespassing signs, but I don't know how you will enforce them unless you are here," she said.

They talked about the price of the land and each of the options. He told her his major's income and about the trust of which he was beneficiary and, at thirty, would be the trustee. MacLachlan included the fact he had no debt whatsoever.

"Think I could get a loan for the parcel and options

on the adjoining pieces? I would be prepared to offer fifteen percent less than asking," he said.

"Could you put 25% down in cash?" He nodded. "Then, yes to the loan. We have a connection with a mortgage lender. I will ask the seller about the offer amount. I should be able to get an answer to that by tonight. Are you staying over?"

"Yes, just until midday tomorrow. I have to get back to the Pentagon."

"Mack, what do you do there?"

"I just do analysis and push papers around a desk," he replied. She did not buy that for a second. This guy was about as far from a paper pushing desk jockey as she could imagine. But she was smart enough to not press further.

"Evie, do you want to take the paperwork back to a restaurant and sign it there? I am getting hungry from all this fresh air," he asked.

"Sounds good to me. I have everything we need except bank loan forms in my briefcase. The bank has Saturday hours, but will be closed by the time we get back, I'm afraid."

"Can they fax me the stuff?" he asked.

"I don't see why not...as long as you have a lot of paper in your fax machine."

"Not a problem," he assured her. His business card had phone, pager and both unclassified and classified facsimile numbers on it.

Later, all the papers were done except the mortgage forms to be faxed on Monday. MacLachlan drove over to Belle Grove, a plantation where the Battle of Cedar Creek occurred in 1864. Following a casual walk around the grounds, thinking about the battle during the War Between the States, he drove to Middletown and his room at the Wayside Inn. Part of the Inn, built in 1742, had been an early stagecoach stop along the valley road. It was added to and has been an inn continually since 1797. The area had such history...the aura gave MacLachlan a sense of continuity. He felt having property in the area would contribute to the stability he sought. Evelina called him at nine o'clock and told him her owners had accepted his offer, subject to his financing. MacLachlan had not told the realtor, but the loan, if used at all, would be a bridge. He planned to request an advance to pay for the relatively moderate sum from the trustee of his moderate trust. If the advance was approved, there would be no loan.

He drove to Arlington, starting mid-morning on Sunday. A call to the duty captain assured him everything in the shop was all right.

The following week was normal with lots of field reports submitted, analyzed and threats assessed. The trustee, a lawyer in Florida, had approved a trust withdrawal for the full amount of the land and the several ten-year options. Closing was set for Friday. MacLachlan cleared with the admiral for another weekend trip to Front Royal. By the following Monday, the major was a Virginia landowner. The land was remote and undeveloped. Precisely as he wanted it to be.

AT SEVENTEEN HUNDRED hours on the following Wednesday, MacLachlan briefed Admiral Howard on the summary of field reports since the last briefing. The admiral listened carefully and asked a number of questions. MacLachlan took notes on the several that would require further scrutiny. The fifty-five-year-old admiral leaned back in his chair.

"Mack, you know what's wrong with all of this?" he asked. MacLachlan had no idea where his boss was going with this line of conversation.

"I'm not sure, sir, could you elaborate?"

"Yes. What we do here suggests there are some very real threats to the United States, even its mainland. Virtually nobody outside the intelligence community is aware of them. In 1947, a distinct line of authority was drawn between the FBI's responsibility inside the US and the CIA's outside. Other than the *Posse Comitatus* prohibition against using the military stateside in a law enforcement capacity, the military's responsibilities are rather vague.

To me, though attacks like bombings and kidnappings break laws, the perpetrators think of themselves more as soldiers fighting a war. They are unlike common criminals in that respect and I don't believe law enforcement is prepared to deal with it. In war, you kill your enemies. You don't try to capture them, protect their rights to the extent police officers do, and try them in a court of law. The Agency, working with our DOD intelligence operations, can follow terrorists to the US border and have to turn them over—by law—to the FBI. The FBI agents are federal, plainclothes cops. All they know is treating the terrorists like cops have to. I don't believe that is adequate.

So, there is a void in our system. This section I head is a meager attempt at filling it, but only intellectually with our analysis. It's the next step that I feel is our point of failure.

Surely one day we will have this all drawn out with proper lines of responsibility. But I don't think we do now. And, it's gonna bite us in the butt if something happens stateside first.

All of this philosophy is leading me to the main context of what I want to say. I am going to turn tables on you. Usually, you provide me with analyzed collateral intelligence. Tonight, I am going to provide you some that was too immediate to pass through the section.

The three-star that heads the Defense Intelligence Agency summoned me up to the DIAC at Bolling today. He had a field report that went straight to him because of its priority. I just got back from a meeting at the White House Situation Room with SecDef, and the heads of DIA, CIA and the VP.

Bottom line: there is credible intel that an Eastern European bad actor has gotten hold of a small nuclear device, a "suitcase" bomb, if you will. He will be delivering it to a buyer, suspected to be Hezbollah, at Český Krumlov in Czechoslovakia, next week. From memory, I recited the history of Hezbollah to them and said I had an officer well-versed in the group. Because of your actions at Beirut, your name was familiar to all.

This is sensitive, as you know. The Czechs are behind the Iron Curtain. We don't know if the Russians are behind this or some rogue criminal organization is selling it. We cannot send a big Agency or SEAL team op in to disrupt this sale and take possession of the object. It could cause World War III. The group collectively agreed to my proposal."

"May I ask what you proposed, sir?" MacLachlan asked.

"I proposed sending one operator in to surveil and perhaps disrupt the plan. If the operator can only surveil, or if he fails, a worldwide lookout would be immediately issued. The operator would act without official cover, an NOC. He would do what he has to do to disrupt or at least report on this plan in such a manner as others could disrupt it along the way," the admiral said.

"Sir, do we know the final destination?" MacLachlan asked.

"We do not. I think it is safe to assume Paris, London, or New York are strong possibilities. At this point, the British Secret Intelligence Service MI-6 and the French DGSE are unaware as far as we know. We will apprise them, based on our man's success."

"How can I help, sir?"

"You are the NOC going in, assuming you accept."

MacLachlan was not expecting this. There were far more experienced field agents than he.

"Sir, why me? There have to be more qualified agents," he said.

"We have one I can name. He's been the DIA agent running our activities in that part of the world. A top agent from Vietnam on. But he took a through-and-through rifle round in the thigh a few months ago in a counter-narcotic op in Columbia. He's not 100% yet. He will be the controller close by. You know Hezbollah firsthand. You even speak some of the language. You have had very personal experience with them. DOD knows about the two in the bar outside Beirut. I know about two others an hour later."

The latter shocked MacLachlan. The only other person who knew that for sure was the DIA man in the debriefing team, though, the others may have figured it out.

The admiral went on. "I have seen your fitness and marksmanship reports. You are outstanding, even for a Marine. I personally know you are bright and resourceful and not one to shirk his responsibility. Your medal recognizes that.

What do you think, Mack?" the admiral asked.

"When do I leave, sir?"

The admiral did not smile at the response. He expected it. He also knew this had a pretty good chance of being a suicide mission or a diplomatic disaster.

"Tomorrow morning, son." He handed a folder to MacLachlan. "Don't take anything from this folder except your travel orders. Everything else is Top Secret/Sensitive Compartmented Information. Give it to the duty o3 when you walk out. Got that?"

"Aye-aye, sir." The admiral stood and extended his hand. "God be with you." MacLachlan shook, did a perfectly executed about face and walked out the door, closing it behind him.

Back at this office, MacLachlan sat, stunned but not scared. This was the type intel operation he dreamed of doing. The danger excited him. He wondered who the controller would be.

A couple of phone calls later gave him the weather, flight plans and schedules and a trip to supply got him the proper military coats and boots. He would have to pick up area appropriate clothes there with the advice of the controller. He did not know what his legend would be. The controller would have that for him to learn...and become.

MacLachlan flew by military airlift into Berlin. A plain sedan met him, and he was taken to the "Mission Berlin," protected by Army military police officers instead of Marine guards in order to not look like a diplomatic facility.

He was taken to a room. Nobody was there. A pack of Kool's and a brass Marine Corps emblem Zippo lighter sat on the table. The address of a *bierhaus* was written on a scrap of paper. MacLachlan grinned. That damned Slickmeister.

He changed into civvies and a leather bomber jacket and left his duffle and briefcase with an MP. The MP gave him directions to the beer house. It was a ten-minute walk. MacLachlan turned up his collar against the cold, blowing rain in late spring. With a light leather jacket and jeans and dark brown hair, he could have been another twenty-something German.

Walking in the door of the German pub, he spied Grafton in the corner, back to the wall. Neither showed signs of recognition noticeable to anyone but them. He went to the bar. A barmaid with dark hair and a lot of cleavage smiled at him. He returned a superhero smile he had been working on. It seemed to work. He ordered a standard choice draft in a mug in German and walked to the corner. Grafton said, "Sit down, you damned Slickmeister," and grinned. The game was officially afoot. MacLachlan handed him his pack of Kool's and the lighter he had given him in Beirut with "Cigarette?"

"Wondered if I'd get my lighter back. I've caught a bunch of crap over carrying a jarhead lighter. Everybody asks about the two small, parallel scratches on it. I say 'don't know. The jarhead must have put them there.'"

"Did the admiral brief you on everything, Mack?" Will Grafton asked.

"He gave me a basic summary. How's your leg?"

"I've had a lot worse, with worse care. It's just bad enough to keep me from doing what you are going to be doing. But I can use my vast knowledge and good looks to guide you through the mire," he said.

"I hope so. I know your good looks will make the primary difference. Time seems to be at a premium. Where can we really talk?" MacLachlan asked scanning the room.

"Enjoy your beer. I have a place. Your duffle should have been delivered there by now."

The superhero grin worked on the waitress again, something not lost on Grafton.

"Can you teach me that?" he asked MacLachlan.

"Hardly, Will. I stole it from you."

"Hmm...it did look kind of familiar," Grafton said.

They stopped and scanned the area behind them in storefront windows every half block or so. Countersurveillance routines were Grafton's life and had become a major part of MacLachlan's also. He enjoyed the firsthand instruction from one who appeared to be a master. This was not classroom. This was Berlin. People would kill an agent of the other side here, or snatch him to trade for one of their own.

At one point, Grafton stopped and said, "No, no. It's behind us." and they turned back and retraced their steps. They crossed the street at the next inter-section and ducked into a doorway of a store to watch. They did not see anyone obvious following them. But in Berlin, the followers would have been senior varsity.

Twenty minutes of such activities brought them to a townhouse whose door and door frame needed paint. The small front border was unkempt.

Grafton quietly said "Lucy, we're home." and unlocked the door. They were no more than four blocks from the mission. But their circuituitous surveillance detection route, or SDR, had taken over twenty minutes to transit the distance from the bar to the safehouse.

MacLachlan snagged his duffle at the landing and followed Grafton up steep steps to the second floor. Two other men awaited them. Grafton introduced them as "Bob" and "Joe" and said they were MP's and provided protection. Joe offered MacLachlan a pocket Beretta .380 with two magazines and a full box of full metal jacket rounds.

"Thanks, Joe. Do I need to sign anything?" MacLachlan asked.

"Sign for what?" Joe responded and smiled.

MacLachlan racked the slide. He made sure it was empty and dropped the hammer. Then, he loaded a mag and stuck it in the butt of the gun. He did not jack a round into the chamber yet. He wanted to fool with the gun a while and fieldstrip it first. He slipped it into his hip pocket. A weak caliber, but not a bad hideaway. It should do up close, anyway. Before putting it away, he noticed several digits of the serial number were conveniently scarred to avoid reading the full number. It was clean gun without being as obvious as a fully ground off serial number would be. "Not bad", he thought.

"Let's get some coffee. A lot of it. And, go into the living room. These two jokers are topflight TSCM guys," Grafton said, signaling they were technical security countermeasures experts. "They scan for bugs several times a day. This place is as clean as your granny's pantry. We can talk openly, but I always like to check with them before getting into anything too sensitive. Bob nodded his laconic all clear and MacLachlan followed the fit black man, now with a slight limp, into the kitchen. Grafton put on a percolator and brewed a pot of coffee. The two MP's each got a cup of black and left. The two officers each poured a cup of the same and sat down at the kitchen table.

"So," Grafton said and paused, collecting his thoughts.

"My source says that a Chechen named Kadyrov, first name unknown, is delivering a small nuclear device to Český Krumlov in four to seven days. He thinks the buyer is called Ekram Khan. Though he works for Hezbollah, we think he is a Saudi," Grafton said.

MacLachlan interrupted. "I thought the Saudis were our friends."

"Some may be. A lot are not. Apparently this one is not. We think some 'freedom fighters' around the Middle East are Saudis with the tacit approval of various so-called pro-American princes. Those same princes would make a big deal of a trial and beheading if they were ever caught. The real allegiance is to the American dollar.

Khan is like 'Smith' or 'Brown' is to us. My personal opinion is that it's too damn convenient and is a cover.

But, since we have no real way to do a background on him, it almost doesn't matter what his real name is. My personal opinion is that Senator Church and his buddies greatly harmed our intelligence gathering activities less than a decade ago. How badly will be determined sometime in the future when we are attacked because we did not have enough HUMINT on the ground to forewarn the country. It's harder and harder to do what we have to do here. If this goes 'way south', you and I are going to be the sacrificial lambs. Or, lamb chops.

But, anyway," Grafton continued, "we have to be there first, identify both Kadyrov and Kahn, neutralize them and take possession of the device and get away. No small task, Mack."

"I guess not. Do we have descriptions of either? Both?" MacLachlan asked.

"Well, kinda. Both are medium height and build, dark haired and likely will be dressed like everybody else in Český Krumlov, including you. Our information is neither speak German. Though both men are Muslims, Chechen is nothing like Arabic. We don't have a clue what the common language will be. With a little luck maybe English." Grafton said.

"Yeah, right. That is unlikely. So, these two guys look like everybody else in this part of the world, we don't know their language. How about modes of transportation?" MacLachlan asked.

"The device is what is erroneously called a 'suitcase bomb.' I say erroneously because it is bigger than a suitcase. Assuming it is the smallest Russian nuke, it should be over two feet long, but maybe sixty pounds or so. It would be a heavy suitcase to lug around yet would comfortably fit in the trunk of about any car. You wouldn't need a truck to haul it."

"Will, how about instability? If I find it, what do I have to do to keep from vaporizing myself and everyone near?" MacLachlan asked.

"Shouldn't be a problem. Remember, these same devices were made to be shot from Howitzers, launched in small tactical rockets and so forth. Probably nothing you could do would be as bad as a vodka-soaked Russian ground crewman."

"Probably?"

"Well, yeah."

"Will, I have not been to Český Krumlov. What's your take on the best place to set up surveillance?"

"That's the $64,000 question. You can't cover every bar. It's unlikely Kadyrov will bring it to the first meet. One idea might be the castle."

"Castle?"

"Český Krumlov Castle is the main attraction in town. Communism has not done it any favors but it overlooks the town and should give a good outside perspective."

"What's my legend?" MacLachlan asked about his cover identity.

"We have complete East German papers for you. Your legend will be graduate student at the Humboldt University in West Berlin. Your major will be the same as your undergraduate and graduate actually were. You are about the right age for a doctoral candidate. As a commuting Berliner, you will be able to show your papers to move through the checkpoint to return home to East Berlin. Clearly, an American could not do that, but for some years, a German has been able to. You will drive a BMW sidecar motorcycle to Český Krumlov. The sidecar will have room for the device, a lead floor to hide your gun and allow you to carry a damn heavy camera and tripod without getting a rupture."

"What camera? And, about how far is it, Will?" MacLachlan asked.

"We have a working old-fashioned Graflex Speed Graphic camera and tripod for you to take on 'vacation'. The camera works with a special large format film. It also has a small, very powerful radio inside you can use to communicate with me. When I'm asleep or whatever, Bob or Joe will monitor our base unit here," Grafton said. "One of the guys will show you how to use the Graflex as a camera and the radio inside. Unless it's an emergency, you will broadcast at specific times with bursts. They'll show you how.

It's about three hundred twenty-five miles. Should take you around six or seven hours, since you don't want to be stopped for speeding."

"No closer way?" MacLachlan asked.

"Not without inserting you covertly into an Iron Curtain country. This was way is plausible. You would be hiding in plain sight."

"Okay, assume I disrupt this transfer and take possession of the device. Where do I take it and how?" MacLachlan asked.

"Part of the answer will be determined by how you came by getting it. Shoot out? Strong arm snatch? Something more subtle? The primary exfiltration will be along a southern route from Český Krumlov to the Danube. We will have a workboat waiting to take you to Melk in Bavaria. This packet has the legend to memorize as well as the map. It will be placed in the hidden compartment in the sidecar. When we get through talking, one of the guys will show you how to use the camera and access the hidden compartment. The gassed-up bike is in a garage in the rear. I suspect you will want to strip the Beretta and familiarize yourself with it. When you are finished, give it to one of us loaded. Include the extra magazine and box of cartridges. Bob or Joe will stash it in the compartment for you. Study the packet, Herr Dieter Maack," Grafton looked at his watch. "It's four p.m. now. Study until chow. We will have a quick dinner and you should study until ten. Then, we will go over your legend until we are both confident your mastery of it is bulletproof."

"Not a great choice of words," MacLachlan said.

"I'm afraid it is the perfect choice so study well," answered Grafton.

———

THREE HOURS and four cups of coffee later, Grafton came and got MacLachlan for dinner.

"How's the study going?" he asked in German.

MacLachlan answered in German that he thought it was going okay. He actually thought several more days prep with the legend, camera and motorcycle would have been optimal. But time did not allow given how fresh the collateral intelligence was relative to the delivery date.

Joe brought in sauerbraten with hot potato salad and sweet and sour red cabbage from a local café. They had cold Beck's beer. The two MP's spoke further about the camera and the BMW 90S motorcycle. Conversation about the latter was need-to-know things like gas mileage and type, top speed, and how fast it could be turned with the sidecar without dumping it. MacLachlan admitted he had never had a motorcycle and was not a big fan. He figured he would get good enough on the over three-hour trip to outrun border police with the hundred twenty mile per hour bike if he had to.

At eight, he resumed studying the legend and directions for exfiltration. At ten, Grafton came in and interrogated him unmercifully for two hours about his cover identity. MacLachlan passed convincingly in German.

The next morning, MacLachlan dressed in jeans, a heavier leather jacket, wool watch and old-fashioned goggles and powered up the BMW. Grafton and the two MP's nodded at him. He nodded back and accelerated off.

Ten minutes later, he came to a checkpoint. MacLachlan couldn't help a few palpitations as he approached the guards and presented his papers.

"You are a student. You should be coming to school at Humboldt, not leaving it in the morning." the young guard challenged him in German.

"I had beer after class. A coed invited me to her apartment. I stayed over. Wouldn't you, sergeant?" MacLachlan lied with a non-repentant wink. The officer looked at him for a minute, then said "Don't do it again. Without inviting me, that is. Get the hell through here."

"I will ask if she has a friend and catch you soon on a trip through. See you."

MacLachlan went through the checkpoint, leaving his new friend behind. He began to look for the route to the highway he needed to take him to the more questionable checkpoint, the Czech one hours ahead.

He drove through the military and truck traffic in East Berlin. It seemed few citizens had private cars. After a half hour of stop and go, he found the highway he needed and accelerated onto it. He had never ridden a motorcycle. The extra stability of a sidecar gave him a little confidence. That turned to bravado as he took the bike up to 121 kilometers per hour. Most vehicles passed him. He pulled in behind a string of mixed cars and trucks. His speedometer steadied on 160 kilometers per hour. He reckoned that to be around one hundred miles per hour. Other than the additional buffeting, it felt pretty good. He held it until traffic slowed for various reasons. After three hours, he stopped for lunch and a restroom break, both much needed. He had not even had coffee before leaving. A brat, some fries, a beer and a trip to a clean but primitive head and he was on the road again. MacLachlan was starting to enjoy traveling by bike.

By three, he approached a sign that indicated the entry and inspection point for Czechoslovakia. Now, the butterflies, added by the greasy brat, started with a vengeance.

He hoped the checkpoint would go as smoothly as East Berlin. It did not. Several guards reviewed his papers, looked at his bike and pointed him to an inspection lane. He rode over to it and stopped. Several storm troopers approached him. Two took his papers and told him to dismount. He did and followed them into a small building. Two others began to search his motorcycle, out of his sight.

MacLachlan answered questions about why he was

trying to enter their country. He told them about his graduate research and need to study and photograph the Český Krumlov Castle. Out of nowhere came, "What is name of your elementary school?" He answered. "Parent's name?" Again, he answered. The border guards did not have anything available to verify answers but kept throwing them at him to for responses. He hoped they would not attempt to verify his answers while he waited behind bars.

Twenty minutes later, the other two guards came in from inspecting the motorcycle and shrugged. Five minutes later, MacLachlan was on his way to Český Krumlov. He felt like he might have aged a couple of years but chalked it up to the costs of the game he was playing.

Because of the poor economies in the socialist countries, MacLachlan could not carry much cash while undercover. He found a hostel and checked in. The wind picked up and it started to sleet. So much for May in Germany. He hoped the Beretta was safe in the false floor of the sidecar. But the small radio hidden in the large camera was more important to him. It was his only method of communications with Grafton. He slung the heavy camera bag over his shoulder.

Using the tripod like a walking stick, he began the walk up to the castle. He walked across the Vltava River bridge and climbed the steps up to the castle. It was not in the greatest shape but was nonetheless imposing in its former grandeur.

MacLachlan screwed a telescopic lens on the camera and aimed it at the town below. He feigned taking photographs, though no 4x5 film was in the camera. The delay of warm weather had left some trees still without leaves. He had a fairly clear view of the town and scrutinized it closely though the four-power magnification. For the rest of the afternoon, he moved the tripod along the wall and appeared to take photographs from different angles. In reality, he was studying the streets of the town below, looking for either Khan or Kadyrov or both. Towards dusk, he packed up and walked down the steps and across the Vltava bridge. He put the camera in the sidecar and padlocked it in before covering the opening with a tonneau. MacLachlan then began to stroll along the streets of Český Krumlov, trying to look like a bored grad student and not like a spy.

At eight, he found a café that fit his legend and its financial status. Though not classically Hungarian, he found a thicker Czech goulash served with a large chunk of freshly baked bread. He had that with Budvar, the Czech Budweiser. Following dinner, he walked the streets of the small city until they were virtually abandoned. He sat with a coffee in the window seat of another café pretending to read a newspaper until the heavyset woman who ran it ushered him out so she could close. It was restful, yet good exercise for someone who had sat on his butt for six hours on the bike. No luck spotting either target though. He was leery about walking around at midnight when only policemen were about. Muggers did not worry him a whit. If his Marine close combat skills were not enough in an altercation, the new Mikov Leverlock automatic knife should even the odds. He had found one with a cocobolo wood grip in a shop in town and spent some of his precious funds on it.

He walked slowly back to the hostel, not seeing

anyone who might be his quarries along the way. At the hostel, MacLachlan unlocked the camera from the sidecar and carried it in. Several people were already asleep in the hostel. He heard the shower running in the bathroom. He quickly opened the Graflex camera and removed the radio. It was like a powerful wireless pager. He typed in "No joy in CK. Continue AM" and it was sent in a microsecond burst. The radio buzzed twice in response. Three buzzes meant warning. Before anyone noticed, he put it back in the camera and stuck the Graflex under his covers.

A quick shower and he rolled up in the sheet and a wool blanket. MacLachlan wore an area-appropriate sleeveless undershirt and German branded boxers. The Mikov switchblade and a small but powerful flashlight were under his pillow. Shoes and jeans were under the rack. He was ready for a fight or rapid departure if necessary. He would risk the gun at the last minute. The knife was legal but the gun represented prison time if he was caught with it. It was quite different from the James Bond films he had waited in line to see since a boy, no Aston Martin DB-5 either, he thought.

One of the several days in the range of the transfer had passed.

The next day, MacLachlan was up early. The other residents at the hostel were Czech hikers. They spoke German as a second or third language, but Slovak among themselves. MacLachlan took a chance. A big chance. He spoke in German to them at the communal breakfast.

"Good morning. I am a student here doing research. I am supposed to meet a professor and cannot seem to find him. He is in his thirties, medium height and dark haired and complexion. Have any of you seen such a gentleman?" he said.

"When I was walking here yesterday, I saw such a man. He was average looking. The only reason I remember him is because he appeared to be watching for someone," an outdoorsy young woman reported.

"Oh? Perhaps he was looking for me. Where did you see him?" MacLachlan asked.

"He was at an outdoor table drinking coffee in front of the Hotel Ruze. It's very expensive. He must be a famous professor."

"He is famous in his field of history. I know he has written several books on the Habsburg Dynasty. Thank you. I will check there this morning," he said. He stopped by the BMW and opened the compartment, pocketing the small Beretta surreptitiously.

MacLachlan had a conundrum to figure out as he walked the several blocks to the Hotel Ruze. Both men had the same general description. If he saw the one the hiker had seen, which one would he be? The man with the bomb? Or, the man selling the bomb?

He played it by ear.

"Hello. I am looking for my professor who is staying here. I am late and may be in trouble with him. He is Professor Kahn Kadyrov," MacLachlan said, using both names.

"I am sorry, we are not allowed to give out guests names," the desk clerk said in a pompous, stuffy manner.

MacLachlan slipped the Czech equivalent of twenty dollars on the desk and slid it over.

"It would be so helpful if I could tap on his door and apologize to him..."

"Two-twelve," the clerk said as he pocketed the money and turned his back to MacLachlan.

MacLachlan walked up the stairs, knowing elevators were tactically dangerous on any op. He saw which way the numbers were trending and walked directly to room 212. It had a peephole, so he stopped short of the door and listened. He heard the shower running. He waited for it to stop and tapped on the door. In bad German, he heard a voice. The accent sounded more Middle Eastern than Eastern European.

"Who is it?" the voice asked.

"It is K. The one you are waiting to meet," MacLachlan said in German.

As the door opened, the man said, "You are early."

He had an aquiline nose and sun darkened skin. His eyes were so dark they were almost black. MacLachlan thought he looked like his first impression, Middle Eastern.

"Kadyrov," MacLachlan said.

The man in the towel nodded and turned to walk to the bedroom, leaving the door open. MacLachlan slipped the Beretta from his right rear pocket and held it behind his right leg. It was out of sight, but ready.

Kahn returned in a minute with one of the hotel's terry cloth robes on. Continuing in German, he said "I expected you to be dark."

"Many Chechens are blonde, though Muslim. Especially in the north," MacLachlan continued, making it up as he went.

"I have ordered tea. It should be here in a minute. I will call and tell them to bring another cup," he said.

"That would be good," MacLachlan agreed, not really caring but playing along to see where this was going. The call was made and after a few minutes of idle talk about the town, MacLachlan heard a tap on the door.

"Excuse me, I have to use the toilet," he said and disappeared before the door opened.

He flushed and ran the water as if washing his hands. As soon as he heard the door close, he reappeared.

Kahn was pouring tea, holding the pot several feet above the cup. MacLachlan had never seen that before and watched with interest.

"Allahu Akbar," Kahn said passing a cup of tea to MacLachlan.

"Inna," MacLachlan responded for "indeed."

They drank the tea. MacLachlan felt it was more ceremonial than for thirst quenching but was not sure.

"I expected you later today," Kahn said.

"I hit less delays than I expected and hoped we could transact our business earlier and each head home," MacLachlan said.

"I take it you have the device?"

"Yes, it is near and available as soon as we are ready to make a simultaneous exchange," the American said.

"I have the bearer bonds. They are all endorsed and worth as much as gold.

"May I see them?" MacLachlan asked.

"What? You do not trust me?"

"Of course, I do. It is Chechen tradition, that is all," MacLachlan said, again inventing as he went. He could see immediately this ploy was raising questions with his adversary.

"I will go get them," Kahn said and stood up. He padded towards the bedroom. As he got in the doorway,

MacLachlan silently stood behind him and saw him push his pillow aside. "Bad sign." thought MacLachlan as he brought the Beretta up to the isosceles position.

"Freeze, Kahn." MacLachlan ordered.

Ignoring the order, the Saudi bent towards the bed. MacLachlan shifted the pistol to his left hand and brought the edge of his right down in a powerfully delivered and immediately re-cocked knife edge hand chop on the back of Kahn's neck. Kahn collapsed onto the bed fully unconscious. He dragged the man into the bathroom. Looking around, he decided the best course of action.

The tub's faucet was heavy duty and stood up in a goose neck about the back edge of the tub. MacLachlan drew the automatic knife and pressed the button. He used the sharp blade to make one longer and two slightly shorter strips from a king-sized pillow-case. He took the robe off the still-unconscious man. He knew from his training that naked people generally feel more vulnerable as captives. MacLachlan tied Khan's hands behind him and tied his feet. He twisted the longer piece of pillowcase and tied Kahn's neck to the faucet. He left enough room to breathe but only as long as the man did not struggle or try to pull loose. Last, he gagged Khan with a washcloth and tied it securely.

Now that Khan was secured and reasonably quiet, MacLachlan had to wait for Kadyrov and the device. He was pretty sure from Khan's reaction that the Chechen was coming to this hotel to meet him, just later than MacLachlan. In meantime, MacLachlan searched for and found a sheaf of endorsed bearer bonds. He thumbed through and closely estimated the value around ten million dollars. A nice contribution to the US Treasury.

The phone rang in an hour.

"There is a gentleman to see you Mr. Kahn. He's says you are expecting him."

"Send him up," MacLachlan said in a gruff version of Kahn's voice and then faked an immediate cough to hint at a reason he might sound a bit different.

A moment later, someone knocked on the hotel room door. MacLachlan peered through the peephole. Damn. These guys really did look alike considering how many thousand miles apart they lived.

He opened the door, stepping aside. As soon as Kadyrov cleared the door jamb, MacLachlan gave him a left jab into the solar plexus. He went "Oof" and folded up. MacLachlan followed up with a hard-right chop on the back of the neck, like he had given to Khan. Kadyrov hit the deck hard. MacLachlan dragged Kadyrov into the bedroom and tied him to the bed spread-eagled. He pushed all four pillows under the Chechen's shoulders to make sure his head tilted backwards. Stepping out the door, he turned the tag on the handle around to what he assumed was DO NOT DISTURB.

Returning, he filled a stainless trash can from the bathroom and a second one from the bedroom with water from the sink. The tub would have been easier, but that faucet was blocked by prisoner number one.

Not wanting to be unfair, MacLachlan stripped the man tied to the bed also and tossed his clothes and shoes into a corner.

The Chechen looked at him with a dark glare of hatred. MacLachlan asked him in German where the suitcase device was at that moment. The man told him to do something MacLachlan knew was impossible. So, instead, he slapped Kadyrov across the face with a fast open hand. He could plainly see his palm print on the man's face. Inadvertent tears ran down Kadyrov's face and he spit at MacLachlan. This time, it was a fist against the point of his chin and Kadyrov was out. MacLachlan soaked a hand towel in one of the trash cans full of water and placed it over the Chechen's face. As he came to, MacLachlan asked again where the device was. No answer. MacLachlan closed the door between the bedroom and the parlor.

MacLachlan poured half a trash can of water slowly onto the hand towel over Kadyrov's mouth. The man gagged and sputtered. MacLachlan repeated the question.

He continued this cycle. Several times, Kadyrov passed out. MacLachlan used that time to refill his water containers.

Twenty-three minutes into to the procedure, Kadyrov told MacLachlan the device was in the trunk of a gray Vauxhall sedan parked two blocks behind the hotel. In response to being repeatedly asked where the device was to be detonated, he responded he did not know. MacLachlan believed him.

MacLachlan went to Khan and subjected him to the same version of water boarding Kadyrov had gotten. He had two questions for the Saudi. Were there other devices? And what were the targets? After a longer period than the Chechen took, MacLachlan found there was more than one device, but it was compartmented on a need-to-know basis. He only knew about his which was destined for London.

When pressed to the breaking point, he still maintained he did not know how many devices there were or when and how others would be delivered to Hezbollah or their targets. Again, MacLachlan believed his prisoner. He also did not have any self-recriminations for his methods of interrogation. The fear and discomfort of one man, he felt, was justified in saving the lives of thousands of innocents. He considered killing both prisoners but decided against it. Probably a mistake, the little hairs on the back of his neck told him.

MacLachlan walked over to the pile of clothes in the corner and fished Vauxhall keys out of the pants pocket he had thrown there. MacLachlan promised himself the next time he had a situation like this, he would have a couple of knock out syringes and several long wire ties to use for restraints.

He gagged Kadyrov and checked on Khan in the bathroom. He was conscious and furious. MacLachlan pulled a Wyatt Earp and buffaloed him. He slammed the flat side of the Beretta along the edge of Khan's jaw and knocked him unconscious.

MacLachlan thoroughly searched the room and Khan's luggage. He found nothing of interest.

He made sure both men were tightly gagged. He wiped the cans he had used for his waterboarding, the teacup, the faucets and anything else he could think of he might have touched.

MacLachlan knew he had been seen by the desk clerk and had an idea. It might or might not work. Bearer bonds buttoned into his shirt and Vauxhall keys in his jeans, he went down the rear stairs and circled the building.

He came back in the front and walked up to the desk. The same clerk he had bribed was still on duty.

The phone rang just before he got to the desk. MacLachlan gently tossed the Vauxhall keys on the carpet beside the desk. The clerk hung up.

"I was here earlier to see my professor in room 212. I knocked, but there was no answer. You were on the phone when I came back down. I think I lost my car keys here. May I look around?"

Without waiting for an answer, MacLachlan began to look around the reception area.

"Aha." He bent down and retrieved the Vauxhall keys.

"Have you seen Professor Khan come down since I was here?" he asked.

"No, I assume he is still in his room," the clerk replied.

"He clearly was. He wanted to see me to discuss my dissertation and I knocked on the door of room 212 and waited. There was no response and I heard a woman giggling inside the room so I came back though here and left. I figured I'd have lunch and come back later.

Would you ring the room for me?" MacLachlan asked. The clerk did, and as MacLachlan knew would be the case, there was no answer.

"I'm getting pretty mad with him showing such disrespect for a student. Wouldn't you be?" MacLachlan said, getting the desired buy-in from a witness. He stomped out, mad.

A middle-aged man was sitting in the lobby, listening. When he heard MacLachlan's set-up about a woman giggling in Khan's room, he smiled inwardly. He rose and walked out the door. At the end of the block, he passed a woman. She was dressed in tourist clothing and fit in perfectly the other people there to see the castle.

The man said "Hooker set-up. Plays into our plans nicely. No witnesses, please." He walked on. The woman ducked around a corner. No one was in sight. She donned a black wig over her dyed blonde hair. Bright red lipstick followed. She unbuttoned her blouse, leaving only the bottom several buttons fastened.

The woman went to the hotel and entered by the rear entrance. She went up to room 212, looking like the non-existent prostitute the American hinted was in the room.

The lock on the door took fifteen seconds with two tools from her lock picking kit. She could have done it with two hair pins but did not have the luxury of time.

She found both men tied, one to the bed, the other in the bathtub. How thoughtful of the American. The one in the bed opened his eyes wide. She pulled her blouse apart and flashed him. His smile quickly disappeared as she withdrew a small dagger, stepped aside and slashed his carotid artery. She gave a wry smile. At least his last view had been quite nice. Nicer than he deserved. She moved to the bathroom. The Saudi did not deserve the view the Chechen received. She drove the dagger deeply into his chest. It penetrated his heart. The muscle grabbed it and she had difficulty withdrawing it. She could not leave it in case it had her fingerprints on the blade. She wiped it on the waterboarding towel and dropped the bloody towel in the floor. She searched the room and emptied both men's wallets of credit cards, identification and cash. The, she walked out the way she had entered. Two dead men. No witnesses. Her uncle would be pleased. Around the block, she wiped off the bright lipstick, removed the wig and placed it in a trash bin and re-buttoned her blouse. She was back to being a very average looking tourist. She met her uncle at a coffee shop and smiled. He did not have to ask any questions. He knew she was the best. He had trained her himself. The man continued to munch on his bagel. He had surveilled MacLachlan and saw the device put into the motorcycle. As soon as he finished his coffee and bagel, the two agents, uncle and niece, would get in his car. He would drive and she would monitor the tracking device he had placed in the American's motorcycle while he was in room 212.

Circling the block, MacLachlan found the Vauxhall just where Kadyrov said it would be. Under the circumstances of their conversation, that did not surprise MacLachlan at all.

He dug the keys out of his jeans and put on his leather gloves. He smudged the keys and unlocked the sedan. Starting, he drove it to several blocks from the hostel. He had prepaid, so he merely got his meager travel bag and started the bike. He rode it to the Vauxhall and popped the trunk. The device was there. Looking around, he did not see any traffic. He loaded it into the sidecar and snapped the tonneau over it. There was no room for the camera with the classified radio. He swung the camera bag strap over his shoulder and dropped the tripod down a hill into some bushes after wiping prints off with his gloved hand. He left the Vauxhall parked with the windows open and keys in the ignition. Anywhere else in the world, it would be stolen in minutes. He hoped that would be true in charming Český Krumlov, as he watched the town disappear in the bike's rear-view mirror.

He wondered what the two conspirators would tell

the police who found them naked in a hotel room. Clearly, they could not have tied one another that way. Perhaps a threesome? After his set-up with the clerk, the part about a woman in the room would surely come out in the investigation. He knew neither would explain they were there to exchange bearer bonds for a nuclear device. MacLachlan did not know that neither could explain anything. Ever again.

MacLachlan dismissed wondering about them and focused on the route to the Danube. At a park along the way, he extracted the radio long enough to have Grafton move the boat to the exfil position on the river for tonight.

All in all, the ride to the Danube was pretty nice. But his mission was only half complete. There was at least one other nuke was out there headed for Hezbollah.

———

MacLachlan reached the ordained spot on the river just after dark. He did not see any border police patrols as he carried the sixty-pound device down to the river. He kept the Beretta and the radio handy. At ten PM, the workboat arrived and idled into the bank at clutch speed. Surprisingly, Grafton was on it. He held an M-16 as the bow touched the bank. MacLachlan handed him the device which he took below. MacLachlan could see a Geiger Counter hung from his shoulder by a strap. When Grafton came back topside, MacLachlan handed him the camera, radio and his small travel bag. Grafton looked relaxed, a clear signal the device was not leaking radioactive waves.

MacLachlan asked the captain for a hundred feet of line. He took one end of the line and secured it to a bollard on the stern. He took the rest and circled the midpart around the forks of the bike under the handlebars. MacLachlan took the rest back to the boat and wrapped the free end around the top of the same bollard. He held the loose, wrapped end as the boat eased out into the fast-moving Danube River dragging the motorcycle behind it into deep water. Once they were fifty feet from shore, MacLachlan let go the wrapped end. It went into the water. When he saw it loose and floating, he pulled it in and coiled it on deck, now freed from the bike.

"In case some shooting starts, you better let me debrief you now," the always practical Grafton said. He propped the rifle out of sight and leaned against the wheelhouse and began asking questions.

A half hour later, as they were heading towards Melk in Bavaria, the debrief was finished. Grafton tuned his radio to a different frequency and sent an encrypted message to the Pentagon. He got a brief response. Grafton opened a chilled bottle of Dom Perignon.

"Should we celebrate a mission only half finished?" MacLachlan asked his controller.

"You may have just saved the lives of thousands of Londoners." So, the two finished it before arriving in neutral Melk, Austria.

As they pulled in to a dock in Melk, MacLachlan saw a van pull up. Several men dressed in civilian clothes got out. It did not take Hercule Poirot to identify them as soldiers from their fitness level, haircuts and demeanor.

Grafton shook his head, deep in thought. "It would take a Slickmeister to snatch a nuke without killing anybody. You sure you didn't kill someone?" he asked. MacLachlan nodded.

Grafton unloaded and pulled the pin on the rifle, breaking it open. He slipped the rifle, now half length, into a musical instruments case. He walked across the gang plank to the shore. MacLachlan followed, carrying the device. One of the men from the van approached him, arms out, and took the sixty pounds and went back to the van. MacLachlan turned and followed Grafton to a VW Jetta. They got in and drove circuitously back to the safehouse in West Berlin. After freshening up, they walked to Mission Berlin and Grafton got on an encrypted phone to the White House Situation room and gave a full report. MacLachlan was present in case his elaboration was needed. The President was in the Situation Room and congratulated both men for a successful operation. He pressed MacLachlan whether his interrogation had revealed the number and target of other devices.

"Regretfully, no sir. Neither man knew. I believe them. Our work is still cut out for us."

"I am sure the people in this room will agree with me when I say 'keep after them'. You and Grafton have the lead. I am not worrying about agency protocol here. I am worrying about averting a massive loss of lives. Do whatever the hell you have to do to keep a terrorist nuke out of an American or any other NATO city."

"We will do our best, sir," Will Grafton replied for both. He mouthed "*carte blanche*" to MacLachlan, who silently raised his eyebrows.

The Director of Central Intelligence advised the

two men on the red phone and those in the Situation Room of several things. First, that the President had called the Prime Minister and apprised her of the target and the mission. The DCI said he was confident the Secret Intelligence Service, AKA MI-6, would have people waiting to 'deal with' Khan and Kadyrov before either reached home. He reported the President had also called the prime minister of Israel and briefed him. Implicit in that call was confidence if the Brits missed the two, the Mossad would not. His last call had been to Paris. MacLachlan knew from the media the President respected France's military and intelligence apparatus. Its government was quite another matter.

"Okay," the DCI said, "anything else?"

"Is Admiral Howard present?" MacLachlan asked.

"I'm here, Mack," came a familiar voice.

"Sir, is there anything coming through our section that gives us a sense of direction about where to look for the next transfer, assuming it hasn't already happened?"

"Not a thing. We are examining every report for the tiniest hint of that. Let me defer back to the DCI for a moment."

"Major," the DCI began, "I have instructed all our intelligence agencies, military and civilian, to start spreading money around to all sources to help. I feel like this will be solved like the average urban murder. That is by putting the word out and paying sources like a detective pays snitches. I believe you two are in the best location. You can have everything you need, except manpower, there with you. We simply have to keep this low profile. I'm afraid if we bulk up your location, somebody will notice. We cannot afford to have that happen. You will know anything we know within minutes. If

you need SEALS, you have them. I have moved operational numbers of both into the region but your location
and your two identities are on the down low. As I
suspect you know, if Hezbollah, the Chechens and
maybe the Russians or their East German boys identify
you, you will be in grave danger. And, I did not choose
my adjective unintentionally."

With that, the call ended. Both men in West Berlin
sat quiet for a few moments, lost in their own thoughts.

MacLachlan spoke first.

"Was it Occam with his razor or Sherlock Holmes
who first said 'when faced with competing assumptions,
choose the simplest one'?"

"Both, I think, in their own way," Grafton
responded.

"So, let's go over what we know. The source for the
weapons appears to be Chechnya, at least for one. The
buyer is Hezbollah. There are unknowns. One is
whether the Russians are behind the supply. Another is
whether it's a Hezbollah deal centered in Lebanon or is
there a strong Saudi influence." MacLachlan said.

"And, the last," he added," is whether the Chechens
stole the nukes and the Russians are ticked off and on
the trail trying to recover them. Maybe our guys need to
be listening to them as well and reaching out to sources,
especially regarding the GRU. I would think the military intelligence would be on this big time and trying to
operate separately from the civilian KGB."

"I propose we ask the guys we just spoke with to
ramp up the NSA listening posts for Hezbollah,
Chechnya and GRU right away, if not already done.
Let's have someone high make a covert contact with the
head of the French intelligence agency with which he

has the most confidence and have them start listening. The Brits, too. Have the FBI start listening in on any Hezbollah cells in the US they have identified with what I believe they call Title III surveillance."

"I concur," Grafton said. "Want to call your admiral and let him honcho it?"

"I will. I can send him a quick message now and try to catch him in the Situation Room. Wait one." MacLachlan took out his pager and sent the message.

The red phone rang within a minute.

"Howard here."

"Sir, thanks for getting back to us so quickly. We have a couple ideas to run past you."

MacLachlan outlined their requests. Admiral Howard stated that several were in process and promised to run the others past the rest of the people in the Situation Room, though noting the President had already left.

"Hang tight. This won't take long."

They waited about five minutes before the admiral came back on the secure line.

"Done. We will advise about any findings as soon as we have them." He broke the connection.

MacLachlan turned to Grafton.

"You are the operational guy. Is it unusual to have such a small contingent running such a large and crucial op?" he asked.

"No rules about that. What we—mainly you—just did was pretty unusual. I guess they are going with what they've got. My experience is too many cooks spoil dinner. I am happy with it like this. If we need, we have SEALS we can use. But, I'd rather not. In 'Nam and countries near it, I went in alone for up to two weeks and performed my missions. I liked it better working lean. Still do, Mack. Think of this as a jungle. Just no damn snakes and bugs. Man, I got real tired of both." Grafton said.

MacLachlan nodded.

"I think I'm going to take a run. Think I ought to take the Beretta?" MacLachlan asked.

"Nah. You are a big boy. You can either out run or out fight muggers. If it's a hit team, that pipsqueak mouse gun won't make much difference. Have a good run. Wish I could join you. Maybe in a couple of months." Grafton said stretching the wounded leg.

MacLachlan put on sweats, a stocking cap and running shoes and walked out the back door. He crossed the alley and looked for surveillance. Detecting none, he started off at a jog, then increased his pace to a full run. He maintained that for an hour, ending up at the front door. Still no surveillance. He had done his SDR's throughout. Nobody on foot, bike or car he could identify. Almost a strange feeling for an American agent in Cold War Berlin. He went in. Grafton was drinking some sort of hard liquor in a small glass. MacLachlan looked at the nearby bottle. It was Té Bheag Scotch.

"I didn't know you were Scottish," MacLachlan commented, grinning at his friend.

"Just because I drink Tea Bag Scotch doesn't mean you are going to see these fine legs peeking out of some plaid mini-skirt."

"You ought to try a kilt. You might like it," MacLachlan said.

"Yeah. I might like a lot of things. But that doesn't mean I am going to try them," Grafton said.

"By the way, in Gaelic, it's 'chey veck'," MacLachlan commented.

"I'm sticking with 'tea bag,' thank you. How the devil can anybody get 'chey veck' out of that?" Grafton asked.

MacLachlan, having no reasonable answer, simply shrugged. Grafton poured him a wee dram and MacLachlan held it up in salute. He did not bother to say Slàinte with its proper Gaelic pronunciation and prolong a useless conversation. Instead, he let the mellow Scotch slide down his throat and enjoyed it with his friend.

Other than twice-daily contacts with the admiral, the four men in the safehouse were like firefighters at the firehouse. They cooked, exercised, maintained their equipment and waited for the bell to ring.

THE BELL RANG four days later.

MacLachlan got a page instructing them to report to the secure phone at Mission Berlin and call the admiral. Thirty minutes later, they were dialing.

The admiral answered the secure phone "yes?"

Both men recognized him.

"Sir, we are both present. What's up?"

"The NSA has picked up some chatter out of Russia. Complaints about Chechen rebels stealing two nuclear warheads. The chatter, coming out of Russian military intelligence instead of KGB, says one is missing and one appears to be on the way to the US. We assume the missing one is the one you got for us. They have no idea where it is. We reviewed and photographed it and gave it to the French. It was destined for Paris anyway and we wanted to show good faith to a NATO partner." Grafton, who had periodically worked out of NATO in Mons, Belgium, nodded.

"The key," the admiral went on, "is twofold: one, there is only one other; and, two: it seems to be headed for the US. The GRU has agents trailing the Chechen with the device. The rivalry with the KGB has flared up and it has agents looking for the GRU agents. There is a lot of encrypted traffic over all of this, with our boys at the National Security Agency getting some pretty good information in bits and pieces. All of this has just popped up overnight. It should be safe to assume the Brits are listening in on the same chatter we are."

"Sir, this is Will. Anything we can act on yet?"

"Yes. The Russians are thinking the Chechens are moving the device overland by truck. The route seems to be pointing towards Dar-es-Salaam in Tanzania. The estimate is they are several days out. It looks like there is a tracking device involved. Expect the Brits, Russians of various agencies and who knows who else to be there. Be there first." The admiral hung up without further instructions.

3

Dar-Es-Salaam, Tanzania

June 1985

THE TRAVEL OFFICE at the official embassy booked MacLachlan and Grafton two different commercial flights to the Julius Nyerere International Airport. Grafton arrived earlier, picked up a rental Toyota Corolla and a room in each of two hotels several blocks apart. He also reached out to his agency and found there was an agent in the area. His name was William Crocker, a second generation American whose parents migrated from Africa. He spoke fluent Swahili, the official language of Tanzania. Many locals also spoke English, some Bantu or a combination of the three.

When MacLachlan arrived at the airport four hours later, a hired driver held a sign for Dieter Maack. He was taken to his hotel. He saw Grafton and another, younger black man sitting in the café as he went to his room. Five minutes later, he joined them.

"Mack, this is William Crocker. He's our guy in Tanzania," Grafton said in a low tone, having already done his surveillance detection procedures in the randomly selected mid-class hotel.

"Hi, William. I'm Mack MacLachlan. Glad to meet you." They shook. The young agent was still in the military. He knew about MacLachlan's CMH and rank and showed polite deference to one no older than he.

"We can expect GRU, KGB, and maybe Israeli activity. We can also anticipate the British will be here as observers. French presence is unknown at this point. Our intel is that the GRU knows the buyer and is tracking him. They have apparently also put a tracker on the device's crate and know where that is. I have already talked with our leadership today and they are good with letting the device go back to Russia. They want us to hopefully capture, or option two, neutralize, the Hezbollah guy. More on him later," Grafton said.

"Mack, interesting news from the brass about Český Krumlov. They wanted me to assure them—which I did—that you did not kill the two guys in the hotel. Because both were found bound as you left them and stabbed to death."

"You're kidding." MacLachlan exclaimed. "I would have killed both, but knew I was seen by at least the desk clerk, maybe others. What do the police think?"

"The information I received is that a female posing as a prostitute or maybe a real prostitute, is the primary suspect. Both men were robbed of all ID and money. The cops have no idea who she is. They are aware of a German student asking about Khan but have no real interest in him. Nor, do they have his identity, other than he may have been on a motorcycle. Not sure how they know that. Good luck to them finding the bike in forty feet of cold, dark Danube water, huh?" Grafton asked rhetorically.

MacLachlan grinned at the part about the bike but was concerned about missing apparent tails that came in and cleaned up after him. He should have seen or felt someone was there. Mistakes in the intelligence world can be fatal. He knew he had to be more careful, paranoid, perhaps. He said nothing. He was pretty sure the savvy Grafton knew exactly what he was thinking.

"Our plan will be to surveil the GRU agents, identify the buyer and take him. We will have to duel with two sets of Russians to get him. Our information is he has several bodyguards, probably not very professional. Our source is one of the GRU agents. We have promised him the world. And, may give it to him," Grafton said.

Crocker spoke.

"The source, codenamed 'Tatra' after a car, called me today. He has setup a drop under a bus stop bench at this location." He gave folded sheets to both men.

"He will leave word about the buyer's name and location there today around five. I will pick it up," he said.

"William has a souped-up taxi we will use for the snatch. I will coordinate from my hotel room. Memorize it and destroy these sheets along with the drop location," Grafton said.

"William," MacLachlan asked, "the Russians have lots of tactical nuclear warheads. And, over the years, lots have been 'lost' one way or the others. What is the Kremlin's impetus in getting this one?"

"I have gathered from Tatra it's two-fold. Certainly, it's a matter of embarrassment to have tangos use one of their warheads on a NATO capital. But more important is they think our president is the butt-kicking cowboy he played in movies. They don't want him thinking they were behind a nuclear explosion in the US or a close friend. They appreciate the proximity of his thumb to a red button that would unleash more than they could respond to," Crocker said.

"They are certainly right about that," MacLachlan said, Grafton nodding his agreement.

"Mack, you and William will grab the guy. If we get away, it's a rendition. If the field gets too crowded, we know what ship the device is on and will just watch the Russians take possession and take the damn thing home. William has a bag for you in under the table. Just take it to your room. It has a small radio for comms and some armaments. I will call you on the room phone with some banal conversation. It is a signal to monitor the encrypted radio for traffic," Grafton said.

Steven Rotenberg arrived on Grafton's flight. He did not know the DIA agent but had a fairly good idea he was some sort of American agent. Too aware of his surroundings. Stopping periodically to peer at reflections in shop windows in the airport. Neither man had checked luggage. Rotenberg went to a different rental car counter. He rented the most innocuous car in their fleet. He was not James Bond. But he was much, much better at his craft.

Yaffa Segal, Rotenberg's niece, arrived on MacLachlan's flight. Both uncle and niece knew him by sight.

Yaffa had already decided the American agent was handsome and likely to check out women his age in specific and pretty ones of all ages in general. Ever the professional, Yaffa got rid of any vestiges of makeup, tied a babushka scarf on her head, donned large sunglasses and hoped he would not notice her level of fitness in jeans and jacket. To further divert attention, she hunched and tried to be as mousey as a lovely woman could be. It worked. He stepped aside like a gentleman once to let her by, looking only at her hands for a threat, as she moved ahead.

Unlike her uncle, Yaffa selected the fastest and most powerful small SUV Hertz offered. It was an Audi. She caught up with MacLachlan at the pickup point and followed him in heavy traffic to his hotel. She was aware of and avoided his tradecraft. Yaffa stood in line two back from the tall American and heard his room number as the clerk gave him the key card. She asked for the same floor once he had gone to the elevator and her turn at the desk arrived. Her room was four doors down the hall from his. She knew it was risky, but it may be the only way she could take advantage of America's superior satellite and other monitoring of intel chatter worldwide.

Once in the room, she showered and dressed in a mini dress, and high heels. She soaked her hair and brushed it back, leaving it wet. Yaffa applied full war paint and looked in the mirror. Hot. She blew a kiss at herself and went to the café. He was there with two other men. She took a table and smiled at their obvious appreciation of the brief time she had spent preparing to get their attention. Yaffa ordered a rare hamburger and a large glass of red wine. She thoroughly enjoyed her meal.

Two sets of other government employees arrived at

Dar-es-Salaam that afternoon, one tracking the other. A team of five Russian GRU agents arrived, having tracked both the device by truck and train and the man by the same modes. They were followed by eight similar looking countrymen representing the more influential intelligence agency called *Komitet Gosudarstvennoy Bezopasnosti* or KGB.

The British Government Communications Head-quarters, based in a building called the "doughnut" in Cheltenham, had heard enough traffic in its Russian surveillance to field an MI-6 team to Dar-es-Salaam to "monitor and report." They were aware of the tactical nuclear warhead the Americans had snatched and given to the French and the existence of a second one. Chatter notwithstanding, the Brits were not taking any chances London was not the target whether primary or second tier.

After a light lunch at the hotel's café, the three American agents separated. Crocker left in his taxi; Grafton walked the blocks back to his hotel to limber his wounded leg. It had stiffened on the flight from Berlin. MacLachlan sat longer and had another coffee, admiring the beautiful young woman who looked up from her table and smiled at him periodically. He did not have time for a meet and greet. The drop was to be made in a couple hours and the phone and radio traffic would commence shortly thereafter. Finally, he picked up the bag. It weighed at least thirty pounds. MacLachlan left money on the table to cover their check and walked towards the door into the hotel.

He said "Hello," and gave his best superhero grin yet to the woman in the thin cotton mini dress. She nodded and smiled. MacLachlan figured her superhero grin beat his by a Texas mile.

In his room, he opened the bag and spread the contents out on the bed. The radio was a very small government-only Motorola. It had an extra battery, belt clip and ear wig set with a mic at second button down level. The channel was marked with a bit of what appeared to be white fingernail polish. Maybe type correction fluid. The largest thing was an AK-47 with a very short barrel. It was probably seven inches instead of the usual 16.3 inches. The wire butt stock was folded, making for a very handy rifle with a lot of fire-power. Three full magazines were included. There was a Kevlar vest, thin tactical gloves and ballistic shooting glasses. Lastly, a commercial blue steel Colt Government Model 1911 .45 automatic with four seven shot magazines and a box of 230 grain hollow points. "Nice," he thought. Again, several of the serial numbers on the Colt were obliterated. The AK did not have any serial numbers, having been finely crafted in a tent in Marrakesh.

MacLachlan field stripped the Kalashnikov and the Colt. Both were clean and had an appropriate amount of lube. He loaded both and filled the pistol mags. He had jeans on and put all four mags in front pockets. He clipped the Mikov automatic knife into his weak hand front pocket. It was too warm to wear a jacket. He pulled his shirttail out and put the .45 in his waistband. He turned several times in front of the bathroom mirror. The big gun did not print. It was in Condition One. Chambered round, hammer back, safety on. Ready for action. The intel said the device and its buyer would arrive in Dar-es-Salaam in a day or two. But it could be anytime. MacLachlan knew he had to be ready to roll with a moment's notice.

It happened less than an hour later.

He heard a tone on the radio and acknowledged. Crocker said "It's going down. I'll meet you out front in five mikes. Full equipment." MacLachlan keyed twice in rapid succession to acknowledge. He took off his loose sport shirt. After putting the Kevlar vest on, he reached for the radio parts

He clipped the radio on the left side and ran the mic and ear wig up his shirt. MacLachlan clipped the mic out of sight near where the topmost unbuttoned button was. He fed the ear wig up behind the left side of his collar before placing it in his left ear. Grabbing the bag with the AK and spare ammo, he walked briskly to the exit and down the steps. As he came out of the hotel, he heard a screeching of tires as an SUV powered by at speed. He was pretty sure it was the pretty girl across from him at lunch. She disappeared in thick traffic, driving like a trained pro.

Within minutes, the old taxi showed up and he hopped in the front. Special Agent William Crocker accelerated into traffic and seemed to be running faster than the SUV had.

"Just heard from the source, Tatra. The ship got in early. The Russians are excited. They expect to get a twofer. One, get the device back. Two, kill or capture a big wig with Hezbollah who is the buyer. He was identified as one Abdel Hariri. I personally think it's a cover name. But the guy apparently is a known entity to the Russian because of having killed so many of them in Afghanistan. They want him badly. Will talked to the brass. They want us to capture him and subject him to rendition or, alternatively, kill him. The Prez doesn't like it when the Evil Empire wins. He would be a gold-mine of Hezbollah intel if we had a chance to talk with him for a few months."

"So, the plan is charge in like the cavalry and snatch or shoot him?" MacLachlan asked.

"Yep. He will be in one of two black Mercedes. That fact suggests his power and importance. The Russians think he might have a total of three body-guards, and they are probably mujahidin's in suits. Not trained security men. They should not be a problem."

MacLachlan was not so sure. At Quantico Marine officer training he had been taught how to plan ops. Reacting by charging in like the Seventh Cavalry at the Little Big Horn might lead to the same result as Custer met.

"Do we know who will get there first? A shoot out with the Russians would constitute an international incident and end our careers, if we survived it," MacLachlan said.

"Unknown."

"Remember the good-looking girl sitting across from us at lunch?" MacLachlan asked.

"The blonde in the flowered mini dress, medium red lipstick and same color high heels? Nope, don't remember her," Crocker grinned.

"She may be competition. She just squealed out of the hotel parking lot a minute ahead of you. Drove like a professional. Going same direction we are."

"Maybe part of the Russian contingent," Crocker hypothesized.

"Maybe," MacLachlan said. "Or, maybe Brit, or French, or Israeli. Or, a local undercover," he said.

"I'd have thought we would have caught her by now," he added. Apparently, she was an even better driver than he had originally thought.

As they neared the port, Crocker slowed down. His AK was on the seat between them. It was short. Identical to MacLachlan's. MacLachlan pulled the operating handle and chambered a round. He placed the rifle, muzzle to the floor between his knees.

Crocker slowly made his way along a road between containers to the docks. There was a number of ships docked. They saw tugs nudging one into dock. They could not see the stern, hence the name, but saw several cars and SUVs waiting for the hawsers to be tied. None were double black Mercedes, so Crocker pulled into a good surveillance point between two large parked and unoccupied trucks. They waited.

With obvious contact with someone aboard ship, the two S-Class Mercedes sped in and aimed towards the dock. One slid parallel to the dock. The second one stopped perpendicular to it.

"Okay, William, these guys are a lot more professional that Tatra predicted." MacLachlan said.

Three men bailed out of the first Mercedes. Immediately, they were dropped by a fusillade of shots from the various cars already at the dock.

"Crap. The damn Russians are overacting."

The rear Mercedes, ostensibly with Hariri in it, blasted backwards at top speed. The driver hit the handbrake and spun the wheel, executing an expert 180 degree turn and accelerated away.

Crocker floored the pedal and aimed the old taxi with the new three hundred horsepower engine at a diagonal course to hit the luxury car as it escaped.

MacLachlan snapped his seatbelt closed and held the AK-47 up left-handed so the muzzle pointed away from Crocker's face.

Crocker aimed perfectly hit the speeding Mercedes just behind the driver side rear tire at fifty miles per hour. The Mercedes spun in a full circle and stalled. MacLachlan, stunned, still bailed out and aimed the rifle from behind the car. He knew better than to lay over the hood like on television. That guaranteed return ricochets right into one's face.

Crocker cranked his own stalled vehicle while the Mercedes driver did his. MacLachlan did not know whether the Mercedes had armored glass. Either way, his controlled pair of 7.62x39 shots into the driver's window sent a pink haze from the driver. Dazed bodyguards rolled out. MacLachlan killed the one on the driver side. The two on the other side commenced firing some sort of unidentified submachine guns.

MacLachlan immediately squatted behind a front tire, guarded by it and the engine block against pistol caliber submachine gun bullets. He leaned around the crunched front bumper and fired a full auto burst under the Mercedes. He heard screams as his bullets hit feet and ankles on the other side. Men fell, writhing. He saw a tall man in a white dishdasha or kandoora. He also wore a red and white checkered keffiyeh.

It had to be Hariri. MacLachlan flipped the selector switch on the Kalashnikov back to one shot per trigger pull. He took careful aim, disregarding a flurry of shots coming at him from one bodyguard and the Russians.

He had a good sight picture and pressed the trigger as something hammered his shoulder. He saw Hariri fall as he fell to the dirty pavement of the port himself.

Off in what seemed a cloudy distance, he heard a car start. Then, another.

"C'mon, Mack. Get in the back of the car." The distant voice sounded like Crocker. He complied in a daze, but on his own power.

Eyes beginning to focus, Mack saw a man with a shoulder-fired rocket aim from behind the wrecked Mercedes. With a "whoosh" it fired, and the center Russian car lifted ten feet off the ground. It landed and exploded, throwing other cars and men through the air.

The rocket-wielding bodyguard dropped the launcher, helped the wounded Hariri into the Mercedes and it began to move away.

MacLachlan's right, upper chest was throbbing from where the bullet hit his Kevlar vest instead of killing him instantly. He slammed another magazine into the AK as Crocker started off, the car clearly in trouble from the steam from the engine and the rattling and bumping as it rolled forward.

He said, "Stop a minute, William." When the badly wrecked car stopped, he stepped out and fired a full thirty round magazine at the fleeing Mercedes. There was no return fire from the Russians this time. MacLachlan's first volley laid a straight line of holes across the middle of both facing doors of the black car. His second volley hit the wheels, tires and pavement below, ricocheting up. The car careened, wobbling from side to side as it slowed. A flatbed truck port truck approached. The one unhurt bodyguard stepped out and fired through the driver's windshield. The truck came to rest against the Mercedes front bumper. The Mercedes driver slid out the passenger side and staggered.

MacLachlan's volley had wounded him and possibly Hariri again. The bodyguard helped both into the flatbed. He pushed the dead driver onto the tarmac. MacLachlan laid down a full magazine of shots from the AK, trying to cripple the truck and hit the Hezbollah operatives. It did not work this time. He tossed the rifle back into the taxi's front seat and ran towards them, .45 in his right hand and a seven-round magazine at the ready in his left. The flatbed started off. Not fast. But much faster than MacLachlan could run. He stopped, dropped the extra mag in his pocket and assumed a two-handed isosceles position. He fired one carefully aimed .45 ACP shot each second with no avail at the truck pulling well out of range.

As he stood in the open, helpless, MacLachlan saw the blue Audi SUV accelerate from behind some containers. The truck stopped again. One man exited and aimed a rocket at the approaching SUV.

"No." MacLachlan yelled. He slammed the second mag home in the .45 and elevated the muzzle, trying to judge Tennessee elevation for the extreme pistol distance.

The two passengers were escaping from the SUV. MacLachlan fired at the rocket wielder. Nothing. He lowered and fired again. Nothing. Another shot and the man toppled as he fired the rocket. The truck sped off, leaving him staining the pavement. The SUV reprised the action of the Russian vehicle, rising before it blew. The concussion knocked the running man from the SUV to the ground. The female, still in the flowery mini dress, waved at MacLachlan, then concentrated on getting to her associate and helping him limp off between some containers. The next thing MacLachlan saw was a woman in a mini dress blowing in the wind. She was driving a lift truck towards the port entrance. A man was on the seat beside her.

MacLachlan could not see her smile, but he saw the wave again and returned it. Turning to Crocker, the two put their weapons except for pistols into the bag and walked away from the taxi. From ten feet, Crocker tossed an incendiary grenade into the open window. He said "Walk fast. Real fast. No, run like hell."

Both men took off and were safely out of range before the car blew.

"Wonder if we should do anything about the device on the boat?" Crocker said.

Sirens were loud now as Tanzanian police and fire authorities drew close to their location.

The two Americans drew between some containers as the horde of vehicles raced by, one stopping at the blown SUV, one at the Mercedes, one at the hulk of the taxi and the rest at the dock carnage.

"My guess is that this will become a diplomatic thing, with the Russian Embassy taking the lead on removing the stolen device," MacLachlan said.

Sometimes, logic can be dead wrong.

4

Dar-Es-Salaam, Tanzania, DC, Shenandoah Valley, Virginia

June 1985

WHILE THE EXCITEMENT was occurring at dockside, Hezbollah operatives were moving the device's case, complete with their tracker, and unknown to them, GRU's tracker.

They offloaded it on the water side of the ship to a small boat, thence to a larger one which left the port. It went to a predetermined site and pulled up to another dock. A box truck waited there. It was loaded onto the truck and the three shipboard operatives joined two more as a second vehicle started and the car and truck left Dar-es-Salaam.

Plan B was in effect.

Later that day, the Americans on the ground and in DC considered their actions may have achieved the purposes of preventing Hezbollah from moving the device further, killing Hezbollah operatives, and putting Hariri out of action. They assumed the Russian diplomats would pull out all stops to recover the device from the ship and take possession of it. Perhaps, surviving GRU or KGB agents already had.

Probably no participants except the mysterious female and her male associate knew that the second shooters were Americans. Nonetheless, Grafton ordered Crocker to take a long sabbatical elsewhere until things cooled down. He obtained transportation for MacLachlan back to DC, where he would join him for a serious debriefing at the Situation Room. All told, the players were happy. For now. Except for ten dead men and their families. Men surely to be reported to those families as being killed in a training incident somewhere else.

MacLachlan turned in his arms, radio, and protective equipment to Crocker.

"You know, Mack. You seem to have an affinity for this .45. It's an off-the-books piece. Do you want me to send it to you by courier bag?"

"That would be great. Thank you. It's the 1970 version with some improvements including a better trigger pull. I really appreciate it, William," MacLachlan said.

Knowing they would likely work together soon, the two shook hands and parted.

MacLachlan's flight out of Tanzania was late, so he packed and went down to the café for dinner. He saw the lovely female was there. Her older associate was not. He went to the desk and obtained a piece of paper and pen. Knowing she was some sort of government operative, MacLachlan was not sure of the tradecraft protocol. But, he did exactly what he feared was the wrong thing. He palmed the note and surreptitiously touched the edge of her table, leaving it, while being led to his.

As he was seated, she read "May I buy you dinner in view of your unfortunate vehicle day today? Mack."

She caught his eye and smiled. Again, her super-hero smile was better than his. He'd better work on it, he thought. She nodded and he got up and walked over.

Proffering out his hand, he said "Mack MacLach-lan." She motioned for him to sit across from her.

She offered her hand.

"Yaffa Segal," she said. Both were convinced the other had given a cover name. Both were wrong.

"How is your friend? Was he injured seriously in the accident? I saw he was limping a bit."

"He's a bit stiff now but not a serious injury. Thanks to you. You seem to be just the person to help out at an injury accident. You must have done it before."

"Thank you. Perhaps. I move around a lot, so I encounter a number of types of situations, as I suspect you do," MacLachlan said.

"Quite. Are you here in Dar-es-Salaam long?" she asked.

"No. Unfortunately, I am flying out to DC tonight. I wish I could stay longer."

"Same here," she responded. He wondered if she meant she was flying out too, or wished he was staying longer.

"Where are you based, if I am allowed to ask?" he ventured.

"Tel Aviv," she answered truthfully. "Are you head-quartered in DC?"

"Yes. I am in the military."

"Oh? Which branch?" she asked.

"The Marine Corps. Out of the Pentagon."

"Ah. You don't seem like a desk bound bureaucrat."

He smiled.

"Sometimes, I get lucky and enjoy some physical activity."

"Like today?" she asked.

"Seldom as active as today. But, sometimes."

"Your pistol shooting bought us enough time to keep us alive. To hit a man and drop him with a 1911 from over ninety meters. As I was running, I watched you shoot for range, then drop the shot right down into his chest. Very impressive. Almost unheard of," she said. He smiled.

"I just do threat assessments."

"'Do' is a broad word, Mr. MacLachlan."

"I guess it can cover a lot of territory. It's Major, but please call me Mack."

"And, I am Yaffa."

"A pretty name. What does it mean in Hebrew?" he asked.

She blushed prettily. Something she almost never did.

"Um...It means 'lovely.'"

"Lovely does not begin to describe you, Yaffa. You are far beyond just lovely," he said, meaning every word. He locked his green eyes into her green eyes.

She took his hand in hers.

"Thank you, Mack. That is so sweet.

"I think I will not ask you what you do for a living, Yaffa."

"I think you already know," she said.

"Yes, I think I do. I'm glad we are on the same side."

"Your President Reagan seems to be very pro-Israel," she said.

"Most good Americans are. You are the only democracy in your part of the world. All your neighbors want to kill you. Americans always respect determination and bravery."

"Yes. They are admirable traits," she said.

They ordered dinner and MacLachlan asked her to pick her favorite wine. She chose a Tzora white to go with their seafood entrée. The hotel had it. MacLachlan, largely a red wine aficionado, liked the Tzora. At this point, he realized he would have liked dishwater had Yaffa Segal chosen it.

After dinner, he said he had to pack. She said she needed to check on her associate. They took the elevator to the same floor.

The situation warranted a long kiss and embrace.

"I wish, Mack," she said.

"Me, too. We will meet again," patting her card in his pocket.

"I am quite sure of that," she said. "And, next time, we will spend more time together." She hugged him tightly.

"Yes," He kissed her again and she disappeared into her room.

He walked to his and packed. He regretted going. He knew he was going to have to report dinner with a suspected foreign agent, even one on the US's side.

Perhaps, he could arrange to convince his leadership she might be an asset. Just perhaps.

———————

MACLACHLAN FLEW the first of several legs that night. He got into Dulles late the next day, deciding Tanzania is one of those places 'you can't get to from here'. But it was where he met Yaffa Segal. That made it very special.

He called Grafton's office phone on his card. Crocker answered.

"Special Agent Crocker."

"William, it's Mack. Where's the Head Slick-meister?"

"Winging his way towards you. He gets in early tomorrow morning. He said to tell you about a meeting. Both of you at White House Situation Room. Eleven a.m. tomorrow."

"Hey, William? You did really well at the cluster at the port. I'd partner with you on an op anytime, my friend."

"Thanks, Mack. That means a lot from a guy who can mow down a tango from a hundred yards with a pistol," Crocker said, using the phonetic letter for terrorist in military fashion.

"Even a Texas country boy gets lucky sometimes. Be safe out there. I'm sure I'll see you soon. What's next on your agenda, if you can say on this line?" MacLachlan asked.

"I'm going to go to the hospital and see a Russian friend in person. Or, Dr. Gabone will. By the way, this line sends encrypted. Unless your home phone is bugged, we're okay talking. By the way, our friend is bringing you the 'present.' No courier bag required."

"Thanks for that, William. Good luck today. Will you let me know how your friend is?"

"I will. I'll leave a voicemail in a couple of hours. Maybe in time for you to check before your meeting downtown," Crocker said.

"Roger and out."

"Yup." The connection was closed.

Crocker had already donned his handball friend's white lab coat with the "Dr. Gabone" name tag, a pocket full of pens and a stethoscope to hang around his neck authoritatively. Gabone did not have visiting privileges at the hospital where Tatra was recovering. Crocker figured he could bluff his way in as a privately hired physician. He hoped no GRU goons were guarding Tatra. He would find out in less than half an hour.

He drove to the hospital in a new rental car. The credit card was real, the backup information was all cover material.

He parked in the doctor's area and put a hand-written sign on the dash identifying himself and stating this was a rental, hence no parking sticker.

Crocker walked in, inquired about the Russian's room in Swahili, using the real name of his source, and walked down the hall to it.

There was a big guy in a suit outside. GRU for sure.

Using a local accent, he told the man he needed to check the patient. As he walked in, the guard followed. Crocker turned and waved his index finger side to side, indicating "no." He closed the door in the man's face and stood there for a few seconds making sure it did not open. The door was solid wood. A low conversation should be impossible to hear from outside. In a louder voice, he greeted the GRU agent in the bed by name and introduced himself as Dr. Gabone.

"Tatra, I am Volchitsa," Crocker said softly, using his own code name, which meant 'wolf'.

Tatra looked at the doctor with surprise. Focused and recognized him.

"How are you, my friend?"

"I am fine. I should not even be here. I just have some scrapes and a strained wrist form falling wrong when the rocket hit. I think I am here so Tanzanian authorities can secure me for questioning for fear my Embassy will spirit me away," the Russian said.

"When will you move me to America?" he asked.

"First things first. Where is the device? Did your diplomats freeze the ship and demand it?"

"Ha. The damned Lebanese are smarter than any of us gave credit. They had a team on the ship and offloaded the device to a small boat during all of the shooting and explosions. They still have not found the tracker we planted. It is on the highway heading west now. I am to be moved out today and will resume as the number two agent following. America?"

"It is imperative that you maintain your position and keep us apprised of the location of the device until we can get it and neutralize the Hezbollah team. Then, we will move you to America in a nice house and under Witness Protection. We will show our appreciation for all you have done. I promise you that." Crocker said.

There was a knock at the door and Crocker opened it. It was a legitimate physician from the hospital and two nurses. The GRU agent was behind them.

"I have examined the patient. As far as I am concerned, he is ready to be released," Crocker said with confidence and authority. I will tell the people who hired me that," he added in Swahili.

The hospital threesome nodded, and Crocker walked past them, nodded at the GRU guard and left.

He called MacLachlan. No need for a voice recording. The Marine answered on the first ring.

"Glad I got you. An onboard team of tangos removed the device to a small boat during the shooting. The Russians searched and, of course, got nothing. The tracker is still good. The device is on a highway heading west. The famous Dr. Gabone told the intern to release Tatra today. I am sure my friend's name is well enough known to carry some weight. Either way, Tatra is well enough to leave. We are back in the game."

"Stay on it, William. I will make sure everyone up to the President is aware of your good work. Gotta go. Leave Will or me everything you can," MacLachlan said. He hung up and finished tying the tie on his class A uniform.

He boarded the DC Metro Blue Line at the Pentagon and exited at Farragut West. It was just a short walk to the White House. He showed both his Department of Defense National Capital Region badge and his Marine Corps ID. Being expected, he was escorted into the waiting area outside the Situation Room, offered coffee, which he declined, and seated.

Shortly Grafton came in. MacLachlan expected him to be rumpled and tired from the long series of flights that ended only about an hour before. He was neither. Grafton had a crisp suit, starched white shirt and conservative tie. He did not have his characteristic grin, however.

"I'm guessing from your expression you spoke with Crocker?" MacLachlan asked.

Grafton nodded.

"I'm also guessing just after our briefing here; we will be back on planes across the puddle. The where part is unknown. We will be giving these guys information that is so fresh they don't already have it," the DIA agent said.

They were called in. The main briefing room was full, and the President sat at the end of the table. He smiled and nodded to the two men as his National Security Advisor directed them to chairs side by side and near the President.

The Advisor started the meeting.

"Gentlemen, we have a quick and dirty picture of what happened in Dar-es-Salaam. Why don't you fill us in with the details?"

Grafton began. When they got to the shooting at the port, he deferred to MacLachlan. The Marine reported in a matter of fact manner and played down his role. He reported how well Agent Crocker of the DIA had handled himself and told about stopping the second black Mercedes with Hariri in it and of assisting the Mossad agents with cover fire. As was proper, he addressed all but direct questions from someone else to the President. It was like testifying in court. Always answer the judge. As he talked about the Israelis, he detected a small nod and almost hidden smile of approval from his favorite President ever. Right up there with Teddy Roosevelt.

"Mr. President, and gentlemen," Grafton began.

"We have news that is less than an hour old. This is the first time it has been shared. Special Agent Crocker debriefed the Russian source in the hospital less than an hour ago. An onboard team from Hezbollah offloaded the device during the firefight and it was taken to another destination by small boat. There, it was put on a truck and is westbound in Tanzania right now. The Russian tracker is still operating. We expect updates as frequently as our source gets them."

"Who knows the participation of American agents in this matter?" the President asked.

"I believe only the Mossad, sir," MacLachlan answered. Grafton nodded.

"Well, they won't be sharing. I will make a phone call in my little breakout office here to assure that. You men, including the one who was not here, did another great job and on the spur of the moment. Now, Admiral Howard concurring, it sounds like you better get back on a plane eastbound." Howard agreed, as expected.

"Here is our detailed report, gentlemen. I printed ten copies once I got here, not knowing the number in attendance. Please note it is classified at the very highest levels when handling or transporting it," Grafton said. The two were dismissed.

Outside, Grafton said, "Read and shred before leaving here," to MacLachlan. "You'll like the gunfight stuff, Wild Bill. So, will the guy at the end of the table," Grafton grinned.

"After you read about your gunfighting prowess, we have a problem."

"I was there, I don't need to read this now. What's the problem?" MacLachlan asked.

"There is a big ocean between Africa and us. We

have no idea what port they are heading to: Luanda; Libreville; Accra; Monrovia; or Dakar for several possibilities. Or, they could turn south and go to Cape Town. It's like we have it narrowed down to Boston around to Houston. Where do we go and wait?" Grafton asked.

"The middle?" MacLachlan queried.

"That would probably be Libreville. Sucky airport connections."

"Will, how do you know all this stuff?" MacLachlan asked.

"I've run Africa for five years for DIA."

"Oh. That explains it."

"Damn army and DIA seem to think I like jungles, deserts and anywhere else hot. Only place I've been that isn't is SHAPE in Belgium and maybe somewhere in the USSR one time. Can't remember," he grinned the famous and charismatic grin.

"SHAPE is NATO, right?" MacLachlan asked.

"Yep. Supreme Headquarters Allied Powers Europe. Operational command HQ for NATO. Only pleasant weather and good food place they've sent me," Grafton commented.

"I'm figuring you are around twenty years since Vietnam. You could retire."

"And, do what? This is my thing. I'll wait it out until the right stateside desk job comes along," Grafton admitted.

"So, are we committed to Libreville, wherever that is?" MacLachlan asked.

"Not yet. I'm still thinking. There's a good deli around the corner. Let's eat and ponder some. Anywhere near here will be loaded with spies. Let's eat without discussing anything sensitive and take a walk after. I know a couple places that are hard to do audio surveillance without a truck full of listening gear."

After lunch, they went to the steps of the Jefferson Monument and sat halfway down. After discussing all the options, they decided to have Crocker and another agent follow the lead set by Tatra and would propose an alternative to the group they just left. The alternative was to have the two of them moved to a navy destroyer positioned to intercept the ship with the device. They would lead a boarding party aboard and confiscate the device. Any Hezbollah operatives would be taken into custody for rendition...if they did not resist and die. Getting to a destroyer in mid-ocean might take skipping from ship to ship by helo several times, but it was doable. MacLachlan paged the admiral. The response was to return to the situation room as soon as possible.

"How DID you get the .45 into the White House," MacLachlan asked Grafton. He squeezed the envelope Grafton handed him earlier. He could tell from the weight and hard shape inside it was his .45.

"I'm a Supervisory Special Agent of a federal agency. They know me."

"Here." MacLachlan handed it back. "I'm just a jarhead from the Pentagon. You take it back in again, okay?"

At the reception area outside the Situation Room, the admiral met them and ushered them to a breakout room to hear their plan before the larger group did.

"I think that is a logical approach. You have my support. It's hard to predict how this group will respond to things, but you guys seem to be in pretty good favor. Mack, the President brought up something about you the rest of us had not thought about," Admiral Howard said.

With more than a little trepidation and curiosity, MacLachlan asked what it was.

"He noted that you are an active duty military officer going armed into foreign countries and engaging in gunfights. He wondered if such a situation could constitute an act of war."

MacLachlan saw Grafton considering, then frown. They now knew one another well enough to know Grafton thought it might be plausible.

"I have a solution. I ran it past the Secretary of Defense and the DNI in the hall. Both said to do it, if you concurred."

MacLachlan nodded for him to proceed, not having a clue where the conversation was going.

"I propose to change your status from Active Duty to Reserve Officer. A promotion to Lt. Colonel comes with it. As a civilian, the DNI will insure you are cleared as a security contractor with all US civilian and military intelligence agencies. You will keep your clearances, subject to normal five-year recertifications. I am thinking that, in view of your being a lead on the boarding party you will need arrest powers. As an intelligence agent, SSA Grafton does not have them. I can make a call to the Marshals Service and have you deputized as a Special Deputy US Marshal with badge and warrant of authority. I had to do it once before and it worked well in the trial that followed."

"Sir, this is all more important than me. But I do

have a housekeeping question. How will I get paid?" MacLachlan asked.

"Ha-ha. Not to worry. The DIA just hired you at a monthly stipend equal to a colonel's pay. It will go through the end of the year and can be extended if this mess is not resolved by then. Keep your pager to me. Think of Grafton here as your direct report and me as the next step up. How does that all sound?"

"Fine, sir. I will start thinking of gigs for the coming year."

"I suspect you will have so many, you can cherry pick," the admiral promised.

"I sure hope so," MacLachlan thought, but said nothing.

"That badge will allow you to carry a weapon anywhere," Grafton noted. "Something most intel officers cannot do stateside. It might prove real handy."

They walked into the Situation Room and were shortly joined by the same group as before, including the President.

Admiral Howard presented the alternative plan and said he would take care of the Navy transportation end and the boarding party. He told the President about MacLachlan's promotion and change in status to civilian. He also mentioned the deputation. The President's face lit up.

"I will take care of that myself," he said. "Stay after, Colonel MacLachlan. I will have the badge and ID sent over and swear you in. I believe I have the authority." The room laughed quietly and the President beamed.

Two hours later, there was an agreed-upon plan, and a new Special Deputy US Marshal leaving the

White House with his friend and direct report from the DIA.

MacLachlan had an 8x10 color photo of the swearing in to put with the similar one of the CMH presentation in a drawer at home. Wherever home was. With luck, he might have some time under this contract to finish the cabin on Cedar Creek. But that would be a getaway, not really home. Ultimately, Casey Key in Florida would be his home. Perhaps sooner than later, as a recent letter from his great uncle said he was likely nursing home bound before the end of the year. As the only kin other than MacLachlan's parents on the ranch in Texas, he would be the one to facilitate the move and prepare to take over his grandfather's home. If he could get through this mission alive, maybe the switch to reserve status and being a contractor would give him some breathing room.

Since nobody said otherwise, MacLachlan decided to try to stay in his Bachelor Officer's Quarters, or BOQ, until the end of the month. He chuckled to himself. Lt. Colonel in his twenties. Unheard of, he thought.

He walked over to a police supply shop and purchased a round badge holder with both a belt clip and a chain lanyard for suspending it around one's neck. He added two belt clip magazine holders. Since they also sold firearms and ammunition, he picked up several boxes of 230 grain hollow points in .45 ACP. MacLachlan's last stop was at an upscale department store to buy three work suits, a blue blazer, both grey and tan slacks, five Oxford cloth button-down dress shirts, loafers and five conservative ties. He would get some Brooks Brothers suits later. He needed some travel suits now.

His pager buzzed. He had a message from Grafton to meet him at Washington National Airport and bring a week's clothes and gear. MacLachlan knew this was related to deploying on a naval vessel. He included Marine fatigues, cap and boots. At the airport, he met Grafton. Grafton gave him a one-way ticket to Norfolk and said he was on the same flight. They separated. This was MacLachlan's first time flying armed. He showed his badge and credentials at the counter. The Continental agent called for an airport police officer, showed her the ID and she walked MacLachlan through to the gate. It was instructive for him. He learned if he was travelling undercover or even just low-key, he should check his gun with a bag and avoid the notice of an escort. MacLachlan suspected if this terrorism thing heated up, such travel would become more difficult.

He carried the loaded .45, holster and magazines and badge in his briefcase so he could sit with his coat off. The flight to Norfolk was less than an hour.

Grafton and MacLachlan met at baggage claim. A Navy non-com in uniform stood with a sign for Grafton/MacLachlan. They showed him ID and the three left immediately.

They were welcomed aboard a carrier getting ready to leave port. The Executive Officer gave them a route and connections via helicopters to various ships. The final one would be the destroyer intercepting the freighter with the device aboard. None of the interim crews were briefed. The destroyer captain and his immediate staff had. They knew they were intercepting a US-bound foreign ship with a nuclear device. This was an act of war and the captain had a great deal of discretion, based on intel provided by MacLachlan's boarding party.

It took less than a day, hopping from ship to helo to ship to reach the appointed destroyer. MacLachlan and Grafton met with the captain, his senior staff and the Marine officer who commanded the destroyer's Marine Expeditionary Unit. He would provide the boarding party members and a captain to back up MacLachlan's leadership.

MacLachlan was recognized as both a Lt. Colonel in the Marine Reserves and Deputy US Marshal with full arrest powers. It had been made clear to the destroyer leadership Grafton and MacLachlan had been sent by the President and National Security Staff.

The ship was a Kidd Class guided missile destroyer, five hundred sixty-three feet in length and capable of almost forty miles per hour.

The interception was planned for 0900 the following day in international waters one hundred miles off Cuba.

Grafton and MacLachlan ate in the officer's mess and turned in early. MacLachlan secured web gear from the Marine captain for his .45. He planned to wear tan slacks with his combat boots, a tan shirt and blue windbreaker and ball cap with no indicia. He would suspend the Deputy US Marshal's badge around his neck in plain sight. From the Situation Room, he was told to start off playing hardball. The two intelligence officers and the destroyer's captain knew they had authority to sink the freighter if it was deemed absolutely necessary to keep the device off the US mainland.

BOTH INTELLIGENCE OFFICERS were up for breakfast by 0630. MacLachlan met the boarding party for a quick physical training or PT session before returning to shower and dress for the op. He and Grafton reviewed their strategy with the ship's Executive Officer, or XO, and the MEU commander and captain assigned to the boarding party. The XO advised satellite surveillance showed the freighter was ten miles out. At current cruise, they should be within sight soon. This was the most serious set of decisions any of them had, or ever would face. To arrest a foreign crew in international waters and put a navy crew about to bring the ship in...or to sink a four hundred foot freighter at sea in the worst case scenario had immediate international repercussions.

The MEU boarding team leader assembled his men in partial battle gear with rifles and life jackets over their vests.

As they stood waiting by the several diesel-powered rigid hull inflatables still on their davits, the klaxon blew. "Battle Stations. Battle Stations. Missiles detected, possibly incoming. Battle Stations."

The Marine captain ushered them to a position behind a bulkhead. They could see sailors in helmets and life jackets manning cannons and preparing to reload launchers if necessary. They saw two flashes and several seconds later, heard two "thumps."

The XO's radio squawked. "The target freighter has

just been hit by two missiles. They have to have been launched by a submarine. It is too far away to determine nationality by signature.

"You can bet it's Russian," Grafton said. "I need to get to a secure line to the White House Situation Room now."

He and MacLachlan rushed behind the XO, who was heading back to the bridge to assist the captain. At the secure communications room, Grafton gave a written instruction to the watch and said, "Get these folks on the line, please."

Seconds later he was reporting what had just happened. MacLachlan hurried back in from the bridge and reported the destroyer was steaming full speed to effect a rescue operations. This was reinforced by the next announcement over the loudspeaker. Battle stations was still in effect until the captain was comfortable no threats existed.

"I'm going to the main deck to supervise the rescue efforts. We will have Corpsmen and a triage set up where we bring survivors aboard. I take it there might be certain people you would like segregated to interview?"

"Yes, sir," Grafton said. "It will be tough to pick them out by appearance, so we might need to do some brief interviews of all who are able to talk to narrow potential Hezbollah extremists down a bit."

"We'd like the boarding party to be with us in case some bad guys act up," MacLachlan added. The XO spoke briefly into his radio.

"You've got them," he said as they followed him down the steps, known as "ladder wells" to the deck where the most action was going to happen.

The Marine captain with the boarding party was already on deck when the three men arrived. MacLachlan took him aside and explained who they were looking for as to ethnicity and language.

"Captain, I see your Marines have zip ties, or flexi-cuffs. Do you have more? The standard five or ten per man may not be sufficient," MacLachlan said. The captain sent a lance corporal off to obtain more from the armory.

They could feel the big ship slowing. The freighter was burning. When they were a mile away, they heard a rending of steel and the ship broke in half. The bow and stern halves both had men aboard. The men slid off as the two halves reared into the air and sank quickly into the deep water. Most of the survivors in the water were treading water without life jackets.

Every small boat on the destroyer was launched. Radiation detection was deployed in case tactical nuclear missiles were used, but that did not appear to be the case.

Navy rescue boats quickly approached men signaling in the water. They were pulled aboard until the small boat was filled to capacity. It then returned, off-loaded onto the destroyer and sped back to the scene for more survivors.

One survivor was screaming in German. MacLachlan understood him and directed a Marine to take him aside and he would help with a written signed statement in German and translated. The man was remonstrating about seeing two rockets coming towards them from the opposite side from the Navy vessel. MacLachlan knew that an eyewitness account would be helpful for the expected partisan Congressmen and conspiracy theorists who would claim the Navy sunk the freighter. He asked the captain to have his men seek out eyewitnesses and take exact reports for the inquiry that was sure to follow.

The captain of the freighter did not believe in going down with his ship. He also saw the rockets coming from the opposite direction of the navy ship and stated it clearly. He also claimed he was unaware of why a submarine would sink his ship. When asked about the device, he pled total ignorance. Neither MacLachlan nor Grafton were sure about that. They knew he was aware delivering a nuclear device to be set off in the US was an act of war, of terrorism and a criminal act. All were punishable in ways he did not want to experience. The two intelligence officers knew the best the FBI had would question him until convinced they had the truth. Or, he would find himself renditioned off to an unofficial prison outside the US for intensive questioning until it was decided to let him go. MacLachlan and Grafton took a quiet moment to speculate about that during the hubbub of the rescue efforts. They agreed *who* took custody of the captain at the dock would quietly determine whether rendition would be involved.

After a long day, the captain of the freighter reckoned he had lost ten men, had another five unaccounted for, and the rest were in varying conditions being treated or fed by the United States Navy. All ambulatory survivors, including the freighter's officers, were sequestered in a gym under Marine guard. Several were in the ship's infirmary, where several Marine guards stood by. Two men were in the brig and had been preliminarily questioned by Grafton and MacLachlan, who were "good cop" and "bad cop" respectively. These were surely Hezbollah. After an hour of intense verbal-only questioning, one admitted to being Hezbollah and said the device was stored with freight and had gone down with the ship.

The destroyer's captain sent the exact position where the freighter sank to his command. He was directed to return to Norfolk, Virginia. The captain advised the two intelligence officers he was sure deep-sea submersibles would be deployed to attempt to find the nuclear device or establish it had been destroyed. He said, based on mission, he would be reporting that the freighter was sunk by an unknown submarine firing two missiles. While, based on the mission, he would think the submarine was likely Russian, it was far enough away that positive identification was not possible. He noted reports such as the one he was going to write were based on facts, not hypothesis. That sort of thing would come out in an investigatory commission, if held, he added.

The two intelligence operatives waited in line to make their secure report to Admiral Howard. They advised they were headed to Norfolk, not Mayport, Florida, which was another likely destination, and would dock mid-morning tomorrow.

5

Norfolk, Shenandoah Valley, Virginia, Afghanistan

June 1985

THE DESTROYER DOCKED AT NORFOLK. Grafton and MacLachlan were first ashore. They escorted the two Hezbollah terrorists. The answer as to whom would pick them up was quickly answered. Four hard men in a dark Suburban took custody. They were not FBI, which was also there to question the captain and the first mate of the freighter and those of his crew not being transferred to Norfolk General Hospital. The Bureau would have agents standing by there to interview all crewmen as their conditions permitted.

Grafton, more familiar with transfers like they had with the terrorists, handled the identification and pass off to the men in dark sunglasses. MacLachlan stood by and observed, learning. The exchange took less than three minutes and the Suburban was gone. A US

Marshal's bus for the crew was strategically positioned to block the exchange from media. The media was cordoned by Shore Patrol officers.

The two intelligence officers speculated whether they would have to appear before a commission on the sinking of the freighter and decided probably not. They were right.

"Looks like our job is done for a while," Grafton observed.

"If it's okay with you, I have to get busy on a place to live on a rural creek near Front Royal. So, I'd like to head that way."

"Keep your pager handy for the admiral and me. Until this is over, it looks like he's my boss, too," Grafton responded. "Is there any telephone coverage available to put on your acreage?" he asked.

"No, it's miles from landline phone wires. Even those new brick-like cell phones would not work there."

"There is a satellite phone system, but it's heavy and may be too expensive for your use. I'll check into it, but I think it may not fly," Grafton said.

"At the very least, Will, I will head back to civilization and call you daily to check in. For emergencies, just use the pager.

"Sounds like a plan, Mack. I guess we didn't have to threaten to have our Navy sink that ship. The Russians, I suspect, did it for us."

"Probably just as well," MacLachlan said. "This time we pretty much know where the device is and it's out of everybody's reach. Maybe even ours. Even if we get a deep-water submersible down, there is no guarantee they will find it. Relative to half a ship, it is pretty small. And, we don't know the condition of the wreckage down there. Is it possible to enter and search it? My vote would be to mine it, get back on the dive ship, back off and blow the wreckage."

Grafton nodded thoughtfully.

"Let's see if we can scare up a military hop to Northern Virginia," he said.

Securing the arrangements took longer than the two-hundred-mile flight. They arrived at Bolling Air Force Base by lunchtime. Grafton went over to the DIA Headquarters and MacLachlan hitched a ride to his quarters, packed and headed the F-250 southwest towards Front Royal, still a bit uneasy over not having a real job after December 31st.

He checked into the Wayside Inn and ran for an hour before showering for dinner. It was one of the few places he knew where quail was on the menu. His grandfather had called Bob White quail, 'Marse Robert', and given it the same respect as the historical figure of the same appellation. Though it the South, he told his young shadow, quail are just called 'birds'. If one had a 'bird gun' it was a shotgun for hunting quail. Young Mack never quite figured out what the other avian beasts were, if only quail were birds. When he asked his grandfather, the learned man replied, "Don't worry about it, Sonny. The other ones don't count anyway." Later in life, he learned that birdwatchers, duck hunters and many other would differ with his grandfather. But, even as an adult, he would stick by the old man.

After dinner, he went back to his room and called his answering machine at the BOQ. He had a message from the trust officer who handled his grand-father's trust. The man, John Bonney, said it was urgent and left his home number. MacLachlan called it.

A woman answered and MacLachlan identified himself. She said she would get her husband, who was out in the yard.

A moment later, John Bonney answered.

"Mack? How are you?"

"Fine, sir. And, you?"

"I'm okay, but I am afraid I have some bad news. Your great uncle Willard passed away this morning. He had called the rescue squad. They took him to Sarasota Memorial, and he died there of heart failure an hour later. I am very sorry for your loss."

"Thank you. Can you guide me with steps I need to take?"

"There really are none. I have his will. He left his personal possessions to you. I suspect they are minimal. He wished to be cremated and buried back in Texas at the family plot. I understand there is ample space to put him without purchasing more. I had him moved to a mortuary and authorized cremation as trustee. I can send his remains to Texas or you can take them if you plan on going to the funeral."

"As you know, Mr. Bonney, my great uncle and I were not close. He was about as different from my grandfather as two brothers could be. I will take him to Texas and have my mother begin to plan his funeral. He was her uncle, though, again, not close at all. Is there insurance or something to cover the costs?" MacLachlan asked.

"No insurance. But there is a provision in the section of your grandfather's trust that cared for your great uncle. Have your mother plan whatever she wants and call me for a check. No need to go to Florida to pick up ashes. I will express them to the ranch."

There are some things that change about the trust. They all affect you. First, the provision about the trustee. Your grandfather provided that the bank be trustee until you turned thirty or until you were twenty-five and your uncle passed. He did not want you to have to take care of his somewhat errant brother. The second option has been satisfied and you are now trustee. I will have checks for the trust printed and send them and a copy of the trust to you wherever you want. We are still the investment arm, as long as you wish and I am here to guide or advise you whenever you wish. We can continue with paying bills for the property in Florida and whatever items like that you need handled."

"Mr. Bonney, what is the balance of the trust?" MacLachlan asked.

"Well, let me do some addition quickly. You see, your great uncle's car portion moves over to you after his final expenses are paid."

The trust officer estimated final expenses and added the two portions. The amount astounded MacLachlan.

"But how about my mother?" he asked.

"She and your father got the deed to the ranch your grandfather established and which they have been running since you were a boy. I suspect its value equals or exceeds your trust inheritance."

"My grandfather was quite a man," MacLachlan said, filling up and trying to hide it with a cough.

"That he was. I was proud to count him a friend first and client second," Bonney said.

"I will probably be at the ranch for a week starting

tomorrow. Can you get the trust package and checks there in that time?"

"Yes, Mack. Or maybe I should call you Major," Bonney said.

"Mack is fine, sir. But, it's Colonel now, just for informational purposes.

"Congratulations. That is wonderful at such a young age. What command comes with it?"

"It is. No command comes with it. I have been switched to reserve officer and will work as a contractor for the government. Exciting, but a bit daunting as to how it will work out and where my next dollar will come from. But I guess this conversation allays those concerns."

"It should. Plus, I am confident you will succeed contracting for the government. I have watched you develop since you were a boy. Your folks and particularly my friend did a darn good job rearing you right. You are the only person I ever met with a Congressional Medal of Honor."

"Thank you, sir. The medal should have gone to the ones who were murdered. I have done everything I could to make their killers pay. And, I will continue to. Terrorism is the methodology of cowards. Soldiers fight soldiers. Terrorists fight innocents. They deserve no quarter," MacLachlan said.

"I agree, Colonel. And, I know your grandfather would have also. Well, I am going to head in to do some work at home. I am sorry for your loss and stand ready to help however you need."

"Thank you, Mr. Bonney. Have a good evening." MacLachlan hung up.

To say he and his great uncle were not close was an understatement. MacLachlan had been raised to believe everyone who could should be a net positive during his time on earth. Great Uncle Willard was a net negative lifelong. A drinker and gambler, he was always in trouble and getting bailed out by his hardworking brother. His lack of mobility in old age was at least partially due to the application of a baseball bat to his joints by collectors for his bookie years before. Even as a ninety-year-old, he still bet the horses, dogs and anything else he could, though his funds were restricted by the trustee of the trust. He was irascible, foul-mouthed and generally a pain. It saddened MacLachlan that he and his mother were the last people left associated with his grandfather. He would do the right thing by his great uncle, but not weep at his funeral.

He called his mother and gave her the news about her uncle. She was more interested in her son's rare visit. She agreed to plan a simple graveside service. Nobody in Texas was still alive who know her uncle other than her. He had left for Vegas and Atlantic City when she was a teenager and only returned to ask her father for money until Big Jim moved to Florida. After that, she was unsure what their relationship was.

His grandfather had hired a handsome, tall Texas cowboy named Alexander MacLachlan. He had stood by the rancher during some rough times with rustlers. Shooting was involved. MacLachlan quickly proved his worth and became foreman. As was inevitable, he fell in love with the rancher's daughter and they wed with the rancher's blessing. Then, they gave him what he wanted most of all. A little grandson to shadow every step, to learn, and to be a little version of Big Jim Walters.

The little boy had his mother's looks, his father's lean rider's physique and his maternal grandfather's height.

His maternal grandparents vacationed in Florida before he was born. Big Jim and his wife loved it. He was wealthy enough by forty-five to turn the ranch over to his son-in-law and daughter and retire. Big Jim bought land stretching from the bay to the Gulf on then rural and inexpensive Casey Key. Casey Key was a barrier island south of Sarasota in West Central Florida. He built a cedar "cracker house" on it and spent the rest of his days adoring his wife and being the moon and stars to the little boy who followed his every step, summers and holidays.

The boy, named James for his grandfather and Edward for his father, was a high school rodeo star, but went back East for college. Then, into the Marine Corps as an officer. And, now, it looked like he was embarking on the next phase of his life.

———

AFTER LEAVING word for the admiral and Grafton about where he was going, MacLachlan bought tickets on an early morning flight to El Paso, connecting through Dallas.

Both parents were in the truck at the airport. He felt like a prodigal son. The truck cab provided as much privacy as anywhere, so he told his parents as much as he could about his activities. MacLachlan used terms like a "bit of a firefight" to describe the bar and the port incidents. His father, having stood shoulder to shoulder with Big Jim in several gunfights with modern day rustlers, knew what he was leaving out. His mother was impassive. He was not sure about her thoughts.

"Okay, boys. Enough of this shoot 'em up stuff. Mack, have you met any interesting young women?" Cindy MacLachlan asked.

"I did meet one, mom. I have to tread gently though, because she is a foreign intelligence officer. She is cultured, beautiful and dangerous as can be."

"But, son, is she blonde and lovely like your mom?" Ed MacLachlan asked.

"She is blonde. I'd say she is almost as lovely, but not quite," he replied.

"There you have proof, Ed. The benefits of raising a boy right. He knows what to say and says it with conviction." she said.

Ed MacLachlan just shook his head, then asked:

"Did you bring the medal son. I feel awful we couldn't come see you get it. But it was roundup and shots and branding time."

"I know, dad. I did. I really did not have anywhere to leave it. It looks like I will call a yet-to-be built cabin in Virginia and grandpa's house in Florida home. Then, I can have a safe to put it in," he replied.

"That means you have three homes," his mother reminded him.

They arrived at the ranch and he went to his room to unpack his carry-on with the medal, the .45, the badge and a few clothes. He had jeans, boots, a Stetson and shirts there. He put on Western attire, which was in Marine parlance "uniform of the day" at the ranch and walked out to find his father checking horses.

"Son, you soft pedaled with your mom. I'm glad. But for my ears only, have you had to kill anybody?" Ed asked.

"Yessir. I have."

"How many?"

"Mebbe eleven. Hard to tell at one firefight. People were falling and there were several different entities shooting at the same time."

"That's a lot, son. Do you need to talk with Reverend Martin about it?"

"I don't think so. Everybody I shot was shooting at me. It was justified. I have not lost any sleep."

"There's a danger, son. A danger you may evolve to be someone different than who we raised."

"It's already happening, dad. I am dealing with people who want to harm America. Large numbers of Americans. These are not people we can deal with using our legal system. They are fighting a war and trying to bring it here. A small group of us have to kill them first, dad. We have to question them and get answers any way we need to. They don't follow rules. If we are going to win against them, we can't either."

Ed MacLachlan knew his son was right. But he saw a hard edge that was not there before. It scared him.

Picking up on his father's expression, MacLachlan continued.

"Dad, let me draw an analogy, based on a term I'm starting to hear. Think of our citizens as sheep. Clustered in different herds around the country. Think of the terrorists of all stripes as wolves. A small group of us are the sheepdogs. We protect the flocks. We do it however we can. But there are two key things. We are dedicated to doing it and we are the good guys. Like every conflict in history, it comes down to good versus evil."

The father considered that, patted his son on the shoulder and they walked into the ranch house for dinner. As almost always on a cattle ranch, it was beef. Really good beef.

After dinner, MacLachlan said he could use some shooting practice. His father went for a couple of lever action rifles and his revolver. MacLachlan got his .45.

They walked to their old makeshift range a hundred yards behind the main barn.

MacLachlan picked up a fifty-five-gallon drum lid along the way. His father carried a variety of cans for targets.

MacLachlan walked about a hundred yards out from their shooting point while his father set up cans. He propped the lid up against a large rock.

Once back at the firing line, they shot at the cans, using rifles for the farthest ones.

Remembering the port, when Yaffa's life was at stake, MacLachlan aimed a bit above the top edge of the hundred-yard lid. Holding in his usual isosceles position, he fired five rounds with the .45. The lid rang like a gong each time.

"Damn, boy. That's a hundred yards. When would you ever have to do that in your duties?"

"Last week, dad," he answered.

"How did that work for you?"

"Better than it did for the terrorist I was shooting at.

And, it helped out that girl I was telling you and mom about."

"She was there? In a gunfight?"

MacLachlan nodded once, not answering further.

"She must be something," Ed MacLachlan said.

"Yessir. She is."

The next day, MacLachlan did the run into town to check the post office box for the ranch. Nothing from the trust officer Bonney. The following day, UPS delivered packages from a mortuary and a trust bank in Florida. Willard Walters arrived in time for his burial.

The graveside services were brief. Reverend Martin had known Willard for years and was aware of his shortcomings. He kept the service short and more about hope and the hereafter than the man being buried.

The minister had a commitment after the service. Due to the deceased's age and how long he had been gone from Texas, only the three MacLachlan's returned to the ranch afterwards.

"Sad to be buried without anybody but three family members present," Cindy MacLachlan commented. Both husband and son nodded their agreement but did not comment.

MacLachlan retired early. He wanted to study the trust document and see what his rights and authorities were. There being no other beneficiaries should he die, except for his parents, there was virtually no liability to him. He knew now that he could build a modest cabin on Cedar Creek and repair the house on Casey Key. There was already a husband and wife team who did yardwork, minor repairs and cleaning. He would retain them. A phone call should to the man should tell what further repairs should be performed.

For the next five days, MacLachlan rode, enjoyed his folks and visited places he enjoyed as a teen. One was a drive-in restaurant. It still had the best chocolate shakes anywhere.

"Dad, there are some bears around where the cabin is going. You know that short barrel .30-30 carbine you got me when I was twelve? It's youth model, but a really handy truck size."

"It's in the rack, son. Take it back with you if you need it. Lord knows, we have plenty more if the Martians attack the ranch."

They got it and an airport-certified hard carry case for it. MacLachlan took it with him when he left for the trip to Florida the following day.

———————

THE RIFLE and his luggage made it through Dallas and on to Tampa. MacLachlan rented a compact sedan for the trip down past Sarasota to Casey Key.

Seeing his grandparent's home, the site of so many wonderful experiences shot a pang through him. While Chuck and Gloria Meadows always took good care of the house and property, first for his grandparents as they aged, and then Willard, it just did not look the same. Willard was so immobile even before being wheelchair bound and having a visiting nurse every day, it just was not lived in. He entered the alarm—his birthday since installed—and went in. It had a musty smell, though it was clean and neat.

MacLachlan called the Meadows and got Gloria on the phone.

"Hi, Gloria. It's Mack MacLachlan. How are you?"

"Mack. I'm fine. Where are you?"

"At Casey Key. I'm just back from Texas and Willard's funeral. Are you and Chuck up for still maintaining the place? I'd sure like it."

"We were wondering and hoping for that, Mack. That place has been a couple days a week on our schedule for the past thirty-five years."

"Well, let's plan on another thirty-five, Gloria," he said.

"We'll try, son, but that would make me ninety-seven and Chuck, oh, about a hundred and one."

He laughed, "So, what's your point?"

She shared the laughter, "Oh, nothing. Just sayin'."

"What are y'all's days now?" he asked.

"I clean on Thursdays and the following Monday. Chuck does the mowing and trimming as needed. Same for repairs."

"And, you still get paid monthly by the bank trust department?" he asked.

"We do. That works, though every two weeks would sure help."

"We'll change it to that immediately, Gloria," he said. "I will be here for a while. It will be great seeing both of you."

"You, too. We think of you as the nephew we never had. See you later this week."

MacLachlan went to the master bedroom. Luckily, Willard moved in before his brother passed away and took the second of three bedrooms. He stayed there after Big Jim died.

The bed was a double. MacLachlan wondered how his grandparents were able to sleep in such a small bed, especially since his grandfather was "Big Jim" for a reason. He was six foot three and two hundred forty pounds of muscle. He was intimidating to everyone except family, especially not to his only grandson.

Since the bed was not antique, he would have Chuck help him move it to the room Willard used and purchase a king bed replacement. Since the house was built before air conditioning, it had excellent cross ventilation. MacLachlan opened the windows without alarm contacts to air it out and turned on the ceiling fans.

MacLachlan unlocked the garage. His grandfather's pride and joy was there. It was a perfect condition 1964 Jaguar XKE, made when Mack was a toddler. It only had eight thousand miles on it. He was aware of the car's shortcomings, from riding with his grandfather and later driving it with him as passenger. It was sexy and fast. But it could not be taken farther than a reasonable tow from a good Jaguar mechanic with immediate access to lots of parts. MacLachlan determined he would get it running this week. At least enough to drive to a mechanic for a full checkup. He loved the classic aspect, but wondered what performance V8, transmission and electrical system could be installed to improve dependability. In the meantime, he would look for an inexpensive Florida car to replace the rental.

The replacement car was in the drive before the week ended. He bought a black Jeep Wrangler hardtop. It was simple. The only option was the hardtop. Otherwise, it was a stick, and a six cylinder instead of the standard four. He might add larger tires and better off-road lighting later, but for now, stock was good enough.

By Friday, the house was cleaned, yard mowed, and refrigerator stocked. MacLachlan left the house in gym shorts, running shoes, Ray Ban Aviators, and a Marine eight-point utility cover or cap. He crossed the road separating his property and went down to the beach. He turned left and began running. Halfway into his planned run, he reversed and headed back. An hour from the beginning, he crossed the road again, showered under the outside shower by the garage and went in for lunch.

He wondered if Grafton was in DC or back in Berlin. MacLachlan blipped him on the pager and Grafton called a few minutes later.

"Slickmeister." came his friend's greeting.

"Hi, Will. Which side of the pond are you on?"

"I'm not in DC," was the response, signaling he was somewhere he did not want to disclose on an open phone line.

"Anything going on you can share?"

"Eerily quiet, Mack. Think our competitors are regrouping. Probably looking for a new product line. I'll let you know when we get a hint. Are you building that cabin or still in Texas?"

"I am in Florida. Had to do some things relative to the house down here. I will probably stay until you call me and say otherwise, okay?" MacLachlan said.

"Not going to build the cabin on the creek?"

"I have to do some planning. A dual-wheel flatbed can cross the ford. But I don't want a lot of heavy traffic to mess up the trail in. I'm thinking the best plan will be to find a kit cabin and have a construction company bring it in and run the wiring and pipes. For now, the only option is generator and a windmill," he said.

"Don't go falling off any ladders or anything. Might need you with little notice."

"Roger that. I will do my best to stay in fighting shape. I just ran for an hour."

"Good, Mack. I suspect we will be seeing each other soon. Stay safe."

"I'm on an island in Florida. All I have to fear is hummingbird-sized mosquitos. You be safe, my friend."

ABDEL HARIRI *still had his left arm in a cast from where the American shot him. A fragment from the shots when the Mercedes stopped during the getaway had been removed from his side. That ached, too. May Allah curse the tall American. He was worse than the Russians Hariri fought in Afghanistan.*

He was back in that mountainous country, meeting in a safe house in the Nangahar Province. The village was twenty miles from Jalalabad.

Hariri met with the tall young sheik from Saudi Arabia and two senior leaders from his Hezbollah. The sheik, a title of respect more than royalty, was an engineer by education. So was Hariri.

After the requisite religious affirmations and tea, the four men got down to business.

"Brother Hariri, you have done everything possible to deliver a nuclear device to both Paris and an undetermined location in America. It seems too many people are sensitive to the movement of stolen Russian nuclear warheads, including the Russians. I have an idea to share for your consideration," the six-foot five bearded man said.

"I look forward to your idea," Hariri said.

"It is an attack that does not require taking any

device into America, only you and the knowledge we can insure you have. I propose you bring down the power grid in a large part of the southeastern United States. They will panic. There will be darkness, crime, no alarm protection for banks, no traffic lights, airport landing controls, food will spoil. And, the government will fail its people," the man known as the Sheik said.

Abdel Hariri thought for a moment. It was brilliant. I would cause widespread crime; the citizens would blame the government for not helping them.

He spoke, "There are many benefits to this idea. I suspect the power companies have minimal security. And, for us, since there will be no immediate radio or television to identify us, we will have time to escape to the Middle East to thank Allah and celebrate."

"Do you like this idea?" the tall Saudi asked the two Lebanese. Both nodded vigorously.

The leader withdrew a thick envelope from his brief-case and handed it to Hariri.

"This has one hundred thousand dollars to finance the mission. If you need more money, it can be delivered to you by hawala. It has false credentials for you to use in Florida. If we had more time, I would recommend you supplement your engineering education with university courses on power transmission. The package contains detailed diagrams and commentary on main grid controls and the different SCADA or Supervisory Control and Data Acquisition systems. Your target will be in Miami. Simply constructed explosive devices will be sufficient. It is basically enter, plant device and get out," he said. "The last bit of information is the name and contact for a Hezbollah deep cover agent who is on the weekend cleaning staff at the facility. He will be your

contact there and will let you in and take you to the main SCADAs."

"Thank you, Sheik. I will leave immediately and make plans from my base. I have a bombmaker in America who is better than I. He is devout and I trust him. I used him in Africa a number of times and once in Palestine. How will I stay in touch with you?" Hariri asked.

"Because I move around so much, I am trying this satellite telephone." He took it out of his bag and sat it on the table next to the Browning automatic already there.

"I will give you the number to memorize. Then, chew and swallow the small bit of paper it is written upon. The other way is surer but takes longer. Call the number on this fake business card. It is always monitored. Identify yourself and say you have an urgent message for the Sheik. It will be delivered to me in person, no matter where I am. But know this: it may take days."

"I will go now. I bid you Allah's protection. I will communicate a schedule when I have one. It may take longer than usual. I have to heal where that Marine shot me twice. And, I will move carefully. I do not wish a third failure."

The tall man with the dark beard nodded gravely and raised his hand as a cleric would. The two Hezbollah leaders nodded and said nothing.

Hariri got in the ubiquitous Toyota Hi-Lux truck. His driver already had the engine running. There were two guards standing in back. Both held AK's. They leaned against a rack. Once the truck flew along the rocky road, they would sling the rifles and hold on for their very lives.

His driver was scary looking but an excellent driver. Both characteristics had held Hariri in good stead over the years. He protected the man from operations. He was too valuable in Lebanon, Saudi Arabia, Pakistan and Afghanistan to risk a bullet elsewhere. As his driver and guards had in Dar-es-Salaam. Damn that MacLachlan's eyes. His intelligence identified the Marine from Czechoslovakia. Luckily Hariri delegated that operation to the man using the name Khan and had chosen to be the control.

It was all he could do to get out alive. More than Kahn and the Chechen were able to do. He was unsure whether MacLachlan killed both men or an alleged woman had. A prostitute. A typical uncovered Western woman with no religion and no morals. MacLachlan would pay. Hariri pledged that to Allah. The woman who had killed Khan and the Chechen? He would like to have her raped by all of his men then stoned. But, unlike the Marine, he had to identify and isolate her first.

The objective that overrode all was taking down the power grid. As he bounced along towards Jalalabad, he ticked off the impacts of the grid going down. He did not yet know how many people in populous Florida were within that grid but knew it would be a lot. Traffic signals, police and fire radios, alarms, hospital equipment, manufacturing equipment, air conditioning, gasoline pumps, elevators, electric buses and trains, street lamps, house power, air traffic control. He tired of enumerating; the list was so long. And, so impactful. Americans in Florida would panic. Some would move onto the streets. A portion would be mad that the government let this happen and was unable to help them, others greedy and ransack unprotected stores.

He smiled under his long, black beard. A beard that would be long gone before he sat foot on American soil. He would be dressed as a Westerner. He might even take a drink. Allah would understand it was because of the part he had to play to do His will.

It would be a long week of travel. He laid back on the torn seat and dozed off.

6

Casey Key, Florida, Tel Aviv, Israel, Countryside

June 1985

MacLachlan drove the Jag to a mechanic Chuck recommended. It was running rough and smoking. More and more he was thinking about selling it as a classic and not fooling with the horrendous maintenance. Even his grandfather had said, "Sonny boy, it's just an expensive, beautiful pain in the butt." He figured his grandfather would understand. But he would get it running as well as possible, store it properly and decide over time. He had the truck in Northern Virginia and the Jeep in Florida, so he had transportation.

He doubted either would impress young ladies, but he did not seem to have a young lady anyway. There was one thousands of miles away he thought a lot about though.

Perhaps a letter to her would be in order.

He wrote one in his ugly, but readable longhand. In it, he said he missed her and wished they had more time to get to know one another when in Africa. He was careful not to be too specific about locations. He told her about taking over the property in Florida and sent her a couple of photos of the Gulf of Mexico beach he owned, the cracker house and the new Jeep. He threw in a photo of the Jag for fun.

He put on shorts, tucked the .45 under a fishing shirt, donned a tan ball cap and headed out in the Jeep. He mailed the letter and parked at a waterfront oyster bar restaurant and had a crab cake sandwich and Bud Lite for an early dinner.

He figured he may have as much as a month, or as little as a week, before being called into action. Since he had not had any real vacation since joining the Marines, this was going to be it. Between his colonel's pay through the end of the year and the trust, he was okay for money. Actually, more than okay.

MacLachlan had looked in his grandfather's tackle corner of the garage. The rods and reels were old. At the very least, they needed to be reconditioned and restrung. The easiest and probably least expensive thing to do now was simply to pick up a new spinning rod, have line put on it and buy a few lures and spoons. While his grandfather always liked to take the boy to old bait shops with their characters and smells, MacLachlan stopped at a fishing gear store on Rt. 41, the Tamiami Trail.

He spoke at some length with a guide who supplemented by clerking in the store. He left with a brass and black Penn Reel on a medium action saltwater rod. He also bought a recommended selection of eight lure and gold spoons and some fishing pliers.

The next morning, he took another run. After, he went down to the bay side dock and looked at the skiff hanging from davits. He put grease he found in the garage on the gears of the manual davits, lowered the skiff sufficiently to screw the drain plug in and hand cranked it down until it floated on its own.

MacLachlan looked at the engine. It was a Johnson 25 from the sixties. He doubted it had been started for fifteen years. He unscrewed the clamps from the transom and lifted the engine onto the dock. It had dried grease at the steering point and surface rust on steel parts and pitting on aluminum ones. He carried it up the hill and put it in the back of the Jeep. He traded it at a dealer and purchased a newly introduced gray Yamaha 25. It was lighter and required a fraction of the oil compared to the old one.

He clamped the engine on the boat. The next trip out was to the county tax collector's office to get a current year sticker. He had to take a document showing he was trustee of the estate and the new owner. MacLachlan obtained a new title in his name and the requisite annual registration sticker to put on the bow of the old sixteen-foot fiberglass skiff. He also got a fishing license.

Sticker applied, he put a life jacket, a bucket, an anchor with line and a paddle in the skiff and pulled the rope on the Yamaha.

The engine started on the first pull. He let it run for fifteen minutes, idling at varying speeds at the dock. The tell-tail seemed to be pumping cooling water well.

MacLachlan loosed the lines and nudged the gear

lever into forward. He began to idle out into the bay in the first boat he had ever driven. He was six years old at the time and his grandfather had sat beaming on the middle seat. MacLachlan considered his grandfather would always be sitting there beaming in his heart.

No boat traffic was coming from either direction, so he opened the throttle. The boat rose and settled on top of the water, planning easily. MacLachlan was in the break-in stage with the new engine, so he varied the speed for the first half hour. During the second half hour, he tried bursts of full throttle, pleased at how fast the old open skiff was with the new engine.

He sped across the water, slowed to explore creeks coming into the bay and watch ospreys and other marsh birds. MacLachlan watched the shadows of snook and redfish speeding by below the surface, He realized how important all of this was to him and how much he had missed it. He made a compact with himself to never let his new contract work take preference over living. And, to him, living was on the water and in the mountains.

He thought of Scotsman John Muir. Friend of Teddy Roosevelt. A lifelong outdoorsman who said "And into the forest I go. To lose my mind and find my soul."

MacLachlan smiled. He took a deep breath and smelled and felt the salt water, the mangrove trees and heard the call of a hunting osprey. He had not been this relaxed in a long time.

He fished the next several days, continuing to break the new engine in. A snook with its side racing stripe provided dinner. The next meal was a mess of small, sautéed mangrove snappers. He was supplementing the fish with fresh vegetables and salads. He ran the beach four days a week, toughening to the point of running barefooted in the sand.

Over the weekend, he drove the Jeep the several hundred miles north to the Ocala National Forest and hiked all day. He preferred mountains and Eastern woodlands more than tropical flora and fauna but sauntered with a walking stick. He usually hiked with one to test steam depths before forging forward, to keep venomous reptiles at bay, and if necessary, use as a weapon.

He stopped in Tampa on the way back for an informal Cuban dinner at a café.

MacLachlan believed he was in the best physical condition he had ever been in, including Marine Officer Candidate School at Quantico, Virginia.

He spent half a day at the Selby Library in Sarasota researching self-defense. In Marine training, elements of krav maga were used. His close combat instructor said it was probably the best single method. It did not have the sport rules of karate and other martial arts. "The street and the battlefield only have one rule: win." he said. MacLachlan found krav maga was developed by a Slovakian Jew, Imi Lichtenfeld. He migrated to Palestine and became an Israeli once the country was formed. He became a close combat instructor for the Israeli Defense Force and refined krav maga over the years.

MacLachlan determined the best way to learn the method was to go to its home. Israel. Yaffa Segal was based there, too. MacLachlan thought that was rather providential. He wrote a note to the school Lichtenfeld founded and wired it that day. He heard back in a day and checked with a travel agent.

His next call was to Grafton.

"Yeah, Mack. I not only have heard of krav maga, I had a couple days training in it. It is serious stuff, better for folks like us than the sport stuff. I suspect you will be closer to where we'll need you when the dirty stuff hits the fan," Grafton said.

"Anything happening we know about on that?" MacLachlan asked.

"Not a thing. Nada. We have every electronic and real ear we have listening for some hint. Hariri has gone to earth. We don't have a clue where he is or if your bullets caused him to bleed out during the escape from the port. So, if you can get a ticket for Tel Aviv, go. Just stay in touch, Mack."

MacLachlan called the travel agent back and sent confirmation a wire to the Krav Maga school. The following day, he heard from Yaffa, who had gotten both of his letters at the same time. She said she wanted to see him badly but could not guarantee being in Israel consistently during his stay. She hinted she could instruct him in krav maga also, having instructed for the IDF and 'other organizations'.

He made sure Chuck and Gloria were aware he would be gone for an indeterminant period of time. It was a part of being a traveling homeowner to which he had to become accustomed.

MacLachlan believed in blending in. He took a small duffle with toiletries, socks and underwear and a windbreaker. He planned on buying basic local clothes and needs. With any luck, since he detested clothes shopping, a certain blonde might tag along and enhance the experience.

The flight took fourteen hours in the air, not

including one connection in New York. MacLachlan devoured several paperbacks and a travel guide for Israel.

He arrived at Ben-Gurion Airport tired but anxious to see Yaffa, the Holy Land, and start the several weeks of krav maga training.

MacLachlan walked through the airport scanning everyone behind the Aviators. He had let his Marine haircut grow out to a businessman's length, but his build and confident stride screamed "cop" or "military." There was little he could or would do about that for now.

"Mack." cried an excited female voice. Then, Yaffa had both arms around his neck and the most beautiful woman in a city known for beautiful women began to hug and kiss him.

Once she came up for air, he asked, ""How did you know what flight I'd be on?" She just rolled her eyes like it was the silliest question she had ever heard.

She took his duffle hand, respectfully leaving his strong hand free, though he had no weapon to present in the face of danger. He chuckled to himself. If he needed one, she would probably pass him her backup. And, he bet it was not a Browning .25.

"I have a car and will take you to your apartment hotel in the Jaffa area. You or your travel agent did your homework well. You are near the beach, the port, and in the historical district. Are you hungry?"

"I could eat something. What do you recommend?" he asked.

"Seafood and vegetables. Fruit for dessert. I will send you home healthy, Major. Though you look pretty good now. I will perhaps take a closer look later.'

"It's colonel, kinda. Long story for later, okay Yaffa?" She gave him a dazzling smile and pulled her Volvo turbo into a parking place in front of a seafood restaurant.

He got the door for her and they walked hand-in-hand to the door.

"I feel naked, being unarmed," he observed.

"Not to worry. I have an extra." He knew it.

"The problem here is not so much one you can handle with a gun. It is more about rockets and idiots who blow themselves up right in front of you. We have very little crime, actually. Just terrorists," she said.

He let her order, but he specified Tzora white wine. She smiled and said nothing but was clearly glad he had remembered.

They ate and he told her his schedule for the krav maga training. He also mentioned that he needed to get clothes and shoes today. Yaffa promised to help him with that and approved his idea of fitting in with local wear.

"I have another idea to run past you when we are in a more secure spot," he said.

The meal was excellent and followed with fruit and cheese as they finished off the wine.

"Did that satisfy you, Mack?" she asked.

He locked eyes with her. "Almost. But, not quite."

"Well, for now, let's get you some clothes and gear." He wondered about 'gear'," the embattled country having some of the most restrictive weapons laws around.

She helped him pick out running shoes, which she called trainers, some cotton slacks in tan, gray and navy and short sleeve shirts. The shirts were mainly white. He picked up a tan baseball cap.

"The car is clean. We can talk openly. Mack, you said you were now a colonel and suggested there were more changes you had to share. This is a safe time if you want."

"The government shifted me from an active duty major to a reserve lieutenant colonel. I am now a security contractor, cleared with the Department of Defense agencies and the civilian intelligence agencies for 'special jobs'," he told her.

"So, you have become what is called 'plausibly deniable'/" she asked.

"Yes. I wanted to pick your mind about actions I should take in preparation for this new career. For example, should I have a cache of money identification and weapons in key locations?"

"You should for sure. What color passport do you have?" she asked.

"A maroon government one, not a blue civilian one," he said. They were in her car driving to the hotel.

"You should go to the US Embassy and request a blue one. I do not know how long it may take. Much of the time, you will want to appear as a tourist. I will take you somewhere to get another passport or two. It will take some cash. At first blush, knowing what part of the world most of the future threats to America will come from, I would think lock boxes here in Tel Aviv, Paris, London to start. Maybe add some others as you see the need. Can you still send things by courier pouch?"

"I believe I can arrange that," he responded.

"Good. We should get you things here, where I can help, and have your embassy send them to your Paris, and London Embassies while you are still here. Then, you should stop at those cities on the way home and set up your caches," Yaffa suggested.

"Mack, for now, can you get your hands on twenty thousand dollars in cash?"

"I think so."

"That way you can have a safe deposit box with several passports, a gun, holster and ammunition, a knife and maybe four thousand in cash and one thousand in local currency in each city. I would recommend a nine-millimeter pistol of a brand the police or military carry in the respective country," she said.

"I will make a call and have my banker transfer the money here. Where, do you think?"

"Try Bank Leumi first. I know it has some branches in America. A wire transfer to a new checking account. Then, you can write a check for cash in pounds sterling, francs and shekels."

"And, the guns, Yaffa?" She just looked and smiled. "Give me a thousand dollars in shekels. I will take care of them. Very quickly. I have sources."

"Of course, you do. I bet they will not have traceable serial numbers. What would I do without you?" he asked.

"You would be a miserable, but very sexy schmuck, I am sure. You seem to have gotten along pretty well in life up to this point in life without me, but the rest of your days will surely be blessed since I am here."

He did not doubt that for one minute.

They arrived at his hotel.

"Will you come up?" he asked.

"I will come up when the time is right. After a romantic dinner perhaps," she said.

"Do you have dinner plans tonight?"

"No, but I have a number of things to put in place for you, that may take precedence over more...carnal...needs. I also need to decide whether to introduce you to my boss."

"Your boss?" he said.

"Yes. He is also my uncle by marriage. His wife is my mother's sister."

"Hmm. How does that work?"

"It would not work with anyone else but him. He has taught me everything I know. He is the best. Maybe in the world. I want you to meet him for your future endeavors, not as my uncle. So, do not get worried. This is not the 'meet the family' thing," she said.

"I was not worried."

"Are you still in your twenties?" she asked.

"Yes, but barely."

"Your demeanor is more mature. That may just be because you have lived on the edge of danger. I read about Beirut and your medal. I also know you have killed at least ten men, probably more."

"You seem to know a lot."

"It is important in my business and my life."

"I understand about your business. Why your life?"

"Because, my dear James Edward MacLachlan, I do not just hop into bed with someone I have just begun to know. Bye," and she pushed him toward the passenger door with a light shove and a smile. He got out and fumbled with his bags. And, his thoughts. The drive wheels of the Volvo squealed, and the red-orange car sped away.

MacLachlan checked in and carried his duffle and the several shopping bags up to his room. He always tried to stay on the third floor. It was generally too far up for robbers, yet a close enough run downstairs in an emergency. It gave him the extra incentive to use the stairs instead of the elevator.

He was a neat hotel guest. He was a Marine. He hung his new slacks and unpinned the new shirts to have cleaned and pressed by the hotel. Toiletries placed neatly in the bathroom and a powerful small flashlight on the bedside table, he set out to check the room subtly for surveillance. He closed the curtains to make it as dark as possible and searched for pinholes of light. Taking a small screwdriver secreted in his toiletries case, he removed the plates on electric plugs. He unscrewed and lamp bulbs. He unscrewed and looked behind air conditioning grills. The room appeared clean.

MacLachlan smiled. There was a long blonde hair on his shoulder. He took it off and carefully saved it to put towards the bottom of the door jamb when he left the room next time. He would put up the Privacy door hang tag and control when housekeeping came to his room. If the hair was not there upon his return, he would know someone had entered the room in his absence. He looked at the bottom of the door. Good. There was a bit of space. He would get a small rubber door stop as a wedge for when he was in the room. Not a bad thing to carry on all his travels, he thought.

The room also had a safe in the closet. It could stay there as far as MacLachlan was concerned. He did not trust it as far as he could throw it.

Satisfied, he showered and went to bed. He had

slept on the plane, but fitfully. The next thing on his schedule was the krav maga class after lunch tomorrow.

The next morning, he had breakfast of nova salmon and cream cheese on bagels, chopped tomato and cucumber salad and rich coffee. Wearing running clothes, he walked around the old district for an hour to let breakfast settle, then ran along the waterfront for a half hour. He went back to the hotel and showered. His uniform of the day would be sweats for the krav maga camp, as it was called. A week of intense training at the home of the method of self-protection.

MacLachlan knew from the research and the materials the school sent him the instructors had known creator Imi Lichtenfeld, also known as Imi Sde-Or. Some of their fathers and uncles trained under him when he was the lead close combat instructor for the most elite units of the Israeli Defense Force.

Much of his first day was classroom discussions on the philosophy of krav maga and learning basic positions and strikes. He liked what he was learning, to fluidly incorporate an aggressive attack into a defensive maneuver and to disable quickly by dislocating a shoulder or a similar attack and leave. MacLachlan agreed with the targets: eyes; throat; testicles. As a Marine, he felt comfortable with the no-rules, street fighting aspects. By the end of his first day, he was sore and bruised in places different from his other regimens. But he had made great strides.

MacLachlan's hotel room phone rang about six.

"How was krav maga?" Yaffa asked.

"Great. I am beginning to get the hang of it already. There are elements familiar to me from the Marines. I also took karate as a kid. There is little there. Rules, bowing and so forth. Great sport, not as great on the street. I suspect I will be going as I did earlier this year, into harm's way unarmed. I suspect this camp will be a worthwhile endeavor."

"Mack, you have a relatively short time here in Israel. We need to maximize it personally and professionally. I mentioned my uncle. Would you like to join the two of us at his house for dinner tonight? I will give you a ride back to your hotel and update you on some of the things I promised to arrange yesterday."

"I would be honored, Yaffa. If you give me his address, I will take a taxi over."

She did, adding "I will send a taxi with the address for you at seven and give you his name at the door. It's better that way."

"The driver will recognize you and call you Mr. Mack, okay?" she said.

"Okay. I will see you shortly after."

He cleaned up and put on gray slacks and the new blue blazer over an open-neck white shirt. His loafers were polished, albeit not to a Marine Corps spit shine level.

Just before seven, MacLachlan went downstairs and watched the street from within the hotel. A taxi pulled up. MacLachlan stepped outside. The driver said "Mr. Mack?" through the open passenger window.

"Yes." He got into the rear seat. The driver was taciturn and very fit looking.

MacLachlan positioned himself to have a good view out of the passenger side rear view mirror. After about six blocks, he noticed a non-descript Volkswagen that had been behind them the whole way.

"Driver? Indulge me and take the next two right

turns. I want to see if a car behind us follows," MacLachlan said.

The driver grinned broadly.

"Not to worry. I will have fun busting my friend Ari's chops about following too closely," he said.

"In that case, disregard my request and give Ari my regards," MacLachlan said.

"Just don't tell Steven, okay?"

"Steven is whose home we are going to?" MacLachlan asked for confirmation.

"Yes."

"Don't worry. Ari's driving will stay between you and me."

The driver nodded.

Fifteen minutes later, the driver pulled into the drop off circle of a five story, plain apartment building.

"Here we are."

"What is the fare?" MacLachlan asked.

"On the house."

"Thanks, then," he said as he exited.

"Ring the buzzer for apartment four sixteen." MacLachlan nodded and went in.

He rang the buzzer for the apartment.

"Don't you look nice in your new sports coat," Yaffa responded. MacLachlan mentally kicked himself for not looking for the camera as he walked in.

"Thanks."

He heard a "click" as what he determined to be a heavier than usual apartment house entry unlocked.

Entering, he went to the elevator and chose the button for the fourth floor. The door opened and a petite blonde grabbed him and pulled him off the elevator smiling.

She whispered "There's a camera on the elevator, but none in the hall.

With that, she drew him near and gave him a long and passionate kiss.

Taking his hand, she walked him down the corridor to the apartment and in the ajar door.

"Mack, this is my uncle, Steven Rotenberg and my aunt, Miriam Segal Rotenberg. Mack MacLachlan."

Hands were shaken all around. Rotenberg was probably in his late forties. He was a medium height man with thinning hair and appeared to be very fit. His wife was a short, plump woman with blonde hair and an engaging smile. MacLachlan guessed she was the actual aunt from her maiden name and Rotenberg was the uncle by marriage. Unless, Yaffa had been, or was married, since her surname was Segal.

Yaffa did not hold his hand as they followed the Rotenberg's into a den, where wine, fruits and cheeses were set out on several platters. While the building itself was plain, the furnishings in the apartment suggested a fairly senior government official. MacLachlan kept his mouth shut and his eyes open.

"So, Mack," Rotenberg began. "You have risen from major to lieutenant colonel since Český Krumlov." MacLachlan tried his best to keep a straight look on his face and not show surprise at the mention of the Czech city.

"Do not worry. My apartment, my whole life, is swept daily. We can talk here. I promise to let you know when I switch from your government title to you as a contractor. It is rather convenient, you see. There are things I can share with a foreign government intelligence employee that I cannot with a contractor. So, in our dealings, you must keep both hats handy."

"Indeed, sir," MacLachlan responded politely but without commitment.

Miriam suggested each fill a plate with fruit and cheese while she prepared to plate dinner.

They did.

"I have to thank you for buying my niece and me time in Dar-es-Salaam by shooting that idiot with the rocket launcher."

"It was my honor, Steven. I only wish I had not had to fire once for range before I hit him. It may have saved your car."

"Not to worry. It was a rental."

"That was a pretty dramatic escape with your commandeered vehicle," MacLachlan observed.

"When in dire straits, improvise." Yaffa said.

"Tell me about yourself, Mack. Your childhood and so forth," Rotenberg said.

"I was born in Texas and grew up on a ranch. I was a rodeo contestant in high school. Most of my summers were spent with my grandparents in Florida. It had been his ranch, but my maternal grandfather was successful buying and selling ranch land retired to Florida in his forties, leaving the ranch for his daughter and top hand, who is my father."

"You rode and competed in rodeo in Texas. What did you do in Florida?" Rotenberg asked, his niece clearly listening closely.

"I fished, swam and hunted. I spent every minute I could on the water. I inherited the house in Florida and it's my official home now."

"You have moved away from DC and the Pentagon?"

"Not totally. I bought some wooded acreage in the Valley of Virginia. It's on a whitewater stream and protected by natural forest land adjacent. I will build a simple cabin there and alternate my time between Florida, Northern Virginia and wherever the job takes me."

"No wife, present or past?"

"I think I was married to the Marine Corps, Steven. My wife is in the future. Maybe," MacLachlan said.

"What do you think of Israel?" Rotenberg asked.

"I am spiritual, but not the churchgoer my mother wanted me to be. But it is the Holy Land. All Christians and Jews should protect it. It's also America's one friend in the Middle East. I believe I will find it to be beautiful, but after one day, that's only speculation."

"You said one friend. Your government has always had ties to Saudi Arabia," Rotenberg said.

"My suspicion is it's a 'friendship' based on oil and money. I do not trust the Saudis to act on anyone's behalf but their own," MacLachlan said.

He was clearly being questioned. What he was not sure about was the reason. As the plain talking uncle of a beautiful niece? Or, was it official? Was he being assessed whether he was a threat to Israel? Or being solicited by Mossad? Or something else, with elements of each? He would let this play out, being careful. Very careful.

Steven Rotenberg got out his pipe without considering time and began to tamp tobacco into the bowl. Miriam walked in and told him to put it away and come to dinner. Obediently, he set it aside and got up.

MacLachlan and Yaffa followed him into the dining room. From behind, MacLachlan squeezed her hand.

The meal was excellent. They had fish and salad and *malabi*, a delicious rosewater pudding with cocoanut for dessert.

After, the Rotenberg's, Yaffa, and MacLachlan sat in a small study and drank coffee. The questions appeared to be over for now.

"Miriam and Steven, thank you for the hospitality and wonderful meal. I have a week of krav maga training. Today was only the first day. I fear I should get back to the hotel early and get some rest."

"We enjoyed having you here. Perhaps we will meet again, either for a meal or out in the world somewhere," Rotenberg said.

"The meal would be wonderful, and a chance meeting would not surprise me at all," MacLachlan said.

"Instead of a taxi, Mack, I will drop you at your hotel," Yaffa offered.

"That would be great. Thank you."

Hands shaken, hugs from aunt and uncle for Yaffa, and they got in the Volvo and left.

"What did you think?" she asked.

"You mean about having an agent driving the taxi and your uncle's questioning? Or your aunt's wonderful cooking?" he responded.

"I guess all of the above. You picked out the driver, huh?"

"Unless he is Mossad or an IDF spec ops guy moonlighting as a taxi driver, yes." He said.

"My uncle by marriage and supervisor at work has been in the business so long, his conversation sounds more like an interrogation. You seemed to sail through pretty comfortably though."

"I kind of expected being checked out. Stepping away from personal relationships for a moment, it could be useful for your agency and my new career to be friends and help one another sometimes, like in Dar-es-Salaam. But do know this, Yaffa, I will not spy for another country, friend or not. That is an absolute, okay?"

"Message understood. I will make sure my uncle understands also. I really don't think that was his objective. I believe 'trusted friends' was more what he had in mind," Yaffa said.

"That was what I hoped for also, Yaffa. Let's go with that and see how it works. Back to the personal for a moment. Will you come in for another coffee or a drink?"

"Is that a prelude to 'will you spend the night?'" she asked.

"Yes."

"Then, that is my answer too," she said. Eschewing valet parking always, she self-parked at the hotel and they went into the café for expresso.

Half an hour later, they walked up the stairs to his room. No time was wasted and the two went straight to bed.

"You know, Mack, I thought about us doing that when I first saw you and your associates at lunch," she said as she rested her head on his shoulder and ran her fingers down the washboard ripples of his stomach absent-mindedly.

"I did, too, Yaffa. And, about every day since."

"About? There was a day you didn't think about it??

"Okay. No, there was not. I just did not want to appear too needy."

"How could you not need me?" she asked seriously.

"You are quite confident, aren't you?"

"Well...yes." she said emphatically.

"You have every right to be, dear Yaffa," he said, lifting her for a long kiss.

They had a light breakfast just after dawn and MacLachlan walked Yaffa to the Volvo. They circled it, then she motioned for him to follow her back to the entrance. She hit a remote starter and let it run several minutes before giving him a quick kiss, saying "Love ya." and leaving.

He looked at the scarred old stainless Rolex Oyster Perpetual Datejust. It was a piece of his grandfather he kept with him twenty-four seven. He had enough time for a quick nap before getting ready for his class. Four hours sleep last night was not quite enough.

MacLachlan walked into the school on time. It was an intense session. If he had seen any of his instructors on the street or in a store or restaurant, he would not have considered many of them dangerous. A couple looked like him, short-haired hard bodies with a military or cop look, but most of the staff looked like they could be the guy next door. But at this point any of them could put him flat on his back with very little effort. There was a lesson in that. One he would add to his tradecraft. You can never, never tell a book by its cover. Mom was right.

Because of his natural and Marine Corps level of

fitness, his training was accelerated quickly into combatives. Today and he would find, for the rest of his time there, he would practice blocks followed immediately by punches, head butts, elbow blows, kicks and the short series of moves to dislocate a shoulder and disable an attacker sufficiently to escape from him. The training was based on practical logic, not some mysterious algorithm. It was reiterated that just because one disabled an adversary, there was no guarantee he would not rebound, or draw a weapon or have an accomplice appear. Expect the unexpected. Attack aggressively and leave the field of battle. Do not use one's knowledge to punish the adversary, but only to neutralize his ability to harm you or someone with you.

During a quick lunch break, MacLachlan slipped over to a Bank Leumi branch. He gave them a check to open an account and a safe deposit box. He used trust officer Bonney as a reference. With the difference in time, he had already prepped Bonney to wire twenty-one thousand to the bank once he provided an account number. The bank wired Bonney instead and the funds were scheduled for tomorrow.

Fit or not, MacLachlan was sore and tired when the last of his training iterations for the day was complete.

He took a bus back to his hotel and, tired or not, sprinted up the three flights of stairs. It was the Marine Corps way. And, he would follow that way as long as he possibly could. Beyond that, his tradecraft gave him an implicit distrust of elevators. They could be controlled, rigged with explosives, and be a deathtrap when the door opened to waiting gunmen.

MacLachlan cleaned up and laid down for a

minute. The minute turned into an hour, which was interrupted by the telephone by the bed ringing.

"Yes?"

"It's me," Yaffa said.

"The very special me?" he asked.

"The most special ever me. Can you take the afternoon off from your training tomorrow to go somewhere with me?"

"I believe so. What's up?"

"Oh, I just need your help in some shopping."

He was sure the shopping was for him. She had promised help in getting several pistols, ammunition and holsters. She would also need his photo for fake passports.

"Do you want to pick me up at the school?" he asked.

"No. I am known there. Walk left out of the entrance to the school. Turn right at the second block and halfway down is a very nice café. I will be there at one o'clock, okay?"

"Are you available tonight?" he asked. She told him she had a work assignment.

"Roger that," he said. "See you at the café at one tomorrow, then."

MacLachlan walked down to the lobby and ate a light dinner at the hotel. He liked the Israeli way of eating and thought it was healthier than hamburgers, hot dogs and pizzas by quite a margin. As much as he enjoyed fast foods, he decided to take them out of his diet to the greatest extent possible and eat sit down meals of seafood and vegetables as much as possible.

After dinner, he took a forty-five-minute walk around the neighborhood. There was virtually no old architecture in the area. Everything was built in the late forties or the fifties.

He apprised the lead instructor of his schedule the next morning. He worked harder to make up for the time he was going to lose from just before lunch. He showered at the gym and strode out dressed like any other Israeli. Five minutes and two turns later, he walked past a red-orange Volvo parked at the curb and into a café.

Yaffa was already sipping an ice water with lemon. One awaited him and he drank after kissing her cold wet lips.

"This is exciting. It's almost like having an affair, sneaking around in public."

"If you say so. I never had anyone I had to hide somebody else from," He said.

"Well, if you must know, neither have I. But this is just like in the movies."

He just smiled at her and she returned a dazzling smile.

"We only have about thirty minutes to eat. Our appointment is in an hour, but we need to stop by your hotel and pick up a tie and your blue blazer. You can keep the jeans and trainers on. You also need to pick up fifteen thousand in US dollars from Bank Leumi."

That confirmed MacLachlan's thought that today he was going to have photos taken for his new multinational passports.

"I hope the funds are there already. I just requested the wire transfer yesterday," he said.

After lunch and a quick run to the hotel to get the jacket and tie on, they went to Bank Leumi.

The funds were en route. The manager agreed to

advance fifteen thousand US dollars in view of the confirmation from the Florida bank. That should cover the passports, cash for the safe deposits and the three pistols and their related ammo and holsters.

In the car on the way to the meeting, MacLachlan asked about the passports.

"For the nine thousand dollars, you will be getting three copies each of Israeli, French and German passports. A set for each planned safe deposit box. It is a bargain, I assure you," she said.

To MacLachlan, it was the price of a really good used car. But probably a necessity that would be difficult to replicate in the future without Yaffa's connections.

They went to the Shuk Karmel Bazaar. They walked around like tourists. Yaffa stopped at a display of earrings and MacLachlan bargained the seller down by fifty percent and handed them to her. She was delighted and tucked them in her bag. She took his hand and led him through a maze of stands selling a wide variety of items.

They came to a stand with some photo frames and an old man seated behind the table. He kissed Yaffa lightly on both cheeks and ushered them behind the curtain to an area that was akin to a dressing room in other booths. A single lens reflex camera was on a tripod. There was a flood lamp on another stand and a screen behind a four-legged stool. It was a miniature photo studio, MacLachlan realized.

"I will take three sets of photographs and use different backgrounds," the old man said in English tinged with what MacLachlan thought was a Brooklyn accent.

He used a buff background for the Israeli, light lavender on for the Canadian, and a mottled blue gray for the German one.

Yaffa nodded to MacLachlan and he handed the man an envelope with nine thousand in cash. The man opened the thick envelope and counted the money.

"What names do you want on each?" he asked.

"Joel Mencken for the Israeli," Yaffa suggested.

"How about Dieter Maack for the German?" MacLachlan asked. "It is a name I am familiar with," he said. He continued, "I thought the third one was going to be French?"

"Canadian is one of the handiest to have for quiet activities," the old man said. "Better than French." MacLachlan looked at Yaffa who nodded.

The old man got out a book and looked through several pages.

"I will make you Paul Dusay, of Montreal," he said. "You can speak English or French at your choice."

"*Oui, Monsieur, merci, qui serait parfait,*" MacLachlan responded, thanking the man and indicating that would be perfect. His French surprised Yaffa. Their files showed him speaking English, Spanish and German only. She looked at him with raised eyebrows. He just grinned back.

"You can pick up the nine passports the day after tomorrow from my photography studio. You know where it is. This booth will be empty later today. I assure you; they will fool even the Immigration officers of the countries that 'issued' them," the man said to Yaffa.

"Thank you, my friend," Yaffa said. MacLachlan noticed that, while she obviously knew the man, neither had used names. He suspected canvas walls were the reason.

They walked around the bazaar a bit more for cover, then left.

"I will bring you the passports in exchange for dinner in two nights, okay?" Yaffa asked.

"That would be fine," he said, adding "but you know I'd buy you dinner every night I possibly could."

She flashed perfect white teeth and continued,

"You should use the Canadian one to open a credit card account in London or any bank in Paris, and the Israeli one for a different bank in Israel, perhaps Bank Hapoalum here."

"I guess the German passport is like my orphan one," MacLachlan said.

"True, but you have personal knowledge of Germany and speak the language. It may be a useful cover there, or about anywhere. Where did you learn to speak French?" she asked.

"In high school. For some reason, I kept the fluency. Languages have never been a problem for me."

"Except that you speak them with a Texas drawl," she said, smiling but speaking the truth.

"There is that, I guess," he responded.

"We are going to pick up the car and take a little drive out into the countryside. We will see a few places of religious importance along the way. I'll tell you what I can as we pass. We can afford an extra few minutes if you particularly want to check one out a bit closer," she said. They headed north out of Tel Aviv.

Later, she said "We are in Armageddon Valley. That is Mount Tabor. You may know it as Transfiguration Mount. After Jesus came back from the dead, he took some disciples up the mountain. They saw him transform and talk with Moses and Elijah there."

The MacLachlan felt the very aura of the place. He knew climbing to the top would be a fantastic experience, but they did not have sufficient time today. Yaffa was on a mission. He suspected it was related to the pistols.

It was. They arrived at a small village and she pulled into a restaurant. It reminded him of the bar in the Beqaa Valley where he had his first gunfight but better maintained and, hopefully, cleaner.

The sat at a small table and the server addressed them in Hebrew. Yaffa ordered.

After five minutes, the server brought a plate with warm pita bread and two dishes. One had hummus, mashed chickpeas and the other had baba ghanoush, which was a spread made of eggplant. A pitcher of not very cold orange juice and two glasses accompanied it. MacLachlan liked the food from this part of the world a lot. Except for lamb, which he avoided whenever possible.

They ate and spoke in low terms, not discussing anything of tactical importance. He noticed the older restauranteur watching them when he thought they did not see. His idea about tradecraft was good. His skills at it sucked, MacLachlan thought.

Yaffa very subtly watched the two men. She smiled and MacLachlan caught it. "She knows exactly what I am thinking. All the time," he thought to himself as he returned her smile.

When they had finished and the bill was presented, Yaffa explained the amount and MacLachlan placed it on the table with a twelve percent tip added.

Once the tip was picked up, the man behind the bar nodded to Yaffa and she rose. MacLachlan followed her lead as she followed the man into a back room through an exterior door and into a small building. MacLachlan noticed modern security locks well beyond expectations for the building and the area.

He motioned for them to sit at a scarred top wooden table that had two chairs.

Once they were seated, he placed a small gym bag on the table between them. He nodded for Yaffa to open it. She in turn, nodded to MacLachlan.

He removed three pistols. He picked each up and pulled the slide back and locked it open. He was very familiar with the Browning Hi-Power and field stripped it and reassembled it. The second was a CZ-75. Very popular in Israel and indeed, most of the world, though hard to get in the US since it was made in a Combloc country. He quickly figured out how to strip it. Reassembled, he placed it back on the table. The next one was a classic he heard about but had not seen. It was a Sig 210. Though replaced some years ago by the Swiss army, the 210 may have been the most accurate—and expensive military pistol issued in modern times. MacLachlan did not attempt field stripping. Rather, checking again that it was empty, he aimed at the ceiling and pressed the trigger. It was perfect. The best trigger feel he had ever experienced. The ergonomics were also. He sat it back on the table. He had the same expression as one who had just finished a gourmet meal. So much for being a stoic spy.

All three guns were military surplus, used but in mechanically fine condition. Bores were good. The bag also contained three boxes of German GECO hollow points in 9mm and inside the waistband holsters. MacLachlan asked Yaffa in French about the serial numbers. She asked the man in Hebrew, then explained in French they all had original military serial numbers and had been surplussed. Anyone could have gotten them. There was no trail. MacLachlan nodded.

He handed the man an envelope with three thousand US dollars. The man counted it and put it in a gun safe in the corner.

Yaffa stood and nodded once at the man, so MacLachlan followed her suit. They left after putting the objects in the gym bag into a locked safe in the trunk of her Volvo.

"Let's go home, Ricky," she said in a pretty good imitation of Lucille Ball.

During the ride back, MacLachlan said "I usually try to put a couple hundred rounds through a semiautomatic to make sure it works well and, particularly, that there are no magazine problems. Any place we can do that?"

"I assure you there is no need for that. He is under contract to provide certain people fully functioning, tested firearms. I promise you they have been function tested with a variety of cartridges. Further, each is arsenal refinished by the military of the countries that carried, then surplussed them. That would be enough on its own."

"Okay, thanks. Good enough for you is good enough for me," he said.

He looked at his watch.

"Four o'clock here. That means three in Berlin," he said. "How far are we from the hotel or somewhere else I can make a quick call?"

"An hour," Yaffa said.

They pulled into the hotel at four fifty-five. Knowing Grafton would not leave early, except for a meeting, he motioned the agent to follow him up to his room. He dialed a number.

"Yes?"

"Slickmeister, I need a little favor," MacLachlan said.

"I'm listening. Just remember, we're in the clear."

"I am aware of that. I need a small pouch sent from our place here to London and one to Paris. Think you could arrange that?"

"Aw, man. I thought it was going to be something big and you'd owe me. That is easy. I will have one of my guys meet you at your place. Give me an hour," Grafton said.

"Thanks. Later." They both hung up without further conversation.

"Yaffa, I'd like to package these, so the objects won't be identifiable. The shapes are pretty much a give-away," MacLachlan said.

"There's an office supply store around the corner to the left. It's in the next block. Why don't you pick up a couple medium mailer boxes? I will count out the three packs of money and get out a little surprise I got for you in the meantime. Get three opaque envelopes that will hold the money and some tough sealing tape."

MacLachlan bent over and kissed her and left for the store. He was back in fifteen minutes with the supplies. She had three piles of one thousand US dollars each and three wicked-looking folding knives sitting on top of each pile.

He looked down and smiled. Picking one up, he

flicked the blade open and tested the edge and the point.

"You really know the way to a man's heart," he said.

"I do, but you have not seen proof of that...yet."

"You mean our time together," and looked towards the bed, "was not it?" he asked.

"You have not had my cooking. The food would make you want me to be with you forever. That's why I have not cooked for a man. It's too dangerous."

"We could pick up groceries and we could then go to your place," he suggested.

"Too fast. All in good time," she said.

They packaged three pistols, ammunition, holsters, knives and cash in the three boxes. The Israel box would go to Bank Hapoalum, the other two to US Embassies in Paris and London.

MacLachlan put the mailer boxes in the gym bag. He left Yaffa in the room while he went down to meet the DIA agent. There was no need for him to see the Israeli. Grafton knew about her. That was enough.

He sat at a café table near the open entrance to the hotel. With any luck, he could hear the agent asking for him. He could not chance picking an American-looking man or woman and introducing himself.

An older guy walked by. He could have been from anywhere. He went to the desk. MacLachlan could not hear his conversation with the clerk. The man turned and walked out and straight to MacLachlan.

"Mack?" MacLachlan nodded. "Will sent me," he said using a name both knew, but which had not been used on any phone call from his room, in case his phone was being monitored.

He gave the man the duffle bag. "Two packages are

inside. Labels have where they should go and that I will pick them up in a few days. Thanks for the help. Coffee?"

"Thanks, but I have to get back to the office. Maybe next time." The agent left without introduction.

MacLachlan went to the room and was persuaded to take the young woman there to dinner. He agreed it was a brilliant idea.

The next day he locked the box with his alternate identities and weapons and money in his locker at the krav maga school. He skipped lunch and walked to the nearby headquarters office of Bank Hapoalum. He opened a small balance checking account and rented a safe deposit box. Items secured, he went back to the school and went through more evolutions.

This afternoon focused on ground fighting. MacLachlan learned to apply what he had learned standing to fighting after he had been knocked or deliberately gone to ground to avoid shots or other dangers. Implicit in the training was the real-life realization on the street where one would quite likely be knocked or pushed to the ground. Most thugs would not expect the victim to continue to fight effectively there. Krav maga guaranteed them a real surprise.

He went back to the hotel after the class. He knew Yaffa was on some sort of surveillance op tonight and he was on his own. MacLachlan took a run to loosen up a bit. He skipped dinner and turned in early. The next day would stress punches, head butts, elbow blows, kicks and knees. On Friday, he completed the training in Tel Aviv. The Director gave him a letter outlining what he had been taught and his current proficiency level, which was amazingly high for only a week.

MacLachlan suspected, unlike most people who voluntarily took close combat training, he would stay in practice through use, not on a mat somewhere wearing boxing gloves.

It portended to be his and Yaffa's last night for a while. He gave her the opportunity to show off her cooking prowess and she demurred. So, he took her to dinner in the finest restaurant he could find in the city.

The next morning, after very few hours of sleep, she drove him to Ben Gurion Airport.

Both were quiet, wondering about what to say at the parting. Was it temporary or permanent?

"Mack, this has been a wonderful week," she began ten miles into the trip.

"Steven is one of the top intelligence operatives in the world. I think—no, I know—one day both you and I will eclipse his skills. I know you love your country. You chose to be a Marine. That says a lot. I don't know whether it was for adventure or patriotism or a combination. For me, it is a lifetime commitment. Israel and my uncle have put a lot into training me. Everyone around us in the region and many throughout the world want us to disappear. To die. Every Israeli has to defend against that. And, I will. Until my last breath, if that's what it takes. I am a sabra. I was born here. I have an obligation and I will meet it," she said, finishing.

"I understand and appreciate you saying it. I pretty much knew we were not headed for a vine covered cottage with a picket fence. Yaffa, you are right about my reasons for doing this. I don't know any more than you do what the percentage breakdown between adventure and patriotism are. I'd like to think it skews heavily towards patriotism. But you know something? A lot is pure anger. Anger I developed one day at a Marine barracks in Beirut and has never diminished. Maybe one day it will. I'll let you know.

This was a wonderful week for me, too. We will have others. Many, I hope. I suspect we will work together soon and often. I will have your back. If you ever get in a tight spot and there is time for me to get there, call. I will be there."

She had tear streaks on her cheeks as they pulled into the airport.

"Now, get out, before I start crying like a baby, dammit,' she said.

He leaned over and kissed her tenderly. The tears started and she pushed him towards the door. He took the hand pushing him and squeezed it softly as he slipped out and retrieved his carry-on bag.

MacLachlan walked towards the security section without looking back.

The woman in the red orange Volvo silently mouthed "I love you," then smoked the tires as she pulled away from the curb. MacLachlan heard the tortured rubber and smiled, walking on.

7

Paris, London, Casey Key, Florida

June 1985

MacLachlan had booked a flight to Paris with a one-day layover, a boat trip to London, this time with a two-day layover and a flight to Miami. He had not been to Paris, except on a stopover at Charles De Gaulle Airport, so he figured the quickest way to see things was a hop-on, hop-off bus. His first stop required a bit of walking but took him to the US Embassy. He retrieved his courier package and walked to the next stop and waited. When he saw the brightly colored double decker, more suggestive of London than Paris, he got on and rode to the area of Credit Suisse. He went in and opened an account and secured a safe deposit box. He put the courier package's pistol, holster, ammunition, knife, three passports and one thousand US dollars in and departed. At the bank, he stated his address in

Florida was temporary and obtained duly signed change of address forms to complete and return later. He used the business name Highland Services, LLC for the accounts.

He rode past the Louvre, the Eiffel Tower and stopped for a quick meal on the Champs-Èlysées. MacLachlan had hoped to see beautiful French girls in short black dresses promenading by. Instead, he saw mainly tourists from all over. A look at the Paris phone directory gave him the number of a Melia hotel close to the airport. He took a taxi there and settled in for the night. Early the next morning, he flew to Gatwick, London. Checking with a travel guidebook he bought at the airport, he selected a hotel in the Paddington Station area of London. One call and he had a room. A brief ride on the "Tube" subway took him to Paddington. Another three blocks delivered him to his hotel. He took a taxi to the US Embassy, picked up the last courier package and went straight to the Royal Bank of Scotland's largest London branch. As in Paris, he opened an account and a safe deposit box. He used the same business name and obtained a change of address form just as he had done at Credit Suisse.

With directions from the banker, he hopped a bus that took him to Harrod's Department Store. He wanted to pick up a couple of Cuban cigars to enjoy there, since they were embargoed in the US.

MacLachlan walked in and asked a concierge the way to the tobacco humidor. As he walked towards it, a rush of hot air, dust and some broken glass preceded the sound of an explosion. It was a sound he remembered poignantly from Beirut.

He was knocked to the ground, but his immediate

impression was that he was not seriously hurt. Though his hearing was a bit impaired, it was not nearly as bad as Beirut.

As he got to his feet, he saw a medium sized, dark-haired man running towards him and the door. A uniformed security guard was limping after him as fast as he could, yelling "Stop. It's one of the bombers."

MacLachlan threw himself on the man as he ran past. They both staggered against a counter. The man drew a wicked looking blade and MacLachlan grabbed the man's knife hand wrist with his left hand and pushed to the outside. At the same time, he moved in and struck the man in the face with the heel of his right hand. As the man's head recoiled, MacLachlan kneed him in the groin. He doubled over and a hammer fist to the back of his head finished the man's resistance. He crumpled to the floor, unconscious. As the injured guard arrived, MacLachlan kicked the knife away from the prone man. The guard stumbled.

MacLachlan saw he had a wound in his groin bleeding badly. Femoral artery.

MacLachlan unfastened and pulled the belt off the attacker, who was now regaining consciousness. He hit him on the side of his jaw with as hard a blow as he could. Punch soft, chop hard was violated and MacLachlan felt the pain go all the way up to his shoulder. But the man was down for the count.

Flexing his painful right hand, he wrapped the belt around the guard's upper leg. He called for a dress clerk to hand him a wooden clothes hanger. MacLachlan broke the wooden hanger rod off and used it as a lever to tighten the makeshift tourniquet. He tucked the end of the rod under the belt to hold it. The blood flow had stopped. The guard was starting to lose consciousness. Marine Corps style, MacLachlan drew a large, obvious T for tourniquet on the man's forehead for medical personnel to see.

As this was happening, London fire, rescue and police were responding.

MacLachlan saw a pair of uniformed constables running in. He beckoned them over.

"This store security man needs immediate medical care. He identified the prisoner here as one of the bombers. The senior of the two constables spoke into his radio and asked MacLachlan to stay there for questioning.

"I'd like to clean some of the blood off my hands," he told the officer who told him to just stand there until a detective could speak with him.

The prisoner was waking up again. A kick from the constable took care of that. MacLachlan, not the softest souled person alive, still grimaced.

Hearing the part about cleaning the blood, one of the young female employees walked over with a bottle of makeup remover and a box of tissues. A few minutes later, MacLachlan was more sanitary.

A detective inspector identified himself and took MacLachlan's particulars. He told him he would have to come to New Scotland Yard and give a statement. MacLachlan knew the drill and agreed. He saw the employees from the immediate area rounded up and ushered to the door along with him. He left shortly thereafter with a pair of constables in a marked car, perhaps a Rover. He was not sure.

Two hours of questioning and a succession of detective inspectors, detective chief inspectors and a detective superintendent later, MacLachlan was coffee'd out.

One last man walked in. He was a powerful looking man in his early fifties. He was going bald. His suit was obviously more Saville Row than department store.

He sat down across from MacLachlan.

"A hot drink?" he asked.

"No thanks, I have had several coffees. I'm fine," MacLachlan responded.

"My name is Walter Harvey-Smith. I have a few more questions and then we will point you to the Tube station and proper stop for your hotel, all right?"

MacLachlan nodded.

"Thank you for stopping the man. He is a sought-after Irish Provisional Army criminal. A Provo, as it were. He and an associate, who was blown up, brought in the bomb. Luckily, unlike the attack here in 1983, no one died this time. It was rather a botched attempt as the bomb went off in an inventory room while the dead bomber was trying to activate it. The man you stopped was standing guard outside and down the corridor. But we expect to obtain lots of information from him about his prior history and his associates in Belfast.

MacLachlan nodded but said nothing.

"Were you conducting surveillance on these two, Colonel?"

MacLachlan was surprised to hear his rank used as he had not had any reason to mention it.

"No, not at all. I came in to buy a Cuban cigar. Something we cannot buy in the US."

"There is no tie-in to the people you...interacted with... in Dar-es-Salaam?" Harvey- Smith asked.

"None, whatsoever," MacLachlan said, neither confirming nor denying being in Tanzania.

"You seem aware we had people in Tanzania, Colonel."

Deciding to stick with being vague and noncommittal, MacLachlan said

"No matter where in the world one may be, it is prudent to keep one's eyes open for friends and enemies both."

"Indeed."

"Why are you in London?"

"I have a few days before I need to be back home, so I thought I'd play tourist. I did the same in Paris yesterday."

"Do you work for the Israelis?" Harvey-Smith asked.

"No, I do not. Until very recently, I was a Lieutenant Colonel in the US Marine Corps, stationed at the Pentagon. I just moved to reserve officer status and am heading home to develop a career to pay my bills."

"And, what will that career be, Colonel? Mercenary, perhaps?"

"Hardly. A consultant of some sort probably. Maybe a teacher. I really don't know for sure yet."

"And why, Colonel, would one of the most highly decorated Marines alive, one who may be the youngest colonel in the Corps' history, give all of that up?"

"Maybe to leverage a career on those facts. Or, maybe because I am tired of constant travel and violence," MacLachlan said.

"I might buy the former. Certainly not the latter. You appear to relish the violence and be a magnet for it, Colonel."

"I think you give me more credit than I am due, Mr. Harvey-Smith, if that really is your name," he said.

"In fact, it is my name. I am not actually from this building. I am with a group you may well see in the future. Like you did perhaps in Dar-es-Salaam. I will be interested to see how your 'leveraged career' evolves. Here is my card. Call if we can help one another. And, on behalf of the chaps here at the Yard, thanks for capturing the Irishman."

"You are welcome. How is the security guard?" MacLachlan asked.

"Oh, yes. Him. Alive thanks to you. Should recover nicely. Showed good grit. A former corporal in the army. May talk to him about a slot on my team."

MacLachlan glanced at Harvey-Smith's card for the first time. It read Walter Harvey-Smith. Her Majesty's Secret Intelligence Service. A phone number was given. No rank. No address. MI-5 to James Bond fans.

"Perhaps we will meet again, Mr. Harvey-Smith," MacLachlan said pleasantly.

"It wouldn't surprise me a bit." The British spy arose and left the room, without shaking hands or saying anything further.

Ten minutes later, a constable came in with a note having which train to take for his hotel and led him out. On the way, his wallet, passport and pocket litter were returned. MacLachlan was glad this incident occurred *after* he had deposited the contents of the courier bag at the Royal Bank of Scotland. The pistol and different name passports would have been difficult to explain in handgun-free Great Britain. He left New Scotland Yard and walked to the Parliament Square Tube Station and headed back to Paddington and a pint of ale and some pub food. He would go to Stratford on Avon and Oxford tomorrow, playing the tourist one more day. Then, Florida for who knew how long.

––––––––––––

THE FLIGHT into Miami was long and cramped. Maybe one day he would be able to fly first class and stretch his long legs out a bit. He just hoped he would have enough consulting work to fly at all. While, with no mortgage, he could live on the trust, it would be a modest life. But, an appreciated cushion for sure, he admitted.

MacLachlan drove northwest towards Casey Key. Alligator Alley lived up to its name. It may be part of the Eisenhower Interstate System one day, but it was a lonely, desolate drive now. He saw a long branch across the lane and slowed down. No need. It slithered away before he got there. He thought he saw one of the rare Florida panthers in the distance but was not sure. He was sure about the alligators at a boat ramp where he stopped to look around. Where was his .45 when he needed it?

The house and grounds were in good shape, as he expected. MacLachlan unlocked a cabinet and withdrew the .45 and checked it. He stuck it in the bedside table for now.

He did not have fresh food, so he went out for dinner.

The next day, he took the virtually useless rear seat out of the Jeep and bolted a steel box with a hasp and high security padlock in its place. That would be his trunk...and weapons locker. He found an old Winchester Model 12 pump shotgun at a local gun store. They had an onsite gunsmith who he paid an extra thirty dollars to shorten the barrel to 18 ½ inches. It was just over the federal minimum. With a couple five shot packs of oo buckshot and slugs, he had heavy protection that fit in the new Jeep vault and for little expenditure. MacLachlan added a first aid kit, axe and sheath knife, short surplus army shovel and wool blanket. Stopping off as the Publix Supermarket, he bought several day's groceries. He did not dare to buy a week or two worth, since the Hariri shoe might drop any time, prompting him to be away for a while.

Building on the land on Cedar Creek was a project he pushed into the future. He waited, fished, swam in the Gulf and ran the beaches, and waited some more. He likened his life to that of a firefighter. Rest, exercise, maintain equipment most of the time and high stress danger the rest. But he knew this: it beat the devil out of sitting at a desk all day.

The following day, he drove the Jag to a dealer in Sarasota and had it appraised. The amount was not as high as he wished but was like found money to him without hitting the depleting trust or his faster depleting savings account. He told the used car manager he would consider the offer and get back to him.

MacLachlan added another fifteen miles on Route 41 to the new Jeep's odometer and stopped at a phone booth in Ruskin. He checked the Rolex and took a chance.

"Yes?" a familiar voice answered.

"Hey, it's me. I am at a random phone booth twenty or thirty miles from home. It's the best I could do," he said to Will Grafton.

"Not perfect, but reasonable for a careful talk. The navy submersible found a bit of the device we were chasing. Enough to prove it is out of play," Grafton said.

"Good news. Anything on the injured guy from Dar-es-Salaam?" MacLachlan asked.

"An unconfirmed sighting in Pakistan. But he was moving. Maybe Afghanistan?"

"Maybe. There are still some mujahedeen's there whose real mission is unknown. Do you think they have given up on the type product we competed with them on?"

"I do. Can't be sure, but I've got a strong gut feeling they will look for another WMD," Grafton opined, referring to weapons of mass destruction.

"What do you think it could be?" MacLachlan asked.

"Could be anything. WWI mustard gas. Sarin. Some sort of plague. A lot of explosives in a busy place. I just don't know. But it will be something. And, we have to stop it. I was at a meeting the other day where you and I met with all the big boys. The biggest boy said we have to stop these people no matter how. Kinda like that fictional oo status Bond has. But I think we have his go-ahead to take out any threats that present themselves. No worry about waiting for self-defense. Search and destroy."

"So, he'll back us up?" MacLachlan asked.

"I believe he will. He is a man of integrity. The rest of the politicos in the room? I wouldn't trust any of them for a minute."

"Even the admiral?" MacLachlan wondered aloud.

"Even him, if it might impair his next star," Grafton said.

"I'm beginning to think bullets are not our most dangerous threats, Will."

"Welcome to the intelligence world. This is the crap they don't go into in movies. But it is what we have to live with. The mission is worth it. The day you question that is the day to bail immediately," he said.

MacLachlan gave that serious thought. He continued those thoughts as a daily regimen.

"Hit me on the pager. I will keep it close 24/7," he said.

"Will do. Out." and Grafton hung up. The entire conversation lasted a minute and a half. Long enough to trace, if traces were set up for the phone booth. That would be a thousand to one against chance. Or, better. Good tradecraft is built on reasonable threat assessments, MacLachlan knew. He got back in the Jeep and turned south again, thinking about Yaffa Segal. He wondered when he would see her next. At home, he wrote her a brief and sanitized letter. He wished there was an immediate and encrypted way to communicate at will. But, no such luck.

MacLachlan felt like life was on hold. He hesitated to get started on any project around the Florida place or in Virginia as long as they did not know where Hariri was. While there was not definitive proof he was behind the warhead in Czechoslovakia, both Grafton and MacLachlan felt he was. He was the man they had to get. Like the old cop said about a shooting in the 'hood, "the right one may not have been shot, but he sure wasn't the wrong one".

Big Jim also had a probably more quotable line. "When at an impasse, go fishing". So, he got his gear and walked down to the skiff. Without time to get live bait, he did what he did half the time anyway. He decided to use Mirrolures, jigs, and spoons.

He put the drain plug in the skiff and cranked the two winches down alternately until it was floating. Unhooked and gear aboard, he pulled the starter handle and the Yamaha fired up. MacLachlan untied his temporary dock line and idled away from the dock. He entered the main channel of the Gulf Intracoastal Waterway and accelerated up to about thirty miles per hour. It felt faster in the sixteen-foot skiff, driven at the rear by motor tiller. After a mile or two, he spotted an inlet leading into the mangroves. He reduced speed and entered, going down to an idle. He idled for several hundred yards then cut the engine and drifted.

As he came to a stop, he cast a bucktail jig and worked it jerkily back to the boat. He did that repeatedly for five minutes before on his last cast, the water exploded sixty feet away. He knew it had to be a snook with that hit. The reel screamed as the fish ran and took line. He turned the fish a little and was able to recover line. This went on for a while before he got the fish beside the boat. It was a large snook.

MacLachlan knew it was a keeper and would be a good dinner. But he carefully unhooked it and gently moved it through the water at the boat to flow oxygen-laden water through its gills. When the fish wiggled trying to get away, he released his hold. The snook swam away at full speed back towards the mangroves. Seated or not, MacLachlan snapped a Marine salute at the snook.

He fished a bit longer but knew that would be the height of any outing. Motor restarted, he headed home. If the boat had navigation lights; he would have docked at a waterfront restaurant. But he hooked the overhead davit lines and cranked it up. Fastening flushing 'ear muffs', he turned on the dockside hose, started the engine and ran fresh water through the cooling system until the engine had heated it to hot. He turned off the engine and hose, put the gear away at a dockside shed and walked back up to the house.

He had a gourmet dinner. Cheese sandwich and a Coke. Settling into a big leather chair, he read a novel until eleven and turned in.

At four in the morning, his home phone rang. That could not bode well, he thought.

"Yes?"

"It's me," Grafton said. "Pack for a tropical resort and get your butt to Miami ASAP.

Go to the American counter. There is a ticket waiting for you. Leaves mid-morning. Call me from a phone booth and I'll fill you in. Bye."

Grafton hung up without any further words.

Tropical resort? Mediterranean? Caribbean? Well, it did not matter. MacLachlan got up, showered and got out his carry-on bag and maroon passport. They had not requested it back and he still did not have the civilian one. He left the US Marshal's identification and the .45. He packed toiletries in a dopp bag, swimsuit, shorts and a couple of polo shirts and carefully folded a Cuban guayabera shirt. He put one on with his label-free Tel Aviv blazer and khakis, a pair of loafers and left a note for Chuck and Gloria that he would be gone a few days. MacLachlan started the Jeep at four-thirty and took I-75 to the Alligator Alley to Ft. Lauderdale then down to Miami.

He hit rush hour traffic at Ft. Lauderdale and did

not park at Miami International until eight-thirty. Rushing to the counter, he found the American flight would not begin loading for Guadeloupe's Ponte-à-Pitre Airport until ten, giving him plenty of time to get through security and to the gate. From Guadeloupe, he would connect to Lamentin Airport in Fort-de-France, Martinique. He had an open return to Miami.

"Interesting," he thought as he dialed Grafton from the gate a little later.

"I'm at the gate. Thanks for the great vacation, Dad," he said when Grafton answered the phone.

"You are welcome, my son," Grafton said sounding more like a priest than a father.

"When you get there, rent a car and go to Hotel Bakoua Les Trois Inlets. You have an open reservation there. Our friend left the mountains and is heading there by way of France. The French are sending an Interpol agent after him. He knows you will be our person on scene and are familiar—somewhat, ha-ha—with the guy he's following. I don't have his name, but he has yours. Sorry about that. Be real careful, Mack. The French government still has relationships, both governmental and business with Colonel al-Gaddafi. He's as crooked as he is crazy. I don't trust the French. Only with France, its home, does an Interpol agent act like an international agent. As you know, the rest are agents of their country's National Central Bureau and use Interpol just for law enforcement and criminal intelligence liaison only. The rest of the world does not go about flashing Interpol badges and claim to be anything. Their credentials are the ones issued by their respective departments of justice, or whoever issues them in that country.

"I hate for you to walk into something this vague. So, be careful with this damn guy, okay?

"The rest of the story is our boy and his Interpol follower get into Guadeloupe, then Martinique on Saturday. That gives you several days to get the lay of the land," Grafton said.

"Why on earth a resort-only island like Martinique?" MacLachlan asked.

"The only thing Interpol can figure is the guy he is going to meet there to negotiate whatever the weapon is insisted on Martinique. Doesn't make sense to us either. We don't think the weapon is there. We think only the deal will be consummated there and the weapon delivered somewhere else, probably in this hemisphere. Beyond that, who knows? If you get a chance to get the contact first, do so. And, squeeze the hell out of him. If not, but you get a chance to take out H, and get away....do it. But we can't give you much cover. Okay. We can't give you any cover."

"Well," MacLachlan began, "if one has to make lemonade out of a whole bag of lemons, which is what this sounds like, the place is not a bad choice. I've heard the beaches are great.

"Yeah, Mack. The beaches in Vietnam were great, too. Shame I didn't see them. You are on your own. None of the alphabet agency boys are there, as far as I know. I'm not sure whose side the French are on. They have a lot of trade and all their petroleum coming from al-Gaddafi's region. They liked us giving them the device you picked up, but their politics are convoluted as hell."

"I don't mind working alone. Beats our different agencies tripping all over one another. But, Will, just get me as much intel as you can. If no such agency," he said using the nickname of one which shared those initials, "is listening in on transmissions, get them to share, okay?"

"You got it. Fly safely and I will talk to you once you get in. Take your pager so I can beep you if something interesting comes up."

"I have it. I'll with you talk later." Both men hung up and MacLachlan stood by the pay phone for a minute. This whole op was screwed up. If his very experienced boss and friend Will did not like it, he shouldn't either.

He went to a shop and picked up some candy bars, chewing gum, a couple fishing magazines and three paperback Westerns. He studied the people in the waiting area around the gate. From clothes and actions, most looked like tourists going to Club Med or somewhere. The rest seemed to be locals returning home with bags of diapers and hard-to-get items instead of carry-ons. The flight was going to be full and he did not look forward to it. Arriving, even under less than salubrious operations planning, however, excited him. It had every earmark of an adventure. Maybe Yaffa was right about him. He knew he would outgrow that. Perhaps. He was the fittest, most tanned tourist on the flight. So, it was likely he was the only person flying from Miami to the French Antilles. But he was not absolutely sure.

The fight was two magazines and almost a thick paperback long. Four hours.

MacLachlan knew he was walking into the op unarmed and did not like it. As he went through Immigration at Guadeloupe, he realized he could have carried a rocket launcher through. He watched the other side for pre-boarding security. It was about as lax. He would stop at a store before Hariri arrived and at least get a knife.

He went to the Martinique gate and sat down. He had over an hour but was neither hungry nor thirsty. The breakdown of the passengers was in similar proportions to Miami. Tourists and locals. No hardmen. But then, Rotenberg did not appear to be a hardman. Yet, Yaffa said he was deadly.

An hour later, he boarded. Forty-five minutes later, he arrived at Lamentin, rented a car and followed directions to the Hotel Bakoua Les Trois Inlets. He liked it.

MacLachlan hung his blazer, guayabera shirts, and one pair of long pants and set his dopp kit in on the sink counter in the bathroom. He put on swimsuit trunks and a polo shirt and padded on bare feet to the beach.

He had never been to the French Caribbean before and did not realize most young women only wore half a bikini. He was glad for his Aviator sunglasses. MacLachlan saw some of the most beautiful women he had ever seen. Politics notwithstanding, his view about the French was changing rapidly. Where were these women when he was sitting on the Champs- Èlysées so recently?

As he pondered, he spotted one who stood out from the rest walking down the beach. Dreamily, he tried to focus into the bright sun to see her better. She was coming his way.

"Hi. Bet you didn't expect to see me this soon, did you?" Yaffa Segal asked.

MacLachlan was speechless and had no way to hide it as she began to laugh at him.

"What... what are you doing here?" he managed to get out.

"Probably same thing you are, I guess," Yaffa said.

"We need to go somewhere secure and talk."

"Let me go back to my chaise and get my top and towel," she said.

"Do you have to?"

"Not really. Let's go into the water. I doubt if anyone has waterproof listening gear," Yaffa said.

He walked hand-in-hand with her into the warm turquoise waters of the Caribbean. She embraced him for a long time.

"This is what I have dreamed about us doing on the beach in front of my home in Florida," he said.

"Maybe one day. For us, I think we take it when we can get it, dear Mack."

"Umm. So, what can you share?" he asked.

"No. You first."

"Okay. Hariri is on the way here in two days. He is to meet an unknown person who will negotiate the sale of a WMD, located somewhere else. An Interpol agent is on the plane following him. I do not know his name. He is to contact me shortly after landing."

"That's it?" she asked.

He nodded.

"Not very much, I'd say."

"I'd say the same," MacLachlan whispered in her wet ear.

"Squeeze me later. We need to focus now," the experienced spy said.

"Okay. Focused. Your turn."

"I actually don't know much more than you. I know what you said, plus the name of the Interpol agent. It's Leroux Benoit. I know the WMD is plans, not an actual weapon. So, he could have it here," Yaffa said.

"Then, why meet here?"

"I think probably the contact is just squeezing Hariri for a nice vacation."

"But, does that make sense among serious terrorists? Especially Muslims who don't drink, hate non-Muslim women and all," MacLachlan said.

"Maybe it has to do with there being a new Islamic Center here," Yaffa offered.

"That makes more sense. We should find out who the Imam is in the mosque that has to be associated with it. He might be some sort of terror coordinator for this region or something."

"It's late to try to find that out now. Let's put it uppermost on tomorrow's agenda."

"Do you have backup, Yaffa?" MacLachlan asked.

"No. Not this time. We did not have enough intel to plan. So, Steven sent me to observe and maybe adapt and act."

"Did you know I was going to be here?"

"Logically, yes. Who was in Florida who knew Hariri by sight? Plus, you used your real name on the flights," she smiled.

"Yeah. I should have gotten a fourth set of passports."

"Wire me the money when you get back. I think I can arrange that," Yaffa offered.

"Deal."

"If we can get the Imam's name, we should both get our analysts working on him. Steven has people working on the name of the contact here. If he gets it, maybe we can interview him first. I understand you are a very effective interviewer."

"It's odd to hold an almost naked woman I love and ask this, but since you obviously know about the impromptu waterboarding, did you finish the two in the hotel after I left them?"

"I am not sure about something. Do you know if we have a fifth amendment in the Israeli Constitution?" she asked.

"I guess, given your question, I have my answer."

"How do you feel about it, dear Mack?"

"Business is business. I should have done it myself instead of leaving it for you."

"Probably," she whispered. "Can we change the subject?"

"Yes, it's about time to," he said.

She gave him a long kiss.

"Better subject," he mumbled.

After half an hour, she said "We'd better go ashore before we shrivel up." Then added, "Okay most of us shrivel up," and gave him a smile that was positively evil.

They went to dinner in the hotel's restaurant several hours later.

"You know. I need to advise my control that you are here, and we are working together," MacLachlan said.

"Me, too. Steven likes you a lot. I am not so sure he would like us being in this location trying to keep our minds on the job at hand, but I think he would appreciate that I now have backup."

"Me, too. Any weapons?"

"My hands. I picked up a knife earlier, too."

"Hell, we could have brought anything we wanted in here," MacLachlan said.

"Not really. These French are devious. Sometimes they search everybody. You never know."

"Okay. I planned on getting a knife this afternoon, but something came up."

"Yes. Well, we can get you one tomorrow," she said.

They awoke almost refreshed after several hours of sleep. After a shower and breakfast, they took MacLachlan's rental car, a Daihatsu with bright yellow headlamps, to the store where Yaffa bought a souvenir dagger. She waited in the green subcompact while MacLachlan went in and bought its duplicate.

They circled the Islamic Center and adjourning mosque. There was a Catholic Church nearby and they stopped there.

They introduced themselves as Mr. and Mrs. Dusay from Montreal, using the name on a passport that was across the Atlantic at the time.

"Father, this is an impromptu visit. I am a journalist from Canada. I am on vacation here. But, at home, I am writing a series of articles on how Islam is invading Canada and its horrible Sharia law. Now, I come to paradise and see a big center and mosque.

"I will not use your name, but what do you think of this? Who is the Imam? Is he modern or very orthodox in his sermons?" MacLachlan asked.

It was clear the priest had an opinion and wanted to share it. As he spoke, MacLachlan wrote on a hotel notepad with a hotel pen. His beautiful blonde wife nodded her head with each point the priest made as a participative listener.

They learned the Imam's name. His country of

birth. That he was scarily (in the priest's opinion) ortho-dox, the approximate number of members and that he was offended by the loudspeaker calling for prayers.

MacLachlan put his hand on the priest's shoulder and thanked him sincerely. That emotion was not a lie. This information may save the lives of Catholics and those of many other religions. They made a generous contribution to the church and left.

"You are pretty good, MacLachlan," Yaffa said.

"Believing in what I am doing helps. We have to get to phones, and you call Steven and I have to call Will."

He sped the little car along as fast as its minimal horsepower would allow. At the hotel, they separated for now and went to make the calls. He got Grafton on the line right away.

"That could be why they are meeting in Martinique. It did not make sense. But, if the cleric there is a terror leader, it makes perfect sense. Or if he's the money man. I will call the Director of Central Intelligence and have all the analysts in every damn agency that uses alphabet letters for its name cracking on this as soon as I hang up.

"Plus, I will let the admiral know what we are doing in case he wants to clue in the big guy. Let you know as soon as I have something. Mack, I don't totally trust the Israelis. I know you do. I also know you like the girl a lot. Just be careful man, okay?"

"I promise, Will. Too much is at risk here for anything else. I got that, so don't worry. Bye," MacLachlan ended.

The next day was wait and see what the various agencies would come up with. They spent time around prayers to Mecca doing surveillance. Maybe they would recognize who met Hariri when he arrived by plane tomorrow. After, they went back to the beach, pagers close at hand.

Late in the afternoon, MacLachlan's pager went off. He walked to a lobby phone and called Will Grafton.

"You might have hit a bonanza on the Imam. He is a known money man for Hezbollah. So, if the contact has the plans Yaffa referred to, they could do the deal in Martinique and Hariri could go on to the target location. Maybe immediately," Grafton said.

"If I can't get a flight with him, I will try to find the airline and flight number. You could have the Bureau pick him and the plans up if he lands in the US, Agency if he lands outside," MacLachlan suggested.

"Bureau if he lands in US for sure. As to the who for outside the US, it depends on where. Cuba worries me the most. Whether by commercial, which I don't know off the top of my head, or by private plane, I believe you can get from there to Cuba. He'd be untouchable there. He and old Fidel could cook up a deal where Cuban intelligence or special ops could deliver it. And, we would not know who to look for," Grafton said.

"Have we searched airline manifests for Hariri coming to the US over the next week or two?" MacLachlan asked.

"Yep. Nothing yet. If he's booked, it's under another name."

"Maybe I could get a photo of him deplaning or in the airport. That could be useful to circulate at US airports if he flies in incognito."

"It would. I wish we had set you up with a decent

covert camera. I'm pretty sure you cannot get something like that in Martinique or Guadeloupe."

"That would have been good. I may have to develop a special kit for my carry-on bag. There are some pretty upscale shops here with watches and all. I may take a look to see what kind of cameras they have, Will." MacLachlan said.

"Do that. Just remember it's easy to get burned taking a photo. So, be careful."

Later that afternoon, MacLachlan and Yaffa went into Fort-de-France and shopped for cameras. They found a new Sony 35 mm SLR camera and bought two rolls of film with it. One was used to take vacation photos on the beach, the other reserved for intel photos.

They drove past the Islamic Center. There was no traffic in or out. They drove on, camera still in Yaffa's lap. There was a beautiful sunset. Each took photos of the other walking down the beach. Though the roll was far from finished, MacLachlan removed it and put the film back in the small gray plastic cannister. He reloaded the camera with a fresh roll of film for the airport tomorrow.

They drove to the airport with shorts and polo shirts on, the camera strung around MacLachlan's neck. The plan was to look like tourists there to meet someone and take lots of photos. Before the plane landed, they would be ostensibly of Yaffa posing and making faces at her 'boyfriend'. Actually, MacLachlan would aim around and over her and get photos of people in the crowd who did not profile as Caribbeans or tourists. That was pretty easy, as most of the crowd at the outside gate for the flight fit into one or the other category. Nobody appeared to be a terrorist from the Middle East or anywhere else.

As the time for the incoming flight from Paris to arrive neared, the American and Israeli spotted several men with darker complexions join the crowd. Yaffa posed and MacLachlan took several good surreptitious photos of them.

Yaffa's expression changed in her last photo. She ran up to MacLachlan, kissed him and buried her face against his neck. From that position, she whispered into his ear.

"Undercover police are setting up. The damn fool French are going to try to make an arrest. Things are going to go very badly. I can just feel it."

MacLachlan kissed her and smiling with his forehead against hers, whispered "I just noticed that. They are going to blow everything. They might get the target, but not the plans for whatever weapon he's here to get. That will be gone forever, unless we somehow find out who the contact is. Or, do a black bag job on the Center."

The 747 landed and began to taxi towards them. They watched the crowd and MacLachlan took more photos.

The flagman directed it into the gate. Mobile steps were driven up. The door opened. A procession of tourists and Caribbeans proceeded down the steps. After about fifty or sixty people left the plane, MacLachlan saw Hariri. He had on a business suit and sunglasses. No beard. No headwear. Several men seemed to be with him.

He paused on the third step and peered into the gate area. He spotted the ambush, hesitated, and turned to say something to the dark man behind him. That person turned and started back into the plane's door quickly. The men behind him were obviously body-guards. They pushed past Hariri, surrounded him, head down and did a classic 'cover and evacuate the princi-pal' move.

MacLachlan took several good facial shots of Hariri. He and Yaffa heard shots from within the plane. They sounded like pistols, not automatic fire from a rifle or submachine gun. A couple of civilians, men and women, were pushed out onto the top landing of the mobile stairs. A flight attendant with a pistol at her head disconnected the stair.

The 747 began to taxi away. Its wing brushed the mobile staircase out of the way as the big plane began to move much faster than normal for the main runway.

MacLachlan took several last photos and he and Yaffa ran for the terminal and a phone. A man was talking on the one in front of MacLachlan. MacLachlan told him in French he needed it for an emergency. The man shook his head and turned his back to MacLachlan.

MacLachlan spun the man around and decked him. He was unconscious. Yaffa smiled and did the same to the man on the adjacent phone.

Both called their control and reported the hijacking. MacLachlan told Grafton "I think you forecast it. I bet it will head directly for Cuba. I have good photos of Hariri. Okay." He hung up.

Yaffa had just finished. They slipped away and moved towards the car before the two men at the phones recovered consciousness. A couple of witnesses tried to stop them. MacLachlan told them in French they were police with an emergency and to get out of the way or face arrest.

"What are your instructions, Mack?" Yaffa asked in the car.

"To get back to the US with the film so we will have good photos of Hariri for airport and port watch as soon as possible. But I wanted to get out of that airport before the police tried to arrest us for hitting those two guys."

"Mine are similar," she said.

"I will get copies of the photos to you by way of the Israeli main embassy in DC. That's the best I can do."

"Okay. As soon as you can. Actually, I am more interested in the crowds and the guys on the plane helping him. I wonder how they smuggled guns aboard?"

"Co-conspirators on the cleaning crew? False diplomat creds conveniently overlooked by the French? Who knows? Not the first time Hezbollah has hijacked a jet."

"No, not at all. Anything on the possible ID for the contact?" Yaffa asked.

"No. Nothing."

"Me, either," she said, adding "but, I think I have some news we both will like."

"Oh, what's that?" he asked.

"Steven told me to go back to Florida. If we part-nered, he said he would approve it as long as we protected our agencies' equities."

"Yes." he exclaimed.

They both packed and checked out as soon as they got back to the resort.

"I kind of hate leaving this place," she said.

"Before you get too melancholy, wait until you see mine," MacLachlan responded to her.

Though they had to drive to the airport separately to return the rental cars, they agreed they had been seen together on the small island and it would be riskier to try to appear unrelated than to fly back to Miami as the lovers they had portrayed...and perhaps were. They took the quick hop to Guadeloupe, knives in checked luggage, then the longer flight to Miami.

It was late at night before the Jeep turned into the house on Casey Key.

The next morning, MacLachlan paid for a rush job film processing and sent Hariri, crowd, hijack and one shot of the Imam in Martinique to Grafton. The first was by fax, then the originals were picked up by a young FBI agent from the Sarasota Resident Agency office for hand delivery directly to Grafton at the White House Situation Room.

Grafton called MacLachlan at three in the afternoon.

"These pictures are golden. We finally have a great facial shot of Hariri, even though he does have shades on. Every Middle Eastern desk in the US government is studying the Imam, trying to identify him. I think we will have him before you and Yaffa have some sort of sea creature for dinner."

"That would be perfect, Will. I just know he figures prominently into this. I am leaning toward him being the banker more than the control. I think that was why Hariri went to Pakistan or Afghanistan when he went dark on us."

"I agree, Mack. Listen, I have a solution to our communications problem. And, it will be fixed tomorrow morning. I have a couple of my technicians coming to visit you on Casey Key. They are good guys, so don't shoot them or anything. They will do a quick TSCM on your house. Send your guest to the beach while they are there. I want to keep our sources and methods in the immediate family, okay?"

"Lima charley," MacLachlan responded with the phonetics for 'loud and clear'.

"What they will leave you will allow us to have totally secure comms," Grafton said.

MacLachlan suspected it would be a shortwave, burst transmitting radio of some sort. He wondered if it would be portable.

"Mack, do you have an ADT or some sort of alarm on the house?"

"No."

"Okay. The guys will bring you a cash 'expense reimbursement.' Use that to have one installed *post haste*. The thing they are leaving is not the newest possible technology, but it is still pretty highly classified."

"Thanks, Will. I will hang around the house tomorrow and explain to Yaffa she might have to take a swim alone when I have some guests. She is a pro. She will understand. Oh—can she see the thing being left?" he asked.

"I am sure they have the same equipment. From us, probably. Just make sure she does not see the frequency day book or any codes. That would open up our lingerie drawer to them for sure."

"Can't let that happen. I will be careful. I am anyway," MacLachlan said.

He walked out into the yard. Yaffa was sunning in a

chaise lounge. She wore the half bikini he had first seen in Martinique, along with big sunglasses and a straw hat.

"Hi. How did you conversation with your controller go?" she asked.

"Fine. His name is Will. He is going to send a couple guys down tomorrow to put in some sort of communication device. He told me it's okay for you to see it, but not the bands I broadcast on or the day book with codes. During the installation, which I suspect will involve running wires for an antenna, he asked if you would go swimming on the Gulf beach across the road."

"You mentioned you have a beach. Can we walk over to see it now?" she asked.

On the way, she said "I understand the need for confidentiality. We would do the same thing in Israel if the tables were turned. Maybe worse."

"Thanks," he said.

They crossed the road and walked down a slight incline to the sand beach. A chickee hut was there with a couple of chaises in it.

"I know what this is for, but what do you call it?" she asked of the wall-less hut with a thatched roof.

"It's called a chickee hut. My grandfather had a Seminole Indian friend come up from the Everglades and build it for him years ago. I am amazed it has survived the storms and winds off the Gulf of Mexico so well. When things settle down, I will look for his descendants and get it freshened up a bit."

She looked up and down the long, beautiful sand beach.

"This is beautiful. Do you own all of this?" she asked.

"Good question. My grandfather felt he owned the land down to the low tide line with the Gulf. There have been varying state and federal court decisions over the years. There have been cases where the state replenished sand after hurricanes or storms and then claimed the beach they put the sand on as state property. So, I guess it depends on a particular scenario. Nobody ever put sand here. There has been no riparian claim. So, as far as I'm concerned, it's mine to the left and right all the way to my property line and out to the waterline."

"That is a lot of beautiful sand. And, turquoise water. Of course, you want me to stay here forever."

"Of course. Until one or both of us has to go shoot somebody who's a threat to America or Israel," he said.

"Well. There is that. In the meantime, I am going in. Want to join me?" she asked.

He kicked his boat shoes off and tossed his tee shirt over the back of a chaise and took her hand. The water was in the eighties. They frolicked for a long time.

"I have never quite had this much fun on a mission," Yaffa said.

"It does not seem to be textbook. But, then again, I have never really had spy craft training. My training was more intelligence analyst stuff in the Marines. Not black ops, spook stuff like you have had and like our different groups with 'agency' in their names have," he said.

"Odd. I would have thought you would have."

"No. I sort of bumbled into this because of starting with firsthand experience with Hezbollah at the Marine barracks bombing and collecting some collateral intel first from sources I had paid," MacLachlan explained.

"Was the port your first firefight?" she asked.

"No, I had a fight where a source was killed several years ago and after a gunfight in a bar, I was chased by two tangos," he said.

"How many died?"

"My source and the four guys who shot him and chased me."

"That big .45 again?" she asked.

"No, but an issue one with an ugly Parkerized finish, instead of the blue steel one I used in Tanzania. But, same 1911 Colt under the finish," he said.

"Speaking of that. I am unarmed. Can we do something about that?" she asked.

"Absolutely. I am not sure about regular store sales for a foreign citizen. We need to get you something without paperwork. Will you take it back to Israel? I guess you'd need to be near Washington and use a diplomatic pouch from your embassy..."

"No, I would leave it here," she said.

"I will show you two of my grandfather's guns you could choose from. They mean a lot to me. But, so do you."

"I promise to take good care of them. But a throw away that is dependable would be better than an heirloom."

"We'll take care of your needs, Yaffa."

She smiled. "I am quite sure of that, Colonel."

————

THE TWO TECHS from Grafton arrived mid-morning. Yaffa walked to the beach, carrying a bag with a Thermos of water, towels, suntan lotion and a transistor radio.

A much more sophisticated radio was installed in the house after the two men cleared it and proclaimed there were no bugging or camera devices recording on the property. The technology and appearance of the radio they installed was not too far removed from the early part of the Cold War. It took several hours, part of which time MacLachlan walked down to the beach and spent with Yaffa.

The two techs spent an hour after installation teaching MacLachlan how to use the code of the day, compose messages and send them in microsecond bursts. During their screen of his house, they gave him a harmless, small device to use in hotel rooms and at home if he thought he had been breached. They taught him where surveillance devices, both auditory and camera, were frequently hidden and how to detect them. He was to always carry a blade and Phillips head screwdriver in his travels to remove the frames on light sockets, heating and air conditioning louvers and the like.

Upon leaving, they left a thick packet of cash on the table to use having a professional alarm system installed. He would have to include Chuck and Gloria in the password process as they were in and out almost daily when he was not there.

While Yaffa was showering, MacLachlan got the XKE out of the garage and dusted the sleek, polished body with a chamois. He started it and let it settle to a burble while he went back into the house. Yaffa went from towel to sundress and sandals in a moment. He handed her a Colt Agent revolver to put in her purse. It required no manual of arms training to use. Aim and press the trigger. They would settle on something semi-permanent for her the following day.

She smiled at the English Racing Green Jag. MacLachlan just hoped it would get them to the intended waterfront restaurant and back without dying in the middle of the Tamiami Trail.

He drove the Jag fast and hard. That, apparently, was what the car liked because it responded well and dependably.

The Mahi-mahi was excellent as were the crab cakes. MacLachlan bought Yaffa a silk scarf at a gift shop in the restaurant. She tied it on, giving a 50's look as he dropped the canvas top on the sports car for the ten-mile trip back.

MacLachlan was working on second thoughts about selling the Jaguar until it started missing as he turned into his yard. But, that hardened his resolve.

The schedule of radio check-ins was mid-morning and mid-afternoon during ops. Those were times when Grafton was likely to be in his office. MacLachlan knew someone would monitor Grafton's radio since he was on call to the Situation Room, Langley and his own head-quarters at DIA. Otherwise, they used phones for "in the clear" calls as needed. It was not perfect, but hope-fully would work for the current environment. To take advantage of an obscure phone booth in a shopping center, he called Will Grafton.

"Hi, Will. Just a quick check-in. How did our vaca-tion photos come out?" he asked.

"Really clear. Some of our photo enhancement folks did some enlarging and cropping and we have distributed pictures of your buddy to the FBI, DEA, and airport police in Florida and Alabama. We figure he will come into the Southeastern US by boat or maybe small plane with a smuggler, or fly in. If the latter, he may still think we don't have any good likenesses of him. Long shot, but we have to cover all bases.

"That gives me an idea, Will. Can you set me up with a real knowledgeable DEA guy in Miami or the Keys? Wherever he or she is, I'll drive down and meet them. I'd like some idea about where to start looking for him to show up. I am confident he will come in with drug smugglers instead of a commercial flight. When you get a contact, maybe fax him a photo of me for ID purposes. Those guys have to be paranoid just to stay alive," MacLachlan said.

"That's a good idea. Take along that badge and cred pack in case you need something he can relate to, okay?"

"Will do. I'll wait for you to respond back. Bye."

The call to Grafton was on his home number. MacLachlan only knew the enigma lived somewhere in Northern Virginia when stateside, but that encompassed a lot of area. He was unsure whether his associate was married, had children, pets...anything. But he guessed in their business, it was the safest way. One he had better start adopting.

"COULD we look for a pistol for me this morning?" Yaffa asked at breakfast. "It needs to be small enough for me to hide here in hot Florida on my 5'4" form, yet at least a .380. I'd prefer a 9mm if we can find one."

"What do you regularly carry, like when you were in Tanzania or when we were together in Israel," MacLachlan asked.

"I have several. Depends on my outfit." He grinned at that.

"Stop it, now. Do you want me slouching around like an old babushka lady?"

"Hardly."

"Our generation thinks power is everything. Steven killed some of the Munich assassins with a .22 Beretta."

"How about a compromise? That same exact gun is available in .32 and .380. Why don't we look for one of those?" he asked.

"Okay, but not .22 or .32."

"I am afraid we might have to go to a gun store and do paperwork for something that specific. Unless, you will carry my grandfather's Browning .380 while you are here. It's small and flat. I have shot it hundreds of times without a single jam. It should work until we come up with something else."

"May I see it?" she asked.

Moments later, he handed her a small semiautomatic, slide locked back and chamber empty. She checked it, dropped the slide and tested the trigger and safety.

"Perfect for a non-9mm. How about some ammo for this?"

He reached in his pocket and handed her a full box of Remington cartridges and a clip inside the waistline holster. She tried it on with the unloaded gun in it and moved it around to a place it would be comfortable and still not "print" under a shirt or blouse. Yaffa loaded the magazine to capacity and holstered the pistol on an empty chamber, Israeli style.

"Will I be arrested for carrying this?" she asked, more or less rhetorically, since she was going to carry it anyway.

"Nope. Keep your diplomatic passport with you whenever you are packing it. You can always claim diplomatic privilege," MacLachlan suggested.

They took a run down the beach and MacLachlan introduced his guest to the outside shower surrounded by fragrant tropical plantings.

Before lunch, the home phone rang. Will Grafton spoke without identifying himself and hung up.

"Check the other."

MacLachlan went to the radio and, taking out the day book for encryption code, sent "Monitoring."

A burst came through.

It gave the name and contact for a DEA agent in Miami-Dade. MacLachlan wrote it down, then called.

"Hey. This is MacLachlan. A mutual friend in DC gave me your name. When can my friend and I visit you?"

"You are a couple hundred miles north, right?" the man asked.

"I am. Can leave anytime."

"Can you meet me around five, here?"

"We can. Want me to call back from a phone booth when I get within half an hour?" MacLachlan asked.

"Yup." He hung up.

MacLachlan left the bedroom where the radio was located.

"Good news?" Yaffa asked.

"I hope so. We are going to Miami. Like right now. We may spend the night, so pack your toothbrush and jammies," he suggested.

"Ha. Jammies. Right. Ready in two minutes," she said as they walked into the bedroom and she pulled on short shorts, trainers and a top. She tucked the Browning and holster into her waistband and adjusted.

"Printing?" she asked about whether the butt of the small gun was poking the shirt out.

"Nope. Me?" MacLachlan asked turning with the larger .45 invisible at all angles under his guayabera shirt. She shook her head and he picked up his dopp bag and some clean underwear. He put a couple extra mags in his short's pockets. He already had a folding knife clipped in one. MacLachlan wrote a short note for Gloria, who was scheduled to clean, and they left by Jeep.

As promised, MacLachlan called his contact at four-thirty. The man used the name Tom Vasquez. They met in Little Havana at La Caretta, a Cuban restaurant. As the two walked in, they saw a medium height dark-haired handsome man with a neatly trimmed beard. He motioned them to a corner table.

"Hi, I'm Tom. I know from a faxed photo you are Mack and assume the lady is Yaffa." He passed his creds under the table to Mack, who glanced at them and returned them.

The restaurant was fairly loud at the peak of its dinner hour, which played well with their need to speak without people nearby listening.

"Tom, did you get the photo of the guy we want to pick up?"

"I did, Mack, as did every one of my associates from

Atlanta to Miami to Houston. We've got all eyes out for him. When one of us gets something, I'd like for us to tag along with you to pick up the guys he hitched a ride with. I am pretty sure they would be persons of interest to us," Tom said.

MacLachlan considered for a moment.

"As a federal law enforcement agent, that might put you in an uncomfortable position, Tom. We need to stop this guy. If we can pick him up, he will be sent outside the US for questioning. There is very unlikely to be any Miranda rights read or charges filed. If it looks like he may escape, he will be stopped."

"I figured that from the way I was contacted and this meeting with you two was set up. We have no interest in Hariri, only his transportation and what they will be carrying. If you take him, however 'take' works out to be, it's fine. Just leave the boat and drivers to me. And, I guess you know, we have more deadly gunfights than the other federal agencies put together, right?"

MacLachlan nodded, a half smile on his face. Yaffa's expression was beautifully benign.

"I think we can work together just fine," MacLachlan said.

"I have not eaten all day. Want to order?" Vasquez asked.

"I would love to," Yaffa answered, speaking for the first time in totally unaccented English.

"Can I ask, Mack. Are you two feds?" Vasquez asked.

"When we need to be," MacLachlan said.

"Kinda like us, you work in a vague area generally outside the public view?"

"Very much."

In his home turf, they suggested that Vasquez order the food. They ended up with a table filled with ropa viejo (old clothes, the name for shredded beef), pulled pork, chicken and Moro rice and black beans, plantains, and buttered Cuban bread.

With some hesitation, Yaffa said "If things go to hell when we meet up with Hariri and whoever is with him, we may not want to have our presence known after the fact. Is there anywhere around here, we can pick up 'clean' 9mm's or .45's? That might be better than using issued guns that show someone other than your agency was present."

Vasquez thought about that for a minute.

"There was a raid this morning. A couple of 9 millimeters were picked up from two guys. The guns were run through NCIC and had no record. Maybe legitimately bought or stolen and never reported. That happens a lot. We had to let the guys go, but no way we are giving them guns back. The pistols are not evidence, so they have not been logged in anywhere yet. Ultimately, we'd log them in and destroy them or use them undercover ourselves. They'd work for you. It will take me about an hour after we finish here to get them. How about that?"

"That would be very kind of you, Tom," Yaffa said, dazzling him with her smile. Though trying to be stoic, MacLachlan could not help rolling his eyes. Yaffa saw him and smiled at him, too."

He couldn't resist.

"I bet you did that as a little girl and had your daddy and uncles wrapped around your little finger, didn't you?" MacLachlan asked as Vasquez grinned.

"Moi?" she asked, not elaborating further. They finished with café con leche and MacLachlan picked up the tab.

"If you want to have another cup of café con leche, I will slip out a while and meet you either in here or at your Jeep in the parking lot with a package for you," Vasquez said.

Forty minutes later, Vasquez pulled his navy Tahoe up beside the Jeep and passed a package to Yaffa on the passenger side.

"I didn't include ammo because we don't use 9mm's. Their original cartridges are in the magazines, but I don't know I'd trust it."

"No problem, Tom. We will pick up some new stuff. Thanks a million." Yaffa said.

"Welcome. We'll talk as soon as I hear something," he said.

"Tom?" MacLachlan asked.

"If you need us and cannot reach my home number, call my pager or the Washington number for my control. All are on this card. And, thanks for everything," MacLachlan said as he passed the card to Yaffa to give to Vasquez.

It was early enough to avoid getting a hotel. MacLachlan headed back towards home, stopping at a big box store he knew sold ammunition. They picked up four boxes of 124 grain hollow points. Yaffa had checked the pistols: both needed cleaning but seemed serviceable. One was a Sig, the other a Beretta. Both were full-size and difficult to conceal with thick frames and long butts, but classic fighting pistols.

Yaffa slept as MacLachlan drove across Alligator

Alley and up I-75. She awoke from the different road feel as they pulled into the lane leading up to the tin-roofed house.

"Hey, Sleeping Beauty. Want to wake up so you can go to bed?" he asked.

"Umhumph..." was about all she could manage, but he understood perfectly.

The next morning, MacLachlan let Yaffa sleep and took a quick beach run. He came in after the outside shower and smelled coffee immediately.

After her imitation in Tel Aviv, he tried a "Lucy, I'm home," and it sounded just like Desi Arnaz to him. But he got an "Oh, Mack. That was awful," in return. He decided to do no more imitations.

As he had coffee, eggs and toast she prepared, he suggested field stripping the Sig and Beretta and examining them before a quick trip to a local shooting range. Yaffa agreed. They cleared the table and she had both stripped to their major parts before he got back with a cleaning kit.

He looked at the parts laid out on a couple of paper towels in front of someone wearing one of his old tee shirts.

"I'm thinking you might be the perfect woman," he said.

"You just figuring that out?"

He shook his head and sat down. Picking up both barrels and holding them up to the ceiling light, he peered in.

"My guess is these two bozos lucked onto decent pistols, shot them a time or two, probably at a competitor's house, then put them away dirty. A while ago, it appears."

He affixed a brass brush to a cleaning rod, put some Ballistol in the barrels and scrubbed the crud out. Yaffa put the cleaner and lubricant on a cotton patch and wiped the other parts, leaving only the lightest coats on them.

She assembled the Beretta while he did the Sig.

"I'll put some shorts on and be ready in a minute," she said.

"No rush. The range does not open for a couple of hours yet. Besides, you smell pretty hot with that gun oil..." She smiled and walked out. He knew where she was going and followed.

THEY EACH SHOT HALF a box of fifty at seven, then fifteen yards. Then, they switched guns and repeated. Both bulls targets had fifty holes clustered in the black. They packed up and walked to the Jeep.

"Which one do you want?" MacLachlan asked.

"I think the Beretta. The reach to the trigger is a stretch for my small hand, but I have more experience with it than the Sig," she said.

"It's a deal. We'll go home, clean them again and load up for whatever happens," MacLachlan said.

They did. That afternoon, Vasquez called the house line.

"Hey, can you guys get down to Marco Island quickly? A Coast Guard patrol plane just spotted a go-fast heading in that direction. The boat is about two hours out. They can't get a boat there in time from Station Ft. Myers, but we have gotten a couple of Florida Marine Patrol officers to participate in a stop with us. We will be leaving in an hour and a half from Marco Marina, if you can make it in time."

"Man," MacLachlan said, "it's about two hours from here. We will do our best. If you have to leave without us."

MacLachlan hung up, got out his phone book and spent two minutes before dialing.

"Florida Highway Patrol. What is your emergency?"

"This is Deputy US Marshal JE MacLachlan. I need to speak with your most senior officer present immediately, please."

"I have a sergeant here. Wait one."

"Sergeant Mahoney, Deputy. What's up?"

"Sergeant, we have an internationally-wanted criminal coming by boat into Marco Island in two hours. A federal team with FMP boats is going to intercept him. I have been called to help, but there is no way I can get there without your help. Can you assign me a trooper with a full tank to run my partner and me down Code-3?" MacLachlan asked.

"It's a little irregular. Let me call up to Tallahassee and get clearance. What's your number?" MacLachlan gave it and hung up. He immediately called Grafton. Before Grafton's phone started ringing, he said to Yaffa "I am getting ready to tick off the highway patrol big time..."

"Yes?"

"It's me. Can you get someone to call the Florida Highway Patrol headquarters in Tallahassee immediately? A Sergeant Mahoney is calling to get clearance to have a trooper take us down really fast. The guy in Miami called and said a go-fast is coming in and they are going to intercept it. I cannot get there on time without running over a hundred all the way."

"Wait on hold a second, Mack."

The second was three minutes long.

"An Assistant Director of the Criminal Investigation Division at FBI Headquarters just called the director. They are old friends. You should be good to go."

"Thanks, Will. We will advise in a couple hours," MacLachlan said and hung up.

The phone rang.

"This is Sergeant Mahoney of the FHP. My brass turned the request down. I'm a little surprised, actually. Wait. My communications officer has something urgent."

He came back on, "I guess they changed their minds up in HQ. You need a ride or an escort?"

"I think a ride."

"Where from?" MacLachlan thought for a moment, then named a restaurant at the nearest Interstate exit.

"There will be two of us in a Jeep Wrangler," MacLachlan said.

"He will be there in a couple minutes."

"Thanks, Sergeant."

MacLachlan grabbed a carry case for the shotgun on the way out. It had a pocket with about twenty buckshot and slug loads in it.

The two sprinted for the Jeep and spun the wheel all the way down the drive.

Five minutes later, they were at the restaurant. A yellow and black Crown Vic with its blue lights flashing was already there.

The two got out, MacLachlan sticking the short scattergun into the case. He held up the distinctive

Marshal's badge as they got in the car. Yaffa took the front, MacLachlan the rear.

"Hey, guys. Trooper Rob White. I hear you guys have to be somewhere *real* fast."

"We do, Rob. The Marco Marina. In less than two hours. I'm Mack and the deputy up front with you is Yaffa." She gave him her smile and won him instantly.

"Hook 'em up. We're gonna roll."

MacLachlan had driven fast all of his life. But an hour and forty-five minutes later, he knew one thing. Nobody could cover tarmac better than a state trooper. Nobody.

As they past Ft. Myers, the needle was on one twenty-five. They hit a deserted few miles and it climbed to one-thirty.

"I put a chip in it. Don't tell my sergeant. But it helps me catch those Camaros and Mustangs better, since they've got more horsepower. Even if I can't outrun them, my radio can," the hard charging young trooper said.

"Want me to hang out here?" the trooper added.

"Sure, if you have the time. Take this and have lunch on me. You are one helluva driver, Rob. Thanks." MacLachlan said, passing him a twenty.

Yaffa winked and the two ran towards the dock were two twenty-five-foot dual outboard powered police boats were getting ready to cast off.

As they climbed aboard, Vasquez said, "Hey, guys. These are the folks from Washington. They have an interest in the Middle Eastern guy I showed you. They only want him. The drug smugglers are all ours."

MacLachlan and Yaffa Segal nodded at the crew of

DEA and Marine Patrol men and women. They were handed two life jackets and put them on.

The boats cast off and aimed out the channel. The FMP officer said, "Everybody ready?" With nods, he pushed twin throttles to the pegs and the Mako's bow rose as five hundred horsepower propelled them onto plane and to fifty miles per hour.

"We have a Coast Guard jet up high watching them. Since all mariners have VHF marine radios, we have to assume the target can hear our radio transmissions. The USCG plane does not want to be identified by tail number, so we have to be vague in our calls. We've already spoken with the little jet earlier and set up comms," the officer yelled above the roar of the twin outboards and the two-foot chop on the Gulf of Mexico.

"Jet, this is the FMP unit below. Do you still have eyes on the mark?" the FMP officer radioed.

"FMP unit, we do and also on you and your friend. Turn about thirty degrees port and you will be on an intercept. He's five miles out moving at approximately fifty knots. When you get close, I will vector you until you have eyes on," the pilot or first officer said.

"He's cruising almost fifty miles per hour. Depending on his load, he may have a top end today of seventy," the officer yelled to his passengers.

Soon, the two FMP vessels saw the long, sleek Cigarette-style boat moving at high speed on what seemed a collision course. The boat saw them and veered right. The second FMP boat turned a harder right to cut them off. The boat MacLachlan and Yaffa were in aimed directly at the go-fast and held that line.

The FMP officer keyed his mic on channel sixteen, the hailing and distress frequency.

"Go-fast boat off Marco Island, this is the Florida Marine Patrol. Drop off plane and go dead in the water to be boarded. If you continue to try to evade, we will fire on you."

Agent Vasquez reached for the mic and repeated the order in Spanish.

The go-fast refused to comply. Instead, it would aim at one FMP patrol boat or the other, as if it was going to ram.

Vasquez removed a hunting rifle from a case. He took the caps off a Leopold 3-9 power scope and squatted at the bow deck. He waited for a calm between the Mako jumping waves and squeezed off a shot. The rifle, a .338 Winchester Magnum cracked as he sent a two hundred-fifty grain bullet across the bow of the speeding drug boat.

The driver seemed to ignore the shot, so Vasquez put another one into the rear side. Nothing. He fired another in the same area. Black smoke arose from the engine compartment. There were some high-fives from both police boats as the go-fast slowed and came to rest in the water. The officers and agents could see the crew of four attempting to scuttle the boat so it would sink with its cargo. The two patrol boats came up on plane and rushed in from diagonal points off the boat's bow, so as to not fire towards each other if shots were fired.

Which is exactly what happened. Two of the drug runners came up firing with submachineguns. Both patrol boats spun in tight circles and accelerated off. Vasquez fired the magnum rifle again and one of the men with a submachine gun fell. He worked the bolt as MacLachlan fired a twelve-gauge slug at the shooters. His target was not hit but rattled enough with a seventy-two caliber chunk of lead whistling by his ear to drop his submachinegun overboard as he jumped out of line of sight. The other DEA agents and Yaffa fired a barrage of pistol shots, holding the drug runners down as the patrol boats came back around and bore down on the stalled go-fast.

The drug runners had enough. As the patrol boats neared, the survivors' hands were held high. The man Vasquez shot was clearly dead. One of the DEA agents had documented enough of the gunfight on a movie camera to assure, with the testimony of a group of law enforcement officers and the film, Vasquez's shoot was justified. One of the FMP officers marked the location of the go-fast on his GPS in case a prosecutor wanted divers to recover the lost submachinegun from the bottom. The Gulf was shallow enough at that location according to the depth finder to allow a scuba diver to easily recover the gun.

The disheartening news to MacLachlan and Yaffa was the absence of Abdel Hariri.

A DEA agent gave the prisoners Miranda rights so MacLachlan could ask about the terrorist. Nobody waived the right to have an attorney present.

MacLachlan asked if he might ask a couple of non-drug proprietary questions of the men alone. Vasquez nodded affirmatively to his agents and the FMP officers. They continued to document the several hundred large bags of cocaine in the bow and middle of the go-fast, while MacLachlan and Yaffa ushered the remaining three to the stern of the thirty-four-foot boat.

MacLachlan spoke in Spanish. It may, he hoped, give a little more privacy.

"There are two kinds of people who have you in

custody. Most are state or federal law enforcement officers. They have rules. To them, you have rights.

"Then, there is my associate and me. We don't work for the government. We don't have rules. We don't care if you have rights. Our job is to make problems go away. You are problems. We don't care about the drugs you carried. We care about a terrorist," he held up Hariri's photo, "and, since you were involved with him, you are terrorists, too.

"So, I will make you disappear. A black plane will take you on a long flight blindfolded. And, when you get there, you will be a nameless person forgotten to society in a nameless prison that does not exist.

"But the man who tells me where this man, Abdel Hariri, is right now, will get a reduced sentence. I will do all I can to make it as light as I can. Maybe even a nice, high paid life with his family in the US in the Witness Protection Program.

"Who wants to tell me?"

A man stepped forward. One of the others attempted to grab him, but Yaffa kicked him in the patella, probably breaking that knee cap. He screamed out and she punched him in the solar plexus. He collapsed.

She turned to the agents who had been taking inventory and not paying attention to what was happening in the stern.

"He tried to touch my bosom. That was very rude of him," she said innocently. "I think he will need medical attention when we get back to the marina," she added, this time truthfully. The tough agents tried hard to stifle grins at the small woman decking someone who outweighed her by almost a hundred pounds. But they failed.

MacLachlan separated the man who came forward from the others. He told the other two "You should have taken my deal. The information about the man in the picture will not harm the cartels. They will not care if you tell about something unrelated to them."

He asked the man, "Where is the man in the picture?"

"He was moved to a sailboat and they left for somewhere we do not go. It is north. I think it is something Myers," he said.

"You mean Fort Myers?" MacLachlan asked.

"Yes. They were going to go to that place. A friend was going to pick him up and they were going somewhere else."

"Where?"

"I was never told."

"What is the friend's name?

"I do not know."

"Who is the captain of the sailboat??

"His name is Diego. That's all I know."

"What is the name of the sailboat?"

"I do not know."

"Where were you when he got on the sailboat?"

"About an hour southwest of Cuba."

"Where in Cuba?"

"Trinidad. It was just four hours ago."

"I want to write some facts down. Give me a description of the sailboat and your full name and address so I can make sure the prosecutor cuts you some slack."

MacLachlan obtained the information and wrote it all down.

He asked Vasquez how soon he could get back to Marco, that he had a good lead on Hariri.

"Hey, Charlie," Vasquez yelled to the FMP officer. "Can you take Mack and Yaffa back and drop them off at the marina then swing back here?"

The FMP officer waved them aboard. MacLachlan and Yaffa met with Vasquez briefly. They told him Hariri was going to Ft. Myers by sailboat from Trinidad, Cuba. They would compute ETA, but offhand, it looked like a couple days. They would try to scramble maritime assets to find and board the sailboat and take Hariri into custody. If there were drugs on the sailboat, MacLachlan promised to throw the credit Vasquez's way, since this was his case.

THEY FOUND the young trooper still at the marina. He had left and filled the tank of his patrol car, had a leisurely lunch, waiting as he felt he should for these people who were clearly special to somebody.

"Thanks for waiting, Rob. That means a lot to Mack and me. The guy we are after is on a different boat. We need to go to Ft. Myers or back to the Sarasota are as soon as Mack gets finished putting the alert out. We can even go the speed limit. Though I liked the way you drove on the way down here." Yaffa told the trooper.

MacLachlan was finishing on the phone with Grafton.

"No. Only that it was a sailboat. It was captained by a guy named Diego. It left the south coast of Cuba about four and a half hours ago. I'm guessing at about five miles per hour. I checked some charts in the marina. It's about three hundred fifty miles, so that's seventy hours. Almost three days beginning less than five hours ago. We have some time to involve the US Navy and the Coast Guard. That's a lot of water and a small boat, but what other opportunity do we have?"

"Mack, what does our DEA guy think about all of this?"

"Will, he's a really good guy. He ought to be pretty happy. Our mission to try to get Hariri netted him a ton or two of coke. I told him if the Navy or Coasties found drugs on the sailboat, we'd try to associate it with this case and get him the credit. Can you see to that?"

"Sure. It's the right thing to do," Grafton said.

"What's your feeling on where Yaffa and I ought to be for next three days? That is, assuming the maritime assets don't pick up Hariri tomorrow or something," MacLachlan asked.

"I'd say go home. If the Navy gets him, they will turn him and the sailboat over to the Coast Guard. Any ship they have big enough to be that far out will probably go back to Group St. Petersburg to moor. While everybody is all hot and bothered about the drug bust, you and Yaffa can slip our friend Hariri out and hand him over to a rendition team. Just string that Marshal's badge prominently around your neck and get Yaffa to disguise a little so nobody will recognize her. Heck, you could use two badges, so I will express another down to you. She can wear that with a wig and dark glasses and look like a Marshal, too," Grafton suggested.

"Yeah, Will. She would love that," MacLachlan said.

"Good, maybe she will cook you a nice dinner or something."

"Fat chance. Restaurants and I have been doing all the cooking since we met. I did see her knee cap one of the drug smugglers then render him unconscious today," he added.

"Did she use that krav maga stuff?"

"Probably. She is so damn fast; I couldn't really tell. But I think so."

"Lemme share something my old dad used to say: women and cats will do as they please. Men and dogs better just get with the program," Grafton said.

MacLachlan could visualize that broad grin on the other end of the line.

"Okay, dad. I'll ponder that. Oh, could you get the Director of the FBI or the President or somebody to write a nice letter of commendation for FHP Trooper Rob White out of Tampa-St. Pete? We would not have busted the drug boys or gotten the intel on Hariri if it had not been for him. Thank somebody real high for Vasquez, too."

"I agree. Sometimes the guys on the street get just crap. A pat on the back is righteous. And, it builds valuable friendships at all levels. The Prez or Director sends that and that whole police agency feels good," Grafton said.

The trip back to the Jeep was much slower. MacLachlan asked when Rob got off and he said, "About six hours ago."

"Do you have a wife or somebody to get back to?" MacLachlan asked.

"Not a soul."

"How about dinner with us. We'll pick up the Jeep

and head to Sarasota to a good restaurant," Yaffa said, intuitively picking up on where MacLachlan was going.

"You sure? Y'all bought me lunch."

"You risked your life getting us there. We'd all enjoy a calm dinner. How about it, Rob?" MacLachlan asked.

Dinner was good and the two non-feds got back to Casey Key around ten and turned in. It had been a long day for both.

8

West Coast Florida, Onshore and Off

June 1985

Iт ᴅɪᴅ ɴᴏᴛ ᴛᴀᴋᴇ ʟᴏɴɢ for the alert to hit US Coast
Guard cutters patrolling the Gulf of Mexico. Several
more were added from St. Petersburg, Miami and New
Orleans.

The Guard did not have the right assets in the
water for the op off Marco Island and felt it needed to
catch this guy this time. He was only put on watch out
of the intelligence center as a sought terrorist. There
was nothing about why he was coming to the US or
what he had planned. All of which made the matter
seem more secretive and scary. But the truth was US
intelligence had no idea what or where his attack
would be.

Grafton and MacLachlan had even spoken with the
admiral about whether Hariri might be a red herring

and the real attacker was someone else, possibly already in place.

Several days into the search for the sailboat with Abdel Hariri aboard, a Coast Guard C130 flying patrol spotted a sailboat of approximately 35 feet and carrying a yawl rig. It had two persons visible on deck. The C130 radioed in to Group St. Petersburg, based on the position of the yawl. Group St. Pete aimed an eighty-two-foot cutter towards the sailboat.

The cutter saw the sailboat on its radar and, then, visually later in the day. The sighting was radioed to Group St. Petersburg, then to USCG headquarters, then to the Situation Room. The last to find out was too far away to do anything yet. That person was MacLachlan.

Grafton told him the current position would have the sailboat brought back to St. Petersburg under tow once captured.

The eighty-two-footer dropped a RIB or rigid inflatable boat with a coxswain and four-person boarding party of three males and one female. All carried pistols and three had M16 rifles of Vietnam vintage. There was one short barrel pump shotgun of WWII vintage.

The cutter contacted the sailboat on channel 16 and ordered it to standby for boarding. The two men aboard were busy slashing bales and dumping them overboard to drop sails.

The eighty-two-footer fired a five second burst of 7.62 rounds from an M60 machine gun over the sail-boat's bow. The small boat left the cutter at top speed. The burst got the attention of the two men who ceased trying to destroy evidence. They were in the famous hands-up position when the RIB came along side and four boarders climbed onto the sailboat.

The two men were identified as Cuban nationals. Hariri was not aboard. Fifty bales of marijuana were as well as almost a ton of cocaine.

Following previous orders, the law enforcement liaison officer at Group St. Petersburg notified DEA supervisory special agent Tom Vasquez and someone known only as 'MacLachlan'."

MacLachlan thought about the fast run to Marco and having to use a trooper. He suspected he would have to make other fast runs in the near future. The local car rental did not have a Crown Victoria, but it did have its twin, a Mercury Grand Marquis. MacLachlan considered himself lucky. He found a navy one without the giveaway retiree vinyl roof and rented it.

The two men coordinated their trip to meet at a coffee shop in south St Petersburg. Yaffa was with MacLachlan.

They drove in separately. A third DEA car had some of Vasquez's agents to inventory and take possession of the contraband. At the Coast Guard base, Yaffa stayed in the car. MacLachlan said he was going to be confusing enough to explain, another person without credentials would be too memorable for someone in her line of work. She agreed completely.

They presented themselves to the Law Enforcement Liaison Officer, an Ensign, who took them to a Coast Guard Lieutenant who was the Group Operations Officer.

Vasquez showed his creds. His badge was in plain sight on his belt with his unbuttoned suit jacket open.

MacLachlan, in a dark blue suit, white shirt and

maroon tie, did not offer ID. The Ops Officer asked, "Is it Mr. MacLachlan, or...?"

"You can call me 'MacLachlan', Lieutenant. Most people do. I represent national security equities. I'm here to interview the two from the sailboat to see where Mr. Hariri might have gone. The drug case is Special Agent Vasquez's and Hariri is mine." The question was not answered, nor did it appear it would be. The Lieutenant wondered who this guy was.

They heard some yelling from down the hall, then a thud.

"Where are the prisoners?" MacLachlan asked. The two Coast Guard officers looked out the door and in the direction of the noise.

MacLachlan followed Vasquez out the door as a late twenties dark male plowed into the DEA agent headfirst at a full run. Vasquez caught the head in his gut and went down.

MacLachlan hit the would-be escapee on the back of his neck with a hammer fist blow, spun and caught the second man with an elbow blow to the jaw. Both men were rendered unconscious. He helped the DEA agent up and steadied him while he tried to breathe.

"Better check on your guard and make sure he's okay."

The two officers ran to the room where the prisoners were being held. The ensign came out and brushed past the two men now handcuffing the still-unconscious prisoners. They heard the public address system.

"Now. Boat crew lay to ops with a medical kit."

The ensign came out of the radio room adjacent to the operations officer's office. A senior petty officer, who was the Command Duty Officer or CDO, was with him.

"They whacked the petty officer guarding them with a folding chair. Two of the duty boat crewmembers are EMTs. They will check him out and make the ambulance decision," the CDO said.

Vasquez and MacLachlan roughly pulled the two semi-conscious prisoners to their feet and frog-walked them back to where they were being held with very painful come-alongs involving thumbs and wrists being twisted to an extreme.

"How is your petty officer, Lieutenant?" MacLachlan asked seeing the Ops Officer kneeling by a Coastie under arms who was beginning to regain consciousness.

"Which one hit you, MK2?" the Ops Officer asked the downed guard.

"The shorter one grabbed me and the taller one grabbed a steel chair. That's all I remember. I woke up and the cuffs were on the deck along with my handcuff key. Then, I passed out again."

Vasquez twisted the thumb he held to get the taller man's attention.

"You are under arrest for assaulting two law enforcement officers. That's on top of the drug charges. You are going downtown to the DEA office to be advised of your rights and charged formally. Then, I will give you to the man who just whipped your butts in about two seconds. He will have some questions for you. You may go to the Hillsborough County Jail for holding. Or, he might send you to some secret place where you will never be seen again. I'm kinda hoping for that." Both men's eyes widened.

The two Coast Guard officers had odd looks on their faces. All moved aside as two Coasties with a medical bag rushed in to check on their fellow boat crewman.

After a minute, one turned to the Ensign and said, "I think he's gonna be fine, but he should be checked out in the ER, sir." The radio operator called an ambulance while the two EMTs watched their patient.

They walked the two prisoners downstairs and two of the DEA agents took them in custody.

"Lieutenant, do I need to sign anything to take them?" Vasquez asked.

"No, only for the narcotics once a full inventory has been completed with Coast Guard and DEA both observing."

Vasquez nodded, "As usual, we'll rent a box truck and pick up the contraband for destruction after appropriate photos and evidentiary samples for court are taken. Please have your Public Affairs Officer block the faces of any DEA people in photos for release to the media, okay?" he said.

A siren sounded several blocks away. Probably the ambulance. The Lieutenant knew he would have to go back up to Ops when it arrived.

The officer proffered his hand to the two senior government men in suits. He saw MacLachlan wave at someone in a blue sedan and she got out. She was one of the prettiest women he had ever seen. Wife? No. He saw her join the DEA men and MacLachlan. MacLachlan and the woman were interviewing the two prisoners in the parking lot. He wondered if the DEA agent was kidding about a secret offshore prison. No, he thought. Maybe Hariri, but these two guys were just boat drivers dumb enough to attack a Coastie and a senior DEA agent. The mysterious MacLachlan had put both on the floor unconscious while he watched and was trying to assimilate what was happening. Then, it hit him. Two years ago. National news. MacLachlan was the Marine officer at the barracks at Beirut, Lebanon. The hero with the terrifying expression. The guy who got the Congressional Medal of Honor. That is who MacLachlan *was*. But who the hell is he *now*?

He watched as the Marine and the model drove off in the Mercury. The DEA agents and prisoners stayed behind for a while and then left as other agents and Coasties continued inventorying the drug haul. The Lieutenant, Ensign and CDO were reviewing the day later in the former's office. He shared who MacLachlan was after the Ensign commented on how quickly and decisively, he had put the two escapees on the deck.

"And, both were out cold. In a second. I've never seen anything like it. It was smooth. There was no wasted motion. One second they were escaping, another they were down."

The Command Duty Officer, a senior petty officer who was older than the Lieutenant, commented,

"I think, sirs, we have gotten a rare glimpse at a part of government today the public never sees. We have people in military special ops and spooky government jobs who do things to defend us. And, we never know about those things. If any come to light in the news, they are probably spun enough to be credible, but are not what really happened. This mysterious Hariri guy is some sort of terrorist bent on attacking us. He might drop off the radar and we will never know why. Somebody, maybe even MacLachlan, will make him go away. And, you know what? That's just fine with me."

They finished their strong coffee and went back to their normal jobs, always prepared.

———————

MacLachlan and Yaffa rushed to find the "right" type public phone to be able to tell Grafton the results of their interview of the two men from the sailboat Hariri was supposed to be on. They were looking for one that was in the open and generally inconvenient. Ones near corners in depressed areas or convenience stores had more probability of being bugged by local vice cops. No need to arouse interest, even from the good guys.

The priority of the information, however, justified using the first phone available.

"Hey, it's MacLachlan. Is Grafton available?" MacLachlan said as a somewhat familiar voice answered his office phone.

"Sorry, Mack. He's in a meeting right now."

"I need you to pull him out. Now."

"It's at the Situation Room."

"All the better. This is priority. Can you switch me over?"

It took a minute or two, but shortly someone outside the Situation Room answered.

"This is Colonel MacLachlan. I have urgent information that William Grafton has to have right away. Will you get him to step out for me, please?"

Another brief wait.

"If I transfer you in, can everyone hear it?" the voice asked.

"Yes, he would immediately tell them anyway."

There was a click and Grafton answered what sounded like, and was, an open line.

"Mack, it's Will. You have the President and a full complement on the line. Go ahead."

"Mr. President and gentlemen. Ten minutes ago, an associate and I just interviewed two men the Coast Guard picked up on a drug boat. We had information that boat was bringing Abdel Hariri to the Gulf Coast of the United States. They said midway from Cuba, a Cuban submarine surfaced and transferred Hariri aboard. It then submerged and disappeared. They had no information as to its destination. I assume, and it's just a quick assumption, the Cubans were listening to heavy radio traffic from the Coast Guard and realized Hariri would be picked up shortly on a boat leaving Cuba, since that's the location to which he directed the plane he hijacked in Martinique. I believe the obvious go-fast boat we stopped off Marco Island, Florida was just a red herring. Hariri is either here or back in Cuba. My guess is he's here in the US," MacLachlan finished.

There was silence in the room.

"Colonel, this is the DCI," the Director of Central Intelligence began, "I have an idea about maybe checking on Hariri's status. Let us discuss it here and, if all of us are in agreement, I will get people working on it."

"Good luck, sir. Let me know how I can help," MacLachlan said.

"The fact a Cuban sub was involved puts a whole

new complexion on this matter. We need to discuss that ramification after the DCI's idea, too."

The speaker did not have to identify himself. Millions of Americans heard his voice weekly on the news or movie reruns.

"Good hunting, gentlemen. We will stay on it from this end," MacLachlan finished.

"Thanks for the intel, Mack. It was not good news, but news we had to have immediately. I'll be in touch," Grafton said and hung up.

"So, do you chat with the President often?" Yaffa asked.

"Seems like it," MacLachlan admitted. "The Cuban sub helping a terrorist bent on some attack on US soil is probably raising more blood pressure in that room right now than Hariri's whereabouts. That's a heavy implication. Almost like an act of war. We don't need another Cuban Missile Crisis right now."

THE DCI EXPLAINED his idea and, given full agreement, left the room. Grafton was excused and the politicians discussed the ramifications of Cuba's participation in a terrorist plot. Whatever the plot was.

MacLachlan and Yaffa started the drive back to Casey Key to hurry up and wait.

"You know, Mack, this is the first time I have seen you dressed up in a dark suit. I like the tie. Men in Israel don't wear them unless at diplomatic events where others wear ties," she said.

"Thank you, Yaffa. You look pretty official in your pants suit today, too."

"I have a very short and form-fitting dress and some really high heels with me, too."

"I saw an ad for a Pilbolus Dance Company ballet at the Van Wezel Theater in the paper last night. I'll keep the suit on if you put that dress on," MacLachlan offered.

"You are on. I admit I feel a little guilty. You and I have too much fun when we work together," she said.

He just shrugged. He saw in Lebanon how short life could be. His grandfather always lived to the hilt. His father worked hard every day as a rancher. He did not have time for anything else. That is why the grandfather gave up the ranch and ranching. And, why MacLachlan chose another path. He hoped it was the right one.

MacLachlan enjoyed the comedic and athletic ballet. So did his date, who drew many admiring glances. And, no doubt, a number of elbows to husbandly ribs for looking at the Israeli beauty too long.

MacLachlan was far from being a patron of fine art. But he was amazed and impressed at the male and female dancers' level of fitness allowing them to bend and move as they did.

It was too late for dinner when they left the theater. One option was a place that looked like a biker bar but served the best pizza in Sarasota. They chose pizza.

MacLachlan took his jacket and tie off and locked the Sig in the chest where the Jeep's rear seat had been.

"You have the Beretta in your purse?" he asked and she nodded.

They walked in, Yaffa's presence causing a pool shot to fly off the table and onto the floor.

"What kind of pizza do you like?" MacLachlan asked.

"One without pork, maybe every vegetable they have and lots of gooey cheese?"

"Sounds fine to me. You order."

Halfway through, a drunk staggered up to the table. He was well over six feet and very well over two hundred pounds. Closer to three hundred. He did not appear to be obese. Just big and powerful.

"Hey little lady. Want to dance?"

"She is occupied eating her pizza," MacLachlan said, starting to rise.

Yaffa put a restraining hand on his arm, "This one's mine, please."

"Thank you, but as my very special friend said, I am eating. I'm sure there are other ladies here who would love to dance with you." The waitress walked up and shook her head.

The giant guy saw the waitress and elbowed her hard enough to put her on the floor, flat on her back.

Yaffa stood and pushed against the man like she was going to embrace him. Instead, she reached between his legs and squeezed as hard as she could.

The man's scream was piercing and high falsetto. She looked down and saw, unlike the expected biker boots, he was wearing thin canvas loafers. She stomped a stiletto heel down on top of his foot and he replicated the earlier scream. Yaffa shoved his chest hard with both hands and he went down just as the first Sarasota police officer came through the door.

MacLachlan helped him roll the bozo over and cuff him with two connected handcuffs. A backup unit arrived, and the two officers helped their prisoner to his feet.

The manager was there helping his server who had fallen hard. He told the officers what had happened, and that the giant started it all. While this discourse took place, Yaffa demurely munched a slice of veggie pizza.

"Do you want to press battery charges?" the first officer asked the waitress.

"Hell yes."

He looked down questioningly to Yaffa.

"Oh, no. I'm just a tourist. I'll be leaving and cannot hang around for testifying."

The officer had his pad out and asked for her name and address. She gave one MacLachlan had never heard. He wondered if perhaps it may be her real one.

The officer gave her an incident form to fill out and sign. She did so as she was finishing her pizza.

He turned to MacLachlan. "I saw her put him down as I walked in. Who *is* this woman?" he asked.

MacLachlan grinned. "My bodyguard," he said.

The officer looked at the tall, powerful man seated in front of two slices of pizza. The petite woman reached over to his plate and speared one and slid it over to hers.

He grinned back at MacLachlan. There really was nothing more to say. He and his backup walked the big man out, en route to the lockup.

"That was really good pizza, my darling protectee," she said to MacLachlan.

"Glad you liked it, my darling smartass. Ready to go home?" She nodded. "None too soon. I have a pizza stain to get out of my dress. Do you have club soda at home?"

Upon arriving home, Yaffa unscrewed the cap on the bottle of club soda they had bought on the way home. She slipped the dress off. Yaffa stood in five-inch-high heels scrubbing the pizza stain with a dish cloth and soda. MacLachlan stood there mesmerized, burning the image into his memory.

The phone rang at four-thirty in the morning. MacLachlan knew it could not be good. He was wrong.

"You sleep well?" Grafton asked, hearing a soft female voice ask, "Who is it?" in the background.

"Really well."

"Yeah, so I hear. Well, I didn't, but it was all for good. I want you to have this right away, so I am going to talk a little vague in the clear, okay?"

"Go."

"In our call yesterday, one prominent guy had an idea. Remember?"

"I do."

"Well, it panned out big time. We know where our friend is and what he is after.

"I want you both to start for Miami as soon as possible. It is a big corporate site. In view of the type actions you may have to take, you will have to avoid their security. I know that makes it harder, but people outside our line of work don't understand what we have to do sometimes," Grafton said.

"I'm with you. Want me to call from a phone booth along the way? And, are you or some of your guys coming, too?" MacLachlan asked.

"I will be in the area mid-morning tomorrow. I don't

want to involve my guys in a CONUS op," Grafton said referring to an operation in the Continental US.

"We'll be underway in ten minutes. I say 'we,' but I will give my friend here the right of refusal and explain why. I will call you in a couple hours," MacLachlan said.

"Make it by oh-seven hundred to catch me before the flight. If I've left, one of the guys will fully brief you. Drive safely."

MacLachlan and Yaffa packed several days formal and tactical wear for him and everything she had bought for her. They were not sure whether she would come back to Casey Key or get diverted to Israel or somewhere else. He packed the voluminous trunk, including the Winchester hunting rifle and shotgun.

"Here's a little present from Grafton. It may be helpful on this trip." He handed her a Marshal's badge and holder just like his. She even had credentials in the surprise express package Gloria had picked up on the porch and left on the kitchen table.

The Grand Marquis was not as quick or have the heavy brakes and cooling its twin, the police model Crown Victoria had, but was sufficient for the job MacLachlan had for it.

The got in and left. MacLachlan held it above one hundred on the Interstate. They stopped at the Seminole store in the middle of Alligator Alley to call Grafton.

"I can only talk fast. Almost time to head for the airport. Go to this address." Grafton gave MacLachlan an address in Miami.

"It's the control center for power for the electric power for four or five million people in South Florida and further up. They blow the SCADA Center and it's down for a while. Limited security, all considered," Grafton said.

"What's SCADA?" MacLachlan asked.

"Supervisory Control and Data Acquisition. It's the control room where the power is controlled.

"Will, I respectfully disagree with not bringing the power operator's chief of security in. Maybe the Miami-Dade police or FBI, too."

"Mack, it's not going to happen. Your mission is to stop the attack, legally or illegally. Then, to capture Hariri for rendition or to kill him and hope it looks like self-defense or you slip out of Dodge and nobody knows who did it. We bring in security and cops and we get another Martinique screw-up. Or, Hariri gets turned over to the feds, tried and traded for one of our guys. He needs rendition or to be neutralized. End of story. Talk to Yaffa. If she does not want to play by these rules, cut her loose. I gotta go." Grafton killed the connection and MacLachlan held the phone a while longer.

Yaffa walked out of the ladies' room.

"What's the word from on high?" she asked. MacLachlan looked around. Nobody in earshot.

"Hariri is going to blow the electric power for all of South Florida. Think about the ramifications of that. I have to stop the attack, and capture Hariri for rendition or kill him. No help. Security or law enforcement. Yaffa, are you in? This is an attack on the US, not Israel," he said.

"I'm in. Mack, my mission is to kill Hariri. Does not matter which one of us does it. He is to die for crimes against Israel."

"What crimes, honey?" MacLachlan asked softly.

"I don't know for sure. I get assignments, not always justifications or details," she said.

"If we could capture him for rendition and send him somewhere out of the country to be imprisoned and interrogated, would that suffice for not killing him on the spot?" he asked.

"I think so. But that is not my decision. I'm a foot soldier. Not a commander."

"I have to know to keep you with me on this," MacLachlan said.

"I will call Steven. May I tell him the target?" she asked.

"I guess you will have to."

"Want to get a Dr. Pepper? I noticed the machine had your beverage of choice."

He nodded and walked off, fishing for quarters.

She joined him five minutes later.

"My mission remains the same. Rendition by Americans does not affect it. I'm sorry, Mack," she said.

He embraced her.

"I will have to drop you off in Ft. Lauderdale at a car rental. Keep the clean Beretta but give me the badge back. I hate it, us having to separate this way. It would be easier as a team."

She handed him the badge and he pocketed it.

"Don't get in the way when the shooting starts, Mack. It would break my heart to kill you."

"Same here. Let's find you a rental." They left for the last half of Alligator Alley.

They went down Rt. 84 at the end of the Alley and stopped at a service station and were referred to a Hertz. Yaffa slipped out and pulled her suitcase from the back seat. She looked at MacLachlan and said nothing. He saw two tear streaks below her sunglasses. She turned and walked into the car rental and he pulled off.

MacLachlan parked out of sight around the corner and walked into a MacDonald's. He ordered coffee and sat where he could see the Hertz lot. Fifteen minutes later, he saw Yaffa walk out. She was with a guy with a clip board. They walked around a yellow Ford Mustang. After inspecting it for dings, the man handed Yaffa the paperwork, she put her bag in the small trunk and drove off.

MacLachlan called Grafton's office. One of Grafton's agents answered. MacLachlan had spoken with him many times but did not recall his name.

"Hey, it's MacLachlan. I know Will is in the air, but I am almost to Miami and thought I'd pick him up when he lands. Can you give me his itinerary?"

"Yeah. He gets into Miami International in an hour and a half. He's on a United flight from Washington National. I don't have the flight number, but that should be easy once you get to the airport."

"Thanks. If he calls in before he sees me, tell him to hang out at United baggage claim and I'll get him there. Have a good one." MacLachlan said and hung up.

He headed the Mercury south to Miami and west to the airport.

He thought hard while driving. This assignment really sucked. He had a really good chance of being killed or arrested. He might find Yaffa in his crossfire or him in hers. Not bringing company security in was a mistake. Ditto for local police. The Bureau would want to take over the party but would be a tough adversary if they were left out and something went haywire.

He parked in short term and, clipping the badge to

224 G. WAYNE TILMAN

his belt and the Sig right behind it, donned a blue blazer and went in. He badged his way to the arrival gate and stood there. The flight was on time and a handsome black man in a suit was the tenth person through the gate. He was carrying a briefcase and a carry-on bag.

"Damn. Slickmeister, if you are here to resign or shoot me, you can't do either," was Grafton's smiling greeting.

"I considered both but discarded the idea. Figured we needed to talk and then get down to business," MacLachlan said.

"Where's your girlfriend?"

"I cut her loose. Different objectives. That's something else we need to chat about, Will."

They walked. Grafton said he did not have any other luggage and to head for the car.

"Is her different objective going to be problematic for us?" Grafton asked.

"Might be."

"Hit and run?" Grafton asked, somewhat disguising the question.

"Yep."

"That could be...inconvenient," Grafton said.

They got in the car.

"Where to?" MacLachlan asked.

"I have a room at the Biscayne Marriott. Go there and we'll get you a room."

"You know, I think this is a bad plan, Will," MacLachlan said.

"I do know. I don't even disagree. I'm going to partner with you on this, not be control. It's the least I can do. The big guys are set. They would ideally like to get a lot of information out of this guy. We go the legitimate route and he will lawyer up, clam up and get traded or claim diplomatic immunity. We do it the way we are assigned and that does not happen," Grafton said.

"I realize all of that. But, excluding the power officials, local cops and Bureau will tick off a lot of people. And, we could get caught holding the bag," MacLachlan said.

"Risk of the game we play in. But, before you fully make up your mind it's going to fail, I have some additional intel that may help. A lot. There's a deep cover Hezbollah operative who works for the power company. We have his name. With any luck, we can snatch and squeeze him before Hariri hits the SCADA. I'd like to catch him with the plans and explosive device before he gets on the property," Grafton said.

"What are the plans for the rendition aspect?" MacLachlan asked.

"First off, I have several pharmaceuticals and syringes. I have thiopental as a sedative and a so-called 'truth serum', scopolamine. Second off: there is a black ops team waiting to pick him up. They are already in Miami. Here's their phone number," he said, sticking a slip of paper in MacLachlan's outside jacket pocket.

"What's your idea if we have to neutralize him?" MacLachlan asked.

"If he's unarmed, I have both a knife and a clean pistol as a 'throw-down'. We will use the truth. We were tracking him, saw him with what we feared was an explosive, called for him to halt and fired in self-defense."

"And, that will be the truth?"

"Probably will," Grafton answered.

"Do we know when the attack on the SCADA system will be?"

"We have an impression, more than an exact time. The impression is a couple days," Grafton said.

"So, we go after the deep cover tango. What are his living circumstances? Wife, kids?"

"The source did not know details to that level. We need to surveil him today. I have his address. An apartment at a not-so-good part of Miami."

"Great. Think we'll stand out?" MacLachlan asked.

"You will."

They pulled into the Marriott. Grafton checked in and MacLachlan rented a room, then parked the car. He left the long guns in the trunk, along with his .45.

MacLachlan went to his room. He could see Biscayne Bay. Having an hour before he was scheduled to meet with Grafton, he went to the ground floor and walked around the building to the dock. There was a marine shop on the end. He walked to it. The bats with little string bikinis reminded him of Yaffa. He wondered where she was and what she was doing. She knew the target, but not the day or the deep cover guy they were going to look into later. She was flying blinder than they. He watched his rearview mirror all the way to the airport and back downtown to the Marriott. No bright yellow Mustang. Unless Steven was here and trailed them in something else.

MacLachlan was used to competition. He was a Marine officer. He competed with fellow Marines in runs, shooting, pull-ups, almost everything. But he did not want to compete with Yaffa on this. That kind of competition got people hurt...or killed. But she had forced new rules and he had to play by them.

He stood thinking and looking at the water. Smelling it. Listening to waves lap from the wakes of boats going by. He had never fished Biscayne Bay. He planned to come back and do it. Maybe get a guide the first time. Some of the world's best were here in Miami and down in the Keys. On the last happy thoughts, he walked back up the dock to the hotel. He and Grafton had a job to do. And, the first part was to be inter-viewing a deep cover Hezbollah operative. A "sleeper." It was likely to get physical. He walked on.

A few minutes later, he and Grafton were in the Mercury. Grafton was co-piloting with a Miami street map. They went from urban to a city suburb edged by an industrial park on one side and some pretty rough areas on the other. They planned to ride by the house and then circle the block. They would stop several houses down and pull over to watch. They could not tell much about vehicles, because these were working people and virtually nobody was home yet. The Mercury may stand out due to being a shiny, current model year. Or, it may not. Both men were surprised with the cleanliness and good state of repair of most of the houses. This being a Miami suburb, most had black wrought iron bars on windows and doors.

The two watched as the workers returned to house after house. But, no Abdul Hamdi, the name given them as the deep cover terrorist.

At dusk, a five-year-old Ford pickup pulled into the driveway at Hamdi's house.

MacLachlan gunned the big car and pulled in, blocking the pickup as the man began to get out. Grafton has already exited and was holding up creds. His jacket was back and he had a hand on his sidearm.

"Abdul Hamdi. Federal agents. Do not move."

MacLachlan had gotten out of the car and was subtly patting the older man down.

"Clean," he told Grafton.

"Who's in the house?" Grafton asked the man.

"Nobody. I live alone."

"We need to speak with you. Let's go in," Grafton said.

They followed the clearly shaken man in as he unlocked the door.

"Mind if we check?" Grafton asked as MacLachlan continued doing so unbidden.

The house was a two-bedroom, one bath with a living room and eat-in kitchen. MacLachlan swept it quickly and returned to the living room.

"This is about that damn Hariri, isn't it?" Hamdi asked.

"Why do you say that?" Grafton asked.

"He pushed me to give him a drawing of the power center, especially the control room."

"Why?" asked MacLachlan.

"He is an engineer. He wanted to take pictures for his boss."

"Who is his boss?" Grafton asked.

"My worthless cousin in Marseille. He sent Abdel here. Abdel is going to take secret pictures of the control room to duplicate on a construction site back in Lebanon."

"Whoa. I am getting confused," Grafton said. "Your cousin, Hariri's boss, is in France. But the site is in Lebanon?"

"Yes. We are Saudis. But, my cousin Abdullah is an engineer. So is Abdel. They move around and are always getting into some sort of deals. They are not hard-working men. They always take the easy way. Like sneaking in and copying something instead of offering to buy the plans. Which is what Abdel is going to do tonight."

"Why did you help him?" MacLachlan asked.

"My cousin is ruthless. I never liked him. He said if I did not help his subordinate, it would not go well for moving other members of our family here to the United States. That snake of the desert is not above interfering as retaliation. Even my mother, who I want to bring here before she is too old to make the trip, hates him. She said her sister spawned the devil when that one was born."

"When is Hariri going to break in and take the pictures?" Grafton asked.

"When it is totally dark. He said there would be no moon tonight and it would be a good time to do it. He needs to get back across the sea soon anyway, he said." Hamadi explained.

"What sort of car does he have?" MacLachlan asked.

"It is a small maroon Ford rental of some sort."

"Please stay seated on the couch. We need to speak privately for a minute," Grafton said.

They walked into the kitchen. Grafton maintained a clear sight of Hamadi.

"What do you think?" he asked.

"I don't think he's any more of a Hezbollah terrorist than I am, Will."

"My gut says the same thing."

They walked into the living room.

"Mr. Hamadi," Grafton began.

"We believe you are telling us the truth. We also believe your cousin's friend lied to you. He is going to damage where you work, not take pictures. We need to stop him. Arrest him. We want you to drive your truck back to work. I will ride with you and my associate will drive our car. You should point out the control room. That's where the SCADA is, right?" The man nodded at Grafton.

"Then, you will be free to go home in your truck and we will arrest Hariri. Sound like a plan?"

"Yes. But, will I get arrested or fired from my job for drawing the picture of the building?"

"No. You helped us. We will forget your name and address and actions. Fair enough?" Grafton said.

"Yes. We must leave now.

Grafton told MacLachlan they needed to stop at a phone booth along the way and let DC know about Hamadi and Marseille. MacLachlan knew that call was to pass intel in case they were killed.

MacLachlan pulled in behind the pickup as they stopped at a phone. There were a couple of gang-looking thugs hanging around it.

Grafton got out and walked up to them, a .45 in his hand. MacLachlan could hear him snick the safety off from his seat in the Mercury. He was sitting there, unbuckled, the Sig in hand ready for use.

"Why don't you girls vacate the neighborhood? This thing could go off and kill somebody." He looked crazy. The group strutted away cursing him and trying to look like they were tough and leaving was their idea.

Grafton left a message at the admiral's office and got back in the truck. They drove for another thirty minutes in mixed traffic before coming to the power complex. They stopped before going through an unmanned, open gate.

Outside the vehicles, Hamadi pointed out the building and the portion where the SCADA was located. MacLachlan asked about guards. There was one at this time of night. Armed, he was at his desk by the main entrance door. He patrolled once an hour.

Hamadi looked at his watch.

"He is back at the desk for another thirty minutes. Abdel said he was going to enter by a window over there," he said pointing. "I told him I did not want to know anything about it."

Grafton put a hand on the man's shoulder.

"Mr. Hamadi, if this all works out according to the information you gave us, I will come back and buy you the biggest steak in Miami. If you have lied to us and set us up, there will be nowhere you can hide. Do you understand that? Wherever you go, I will find you and kill you. I promise."

From what the two men was in Hamadi's face in the almost darkness, it looked like he understood.

"Now, go home and have your dinner. Leave quietly and do not tell anyone you ever met us."

The power company cleaning man drove off.

The two left the Mercury parked outside and walked the hundred yards to the location Hamadi pointed out.

They saw a car meeting the description they had been told. MacLachlan took out his knife and sliced four off four valve stems.

There was a sealed window. A glass cutter had been used to remove a two by three-foot section. Large enough for Hariri, Grafton and even MacLachlan to climb through. The two hunters climbed in. They had not been prepared for confronting Hariri tonight. MacLachlan had brought a small Maglite from a bag he had stuck in the trunk, but they feared it would be a giveaway and walked in the dark. Their eyes were accustomed to the darkness and bright lights would inhibit their night vision.

They moved quietly, pistols in hand. There was slight noise from a room ahead. It was where they thought the SCADA would be. Looking through a windowed door, they saw Hariri squatting down and doing something with an item on the floor. It was probably the explosive device and he was likely arming it.

Both knew they could not allow that to happen. Grafton raised his .45 and yelled, "Hariri."

When the shocked man turned, Grafton fired a headshot and the man crumpled. They approached and MacLachlan aimed the Maglite on the device. It was basic with a manual alarm clock, batteries and nine sticks of dynamite.

MacLachlan looked at the ticking clock. A minute.

He grabbed it and sprinted down corridor towards the hole in the window. He needed to get it away from the SCADA and into something that would help contain the explosion. It would occur now in forty seconds. He ran as fast as he could, knowing a fall would seal his fate and maybe still cut off power for all of South Florida.

He climbed out of the window and ran towards Hariri's rental car, wishing for a dumpster to contain the blast instead.

Thirty seconds. He drew the Sig and fired a full magazine at the rear side window, taking it out.

From five feet, at fifteen seconds, he tossed the device onto the back seat and turned to run away.

MacLachlan was a runner, but more an endurance runner than a sprinter. He knew he was at a pace to beat his best ever hundred-yard dash. For some reason, he thought about the 9.2 second record set in earlier in the 1960's. But even that would not have been fast enough tonight.

The wall of hot air from the blast pushed him forward faster than his legs could control, and he went down hard. He intentionally rolled and covered his head when he stopped, knowing parts of the car and who knows what else might be flying his way. He felt items clatter around him, and small ones landed on him without causing harm. He did not hear them, because his hearing was temporarily gone. He flashed back to Beirut. He knew the hearing would come back shortly. Beirut had been much more powerful.

Then, the flying bumper of the rental car fell on his back.

MacLachlan laid there stunned and in pain. He turned over on a back that was numb. For now.

He saw a dark figure running towards him in the dark.

Grafton.

He saw a flash of light and felt the concussion of a shot. He did not hear it. The man stopped, then fell forward. Will.

MacLachlan rolled, looking for the gun he had dropped.

He saw a figure coming towards him. He couldn't find the Sig. He pulled his knife and flicked it open.

The figure went past him.

It was Yaffa.

MacLachlan focused. It was Hariri, not Grafton. How? He lost focus again for a second.

Hariri had shakily stood up, gun at his side. Yaffa fired two shots into his head from five feet away.

She walked back to MacLachlan. Her foot hit something. It was the Sig. She picked it up and tucked it in her waistband.

She carefully wiped the Beretta and dropped it beside MacLachlan.

Yaffa tried to smile at MacLachlan laying there but could not through her tears. She turned and disappeared into the darkness. Normally, MacLachlan would have heard a car squeal away. But he would not hear anything for several hours yet.

By then, the agent would be on a flight home to Israel.

Now, he could he heard ringing in his ears. And, his back felt like it was broken.

He saw Grafton limping towards him. He stopped and looked at Hariri. Grafton did not bother to check his pulse. The twin holes in his forehead said enough. He also saw the crease on the left side he had put there.

He proceeded to MacLachlan and bent down. MacLachlan looked up and shook his head. Grafton grinned and mouthed something that could have been "I'll get you an ambulance." MacLachlan was not sure.

The guard was approaching. He was holding a .38 revolver at high ready. He looked both confused and nervous and had the right to be both.

Grafton told him they were federal agents and needed an ambulance right away and probably a fire truck. The guard turned, holstering his revolver and walked back to the building without saying a word.

Grafton looked down at his audibly challenged friend.

MacLachlan mouthed "Yaffa" and pointed to Hariri.

Grafton shook his head and pointed at MacLachlan but winked at the same time.

MacLachlan got it. For the record, Yaffa was never there.

MacLachlan pointed to the Beretta. Grafton reached down and picked it up. Still prone, MacLachlan reached out. He took a handkerchief wiped it again. Now, both Yaffa's and Grafton's prints had been wiped off. He held the grips and trigger. He put his fingers on the slide. His prints were now all over it in the right places. He placed it on the ground beside him gently. The hammer was still cocked.

Grafton knew MacLachlan carried a Sig tonight. He and Yaffa had switched. The Israeli was not officially here. But she had completed her mission. One Grafton would have completed but for Hariri turning and taking a glancing shot.

The terrorist was dead. The power grid was safe. Lots of intricacies, but nobody would be the wiser. All in all, a good night.

Unless you were MacLachlan who lost his girlfriend, his hearing for a while, and would be in pain moving for a while.

For MacLachlan, being alive was the only good thing. The rest was not so hot.

Grafton shook his head and waited for the ambulance. He would call DC once MacLachlan was packaged and on his way.

9

Casey Key, Florida, Marseille, France

August-December 1985

THE WORLD'S power center put a plausible spin on
what happened in Miami. Two Marshals had been
trailing a fugitive bomber. They caught him trying to
blow up a power grid. One deputy had run the bomb
out of the building and tossed it in a rental car which
blew up. The grid was saved. A running gunfight had
started in a control room and ended up in the parking
lot. The bomber died and one Marshal was injured by
the explosion.

In the hospital later, Grafton told MacLachlan
when he was checking Hariri, the terrorist came to and
slugged him. He fell, injuring his bad leg all over again.
He realized only too late that a bloody head wound was
not always as serious as it looked. Grafton told his

younger partner he was kicking himself for a 'rookie mistake'.

The doctor told MacLachlan the bumper from the blown up 1984 Ford Tempo had fallen on his back. He said it was just the full plastic facing. "Darn lucky it wasn't the steel bumper underneath. You'd be looking at months of physical therapy. As it is, you are going to be released with a couple of aspirin in an hour. Your hearing will be back to normal before you get home," the doctor said.

The Department of Justice handled the press releases. There were a lot of questions about the Marshals, especially about the one who picked up a ticking time bomb and ran it out of a building to preserve power and life. The story was they were part of an elite team and their identities had to be kept secret. "Amen to that," MacLachlan said. Conspiracy theorists asked was if the bomber was the Unabomber, which the DOJ emphatically disputed.

After checking on him that night in the hospital, Grafton had gone back to DC to report in person.

In a phone call from a payphone on MacLachlan's way back to Casey Key, Grafton said the men in the Situation Room knew the full story, including Yaffa's contribution. The President was intrigued and called the Prime Minister of Israel. He told him his agent had been the one who brought down the terrorist. The President also said, if she could come back, he would like to give her the Presidential Medal of Freedom. The Prime Minister said that was nice and he would take it under consideration.

MacLachlan knew, diplomatic courtesy aside, the

Prime Minister had no intention of allowing such a ceremony. It would blow the identity of one of his best agents.

MacLachlan could hear again. But his back was still killing him. He felt like kicking the bumper of every Ford Tempo he saw in a parking lot in retribution. The drive was painful, but not half so much as one in the Jeep would have been.

Back home, MacLachlan began to take stock of his life. It was August. He had a lieutenant colonel's pay through December, so he would not have to dip into the trust or his savings for ordinary expenses. He decided the plan to sell the Jaguar was a good one. He would sell the big pickup in Northern Virginia as soon as the cabin was built and building supplies were delivered.

He would drive the Jeep up and secure a storage facility near Washington National Airport to keep it in. And, maybe some gear, clothes and weaponry. He would lease a similar garage or facility near Sarasota Airport in which to keep a Florida vehicle and gear. He would begin to look for that place in a couple days when he was able to walk upright again.

His second day back, he received a letter posted from Tel Aviv. He ripped it open with great anticipation.

Yaffa said she hated leaving him there on his back and hoped his injuries were mild. She said carrying the bomb out of the building took a lot of *chutzpah*. He knew that was a compliment. She went on to say she hoped he was not disgusted with her after seeing her do her job as she had been taught. Yaffa said she missed him and hope he missed her.

MacLachlan was getting experienced enough in the world he found himself operating to understand what she did. He was not repelled by it. Would he want to be married to someone who could walk up to a wounded adversary and put two rounds into his head? He did not know. Would her loyalties always be to her calling and not to one person? The answer was a definitive 'yes'.

He put the letter aside to think about it. He did not want to answer with the wrong words. She deserved more and would get it.

The following day he found a rental garage near the airport in Sarasota and rented it. Electric power was included in the rent. He slowly began hardening it and added a clothes rack and a rolled steel five-gun safe, lag bolted to the concrete floor. He added a ceiling fan to keep air moving and a battery charger for longer term storage.

MacLachlan developed a spread sheet of contacts he had in the intelligence business from his address book and collection of business cards. He put names, organizations, addresses and phones on it. The last column was type work he might offer them, if any.

His next plan was to be simultaneous to selling the Jaguar would be to find a dependable highway car or truck for fast runs to Miami or Tampa airports.

He pulled into his drive the next day after working on the Sarasota storage facility. It was hot, even by Florida standards. It may call for a Gulf swim instead of running. He had been doing that recently, swimming in an ugly, but efficient crawl for a mile at a time. His back still hurt from the flying bumper in Miami, but the water seemed to be easier exercise on it.

MacLachlan sat a couple of grocery bags on the

kitchen table. He thought about Yaffa and him cleaning guns there. He had left the Beretta for the FBI evidence team. Neither his nor Grafton's identities were given to the FBI, something that caused great consternation. The Attorney General had spoken with the Director who had told his people investigating the case the two would remain anonymous and to 'deal with it'.

MacLachlan had slipped into unconsciousness in the ambulance, so upon Grafton's arrival at the hospital, he had booked MacLachlan in as an undercover federal agent to be referred to as 'John Doe'. Grafton's charisma was only exceeded by his command authority when he deigned to use it. John Doe it was. MacLachlan checked out and his bill was already paid in cash.

He sat at the table and groaned as a spike of pain shot up his back. He went to a Sarasota orthopedist once he got home. After X-rays, he was told there was only bruising of muscles and he would be fine after a few weeks if he went to physical therapy. He did his own.

As he was taking the groceries out, the phone rang.

"How's the back?" Grafton asked.

"Been better, but I'll live," MacLachlan said.

"Look. Two things. I had the device we installed in your house surplussed. It's off the books now, so you can keep it despite the fact the mission is over."

"Okay. I suspect that is the good news from your voice. What's the bad?" MacLachlan asked.

"One of the folks we work with heard some electronic chatter. You know who they'd be right?"

"I do," MacLachlan said, indicating he knew such information would only come from the NSA.

"Well, the chatter was between Marseille and

Lebanon. About getting even with a certain cursed infidel in Florida. Payback. You would be the infidel."

"Delightful. I need to get a running shirt with that on it. What's your take, Will?" he asked.

"I think it's serious kimchi," Grafton said, using his favorite substitute for a ruder word signifying manure.

"So, watch your six. Get that alarm installed we sent the envelope of cash for," Grafton said. "But you have to pay the monthly bills."

"Okay, will do. I already deposited the cash so I can write a check for it. How do you think they will do it? One Middle Eastern guy? A borrowed team of *Spetsnaz*?" he asked referring to Russian special forces.

"I don't have any idea. These people are single-minded and patient. If you go to a hidey hole in the woods, they will wait until you come home. It's almost better to sit around and wait for them. Then, ambush the hell out of them when they show up."

"Yeah, Will. I agree. I have a .30-30 and a shotgun. And, the .45."

"Maybe get something semiauto, like a Ruger Mini-14. You might need to shoot a lot of times and fast. I wish there was something I can do to help, but there isn't. I can't put you in a DIA safe house forever," Grafton said.

"Let me know if you hear anything else," MacLachlan said.

"I will. Later."

MacLachlan got in the Jeep and cruised a couple of gun stores in Sarasota and Bradenton. At the last, he found something that fit the bill for him. It was a WWII M-1 carbine. He bought it at a good price and some surplus practice ammo, ten boxes of new production ammunition and four fifteen round magazines.

At home, he thought about it. He would wear the .45 and keep the little M-I carbine close. The shotgun would be staged in the bedroom, the lever action rifle in the garage. It was not perfect. But neither was one person trying to live in a sniper's nest.

The next day's saw him test fire the surplus carbine. He found it was light, balanced and quick. And, utterly dependable.

He parked the Jeep at a small marina less than a mile down the bay for a quick getaway. If he was going to ambush someone at his house, he would come by water. The house was across the road from the Gulf. There was relatively little patrol by police or Coast Guard boats. One could get in quietly, do the deed and get away. By car, one had to deal with being on an island. There were two ways on and off. The Sheriff's Office was pretty darn good at sealing both quickly, he knew.

MacLachlan was as ready as he ever would be. And, he would do it in a style that would become his signature. Alone.

HE WAS WRONG, or more correctly, they were wrong. They came by road. A group of five men hit the property and spread out. Two went to the house while three separated and began to search the several acres of property. They were Cuban special forces, trained by Russia's Spetsnaz. Unfortunately for them, they did not receive the depth of training their trainers had. They had not done appropriate surveillance. They were unaware the property extended across the road to the beach. Which is where MacLachlan sat in the chickee hut with his carbine and .45.

Two approached the house then split up. Each placed a satchel charge against a stilt that elevated the house out of the flood plain. One in front, one in back. They came back around the way they came in and clicked mics for the others to advise the house was going to blow.

Ten seconds later, the cracker house built in the 1930's by MacLachlan's grandparents blew up. The charges were considerably more than was required. The garage twenty feet away was flattened and the Jaguar destroyed.

MacLachlan flinched with the sound. He had experienced explosions in Beirut, Dar-es-Salaam and Miami. All within several years. He was getting really tired of things blowing up. He touched the .45 in its holster and picked up the carbine. With a messenger bag full of loaded magazines slung around his neck, he moved across the road.

He moved tree to tree towards the house he had lived in until a few minutes ago. He saw two men near what would have been the main entrance.

MacLachlan raised the rifle and fired two series of two shots each. Some people called them "double-taps." He called them "controlled pairs." Two men fell dead.

How many more were there? And, where?

MacLachlan had moved as soon as he fired. Shots were returned in his direction from the area near the ruins of the garage. He snapped several shots in that direction.

An old brick barbecue his grandfather had built stood between the house and the road across from the beach. He took up a position behind it and waited. The explosion was sure to prompt police and fire response. MacLachlan had no way of warning first responders, except perhaps a couple of shots in a safe direction. Unless there was already a deputy on the island, he knew he was on his own for a while.

He saw a man with an AK-47 moving between the trees. Looking for him. The trees were thick, and it would be a hard shot, but he took it anyway.

The man screamed and grabbed his right hip as he fell. MacLachlan knew he was still a threat and neutralized the threat with another shot. Three. How many more?

As he moved away from the barbecue, something hit him like a ton of bricks. Or, a two hundred -fifty-pound assassin. He dropped the carbine and both men hit the ground, rolling together. The man got both hands around MacLachlan's neck and began to squeeze. MacLachlan reached the Bowie with his left hand and pulled it. He did not have room for a thrust, so he slashed the man's arm between the elbow and shoulder.

Pressure released on his neck, MacLachlan punched under the jaw. As the man's head snapped back, MacLachlan thrust the big knife into his heart. The man's eyes opened unnaturally wide and his mouth worked, but no sound came out. When he rolled over on his back, the man's eyes stayed open, unblinking. But, MacLachlan did not see that. He was already up and moving, carbine back in hand.

He felt the burn in his left bicep before he heard the shot. His arm dropped but he fired three fast shots with his hand on the carbine's grip and the butt stock held between his right elbow and body.

The shooter brought his AK up to his shoulder for a kill shot. MacLachlan emptied the magazine and the man fell.

MacLachlan looked at his left arm. Since he was wearing a tee-shirt, the wound was visible. It was a through and through. It did not look like the humerus was hit. It was bleeding, but not badly. MacLachlan knew, unlike movie gunshots, real ones usually led to shock. He had a finite amount of time to end this attack. He gripped the carbine upside down between his knees and pulled the mag. He dropped it and slammed in another. The bolt had not locked open after the last shot, so he pulled and released the operating handle.

During the time it took to reload, the fifth attacker moved into position and commenced firing. He was the leader and had in a stupid show of rank carried only a nickel-plated Colt automatic in 38 Super caliber. His rounds flew all around MacLachlan, who repeated his empty the mag, shooting under the arm action. The eighth, eleventh and fifteenth shot hit the lead assassin and he went down. They were only fifty feet apart. MacLachlan slung the light rifle on his shoulder and drew the cocked .45 as he approached. The grouping was not small, but the hits were deadly.

MacLachlan left the carbine slung and moved around the house. They had to have a vehicle somewhere. He would stay with it to meet the arriving deputy. A siren in the distance was closing fast.

A tan Chevy Astro with a rental decal was parked at his entrance lane. MacLachlan did not see anyone and holstered the pistol. As he reached the van, a man with a pistol popped out from behind it and started shooting. Without thought or plan, MacLachlan drew the .45, flicking the safety off as he drew, and fired twice. The man fell. Two holes in his chest. One inch apart. Instinct. Tachypsychia, but still shooting by rote training.

MacLachlan pulled the Marshals badge on the lanyard out from under his tee-shirt.

A white with green trip deputy car was closing fast. MacLachlan leaned the carbine against the van.

The Ford screeched to a halt, expertly slid into a sideways defensive position. A deputy got out, .357 Magnum aimed at MacLachlan over the door. MacLachlan nodded. The deputy saw the badge as the man in the bloody tee-shirt passed out.

The deputy ran around to him and removed the .45 and put it, the carbine and the bloody Bowie on his front seat. He called for rescue and a supervisor then went back to check the man down. Then, he saw the dead Cuban with a pistol in his hand. He moved that and checked MacLachlan.

"I've got a rescue coming. Firefighters are first aid trained and a fire truck will be here in a couple minutes. Unless there's something I don't see, the arm wound isn't fatal and it's not bleeding much," the deputy said.

MacLachlan motioned him closer.

"Write this number down," he said, and the deputy

removed his pen and pad. MacLachlan gave him the 24/7 number for Grafton.

"Tell whoever answers that MacLachlan was attacked. Five tangos down. No. Six. MacLachlan will recover. House gone. And other than checking for signs of life—and there won't be any—don't touch anything. This will be an FBI crime scene. They will want to count and mark shell casings for evidence."

"Who is MacLachlan?" the deputy asked.

"Me."

"Is this your house?"

"It was," MacLachlan said and lost consciousness. The fire engine arrived. Then the ambulance.

MACLACHLAN AWOKE. His sleep was more from the shots he received at Sarasota Memorial than the wound itself. He had lost more blood than he thought. The wound was stitched and bound. He had two young guys in suits sitting there waiting for him to wake up. The Bureau had arrived.

Their initial questions were textbook, but subsequent ones were innovative and tailored to the unusual circumstances of a bombing and one man killing six in self-defense on an upscale residential island.

"I will be wanting my guns back after you do the Quantico lab stuff. I need the badge and creds now."

"How did you come to be a special deputy US Marshal," the shorter one asked.

"I was sworn in by someone in Washington."

"Someone?" he asked.

"I need to have my boss, who is on the way from

DC and should be here shortly, to read you in. He will explain everything. In the meantime, I was attacked by a hit team I believe to be foreign. Every action I took was in self-defense. That includes the hand-to-hand. By the way, that knife is more valuable than either gun. I want it back, too."

"You mean, this is all you are going to tell us until some guy from DC gets here?"

"This is a national security matter, so yes."

The two agents did not like the response. But they were smart and understood the national security implication of a foreign hit team trying to assassinate someone. Especially when that someone was a lieutenant colonel. One their age, which was unheard of. One who won the Congressional Medal of Honor. So, they gave him the benefit of the doubt. At least until the Washington arrival had his say.

"Colonel, we will let you get some rest. As you can imagine, this is a pretty big case. We will be in the waiting room and want to speak with your boss as soon as he arrives."

"Thanks, guys. I really am the good guy here. You will see," MacLachlan said, fighting the injection so he could stay awake to talk with Grafton.

MacLachlan was awakened by someone leaning over talking low into his ear.

"Hey, Slickmeister. Wake up. I have been flying all day and not to watch you sleep."

"Hi, Will."

"That's better," Grafton said. "Sorry about your house. Got insurance?"

"Yes. Don't know if it covers assassins and terrorists, but I guess I'll find out pretty soon."

"I have to talk with the Feebs. Tell me everything they asked and what you answered.

Considering the sedatives, MacLachlan gave him a cogent and complete report on the questioning.

"Will, how are we going to spin this?" he asked.

"Everything I tell them will be truth. Everything the world hears will be truth. Just not the full truth. I am going to tell them you have been tracking international criminals. Terrorists are criminals, kinda, right? That you are sanctioned at the highest levels. I might mention Miami. But I will tell them this is top secret and their Special Agent in Charge will be getting a call from either the Director or higher to keep a lid on this.

"'A government agent investigating international criminal organizations was attacked in retribution. His home was destroyed, but several attackers lost their lives.' End of story. Black out," Grafton said.

"I'd like to hear that," MacLachlan said.

"Okay. No reason why we cannot have you present. I will go get them now, if you are up to it." MacLachlan nodded.

Grafton came in with the two agents. He closed the door and asked them to sit. He removed an object that looked something like a portable Geiger counter. But it was not. He moved around the room, reading the meter. Satisfied, he turned the device off and returned it to his briefcase.

"Gentlemen, I just swept the room for electronic surveillance devices. What I am going to tell you is top secret. It is like a read-in. I will, at the end, give you what can go in your FD-302 reports of interview." The agents frowned at this news and one started to say something, but Grafton held up his hand.

"About now, someone is calling your SAC. I am not sure if it's your Director, the Attorney General, or who. Your Special Agent in Charge will be hearing the same instructions as you are. This is to be handled as national security at its highest levels. Because that's what it is.

Now, continuing, Colonel MacLachlan is sworn as a special deputy US Marshal to facilitate him doing what we task him to do. What is that? To track and capture, if capture is an option, terrorists bent on attacking US interests here and abroad. He and I report to a group of guys at the White House Situation Room. I believe you know who sits at the end of the table there." Grafton paused to allow that to sink in. It did not take long.

"In the past month or two, we have been successful in thwarting two attacks. One was overseas. One was at a power plant in Miami. I suspect you are aware of the bomb attack and mysterious Deputy Marshals who removed the bomb and killed the bomber."

"You?" the taller agent asked.

Grafton smiled and responded, "I can't say, officially."

"MacLachlan has become a veritable burr in the saddle of a large Middle Eastern terrorist group. It is they who we believe sent the wet team to Casey Key. The team was probably on loan from someone nearer who hates us. That has enough diplomatic implications to warrant a total blackout by itself. Are you gentlemen with me?" Grafton asked.

"Yes. Heavy stuff."

"It is very heavy from both national security and

diplomatic perspectives," Grafton said. Then, he proceeded to dictate the mandated FD-302 text.

"I am sure, when your SAC reads this, he will find this is in concert with what he was told on his phone call. Lastly, the gentleman with the bullet wound here and the explosion injuries from last week you can't see is a dichotomy. He is able to kill six guys who came to kill him yet is a pretty decent human. I suspect he will drop you guys some intel every now and then. You should consider it primo stuff. And, if he should ask a reasonable favor, try to grant it, okay? The four of us are all on the same side, America's side."

The agents left, fascinated to be clued into something beyond their experience to date.

"Does that sweeping device really work?" MacLachlan asked.

"Beats me. Looked good though, didn't it?" Grafton grinned.

"I have to get back to DC. Are you going to be able to get home without standing on Rt. 41, hitchhiking in that open back hospital gown? The bruises on your back and your neck will scare the hell out of any young maiden who would normally stop and give you a ride," Grafton said.

"Yeah. Now that the sedatives have worn off, I will call Chuck and Gloria, who take care of the house. Or used to anyway. I will get Gloria to pick up some clothes and Chuck to give me a ride to the marina where I stashed the Jeep. I'm not sure when they are going to let me out of here," MacLachlan said.

Grafton patted him on the shoulder and picked up his briefcase.

"This might not be over Mack," he said.

"I need sanction to go after Abdullah Hamadi, you know that," MacLachlan said.

"Not going to happen. I knew you'd say that, so I spoke with the admiral. He said the potential risks outweigh the benefits to the country."

"What if it was not sanctioned?" MacLachlan asked.

"You get caught and we don't know you. You are just an international murderer to the French police, if you are talking Marseille. And, it might tick off Hezbollah even more."

"I doubt they could hate me more than they already do," MacLachlan observed.

"Yes, but they are the only ones who currently hate you. Don't risk adding to the list. That's not good for longevity."

"You may be right."

"That's what I said to my mother when I listened to her tell me why I shouldn't do something, but planned to do it anyway," Grafton said.

MacLachlan shrugged and Grafton left.

The duty physician told MacLachlan he would be released tomorrow, so he called Gloria and arranged for temporary clothes to be bought and a ride from Chuck. He was not sure where he would live for now. A hotel, he guessed. The next call was to his insurance agent to arrange for an adjustor later in the week.

He did not have as much as a toothbrush in Florida. At this point, he was more concerned about no protection. The shotgun, rifle and the old pistol that belonged to his grandfather were destroyed in the house and garage explosions and the FBI had his .45 and the little

M-1 carbine. He needed a toothbrush, underwear and guns, to start with.

Chuck brought a new pair of khaki's, a sport shirt, underwear and size eleven tennis shoes the next morning. MacLachlan was rolled down to the front door of the hospital. The nurse gave him he local paper in the morning. The attack was front page news as he feared. It featured a photo of the ruins of his house. The text quoted one of the FBI agents, primarily. He said six armed subjects blew up the house with a bomb and tried to kill a resident. It went on to say the six died in the attack and the resident, who was unidentified, was in Sarasota Memorial Hospital. The reporter did her homework though and said James E. MacLachlan was listed on county tax records as the owner. The reporter wrote she had been unable to reach Mr. MacLachlan for comment yet.

MacLachlan knew this reporter would stay on him until she could interview him. He decided to check into a motel in St. Petersburg using cash. He could do his shopping up there. Chuck took him to the Jeep. He asked Chuck to do the initial meeting with the adjustor. He knew the property better than MacLachlan anyway.

On the way out of town, he withdrew a thousand dollars and ordered new checks. He also stopped at the local post office, rented a box and transferred all his future mail there until he could make other arrangements.

He found a motel room with a small kitchen on 4th Street North in St. Petersburg and rented it for a month. A department store yielded clothes, including one tie and a blazer in case he had a business meeting.

A gun shop provided a used snub nose Colt Agent .38 he could manipulate easier than the slide on an automatic with his current one-handed situation. He called applied for a new, civilian passport. The only ID not destroyed was the wallet, badge and creds in his pocket. The fire inspector said nothing in the house was salvageable.

MacLachlan picked up basic items for the kitchen and mailed a copy of the newspaper article to Yaffa, along with his new PO box address.

A Dr. Pepper and a bologna sandwich served as dinner with two Percocets for dessert. Despite the strength of the painkiller, his sleep was fitful with a damaged back and a hole all the way through one arm.

As he drifted asleep, he decided he was going after Hamadi. It would not be in the next several weeks. More like several months until he healed and built his strength and endurance up sufficiently for a one man hit operation. He had a gun, knife, money and passports in London, Paris, and Tel Aviv. He would pick up a passport in London and travel to Marseille without a gun. He knew he had to make Hamadi's demise look like an accident. He fell asleep before he could figure out how to pull it off.

The following day, he crossed the five-mile long, four lane Howard Frankland Bridge to Tampa and applied for a Private Investigator's license and commercial concealed weapons license. He wanted the ability to accept work in the US also and knew some sort of licensing would be helpful, if not necessary. He would reserve the Marshals badge for government work where it was appropriate and not abuse authority given him by the President.

A week later, the sling was off his left arm. The insurance adjustor agreed upon a settlement for the loss of the house, personal items, the garage and the classic Jaguar. It was a lot more than he expected. He drove to Sarasota and met with a contractor Chuck had known for years. They agreed upon plans for a newer, more hurricane-resistant cracker house. Like the original, it was to be on stilts and have a metal roof. While it would have 1930's looks, the mechanicals would be modern and efficient.

The project was large enough for the firm to require four months from permit application to move-in.

So, MacLachlan discussed an idea with the contractor and they agreed on it. The first construction would be the replacement garage. It would have a studio apartment upstairs. Later, he might use it as an office, but now, he could live there. The contractor promised it could be permitted and built and inspected within several weeks. MacLachlan gave him a deposit and told him to proceed.

He stayed in the motel in St. Petersburg until the garage was finished, bought furniture for the upstairs with an immediate but partial insurance check and had it delivered. Home again, more or less. The FBI returned his guns, knife, and magazines. Now, it was time for the next part of his plan. He was going to drive to Northern Virginia with the Jeep, call on his list of initial contacts for consulting, instructing or more dangerous contracting. He would meet with Grafton, then leave the Jeep at his Washington National area storage facility and fly home.

Once home, he would buy a vehicle to keep in Florida. He had settled on a Volvo 740 Turbo sedan. Blame it on Yaffa with her Nordic hot rod.

———————

TIME PASSED and the sultry Florida summer turned into the sultry Florida winter. It got a few degrees colder. All the snowbirds had flown or driven down from the North.

MacLachlan considered he was at least seventy-five percent back physically from his injuries in August. He was running the beach and swimming the Gulf. He went to the range weekly and practiced at varying distances. It was time to go to Marseille.

He bought a round trip ticket to London with an open return. If he was going to kill a French business-man, he aimed to get out of France as quickly as possible and make sure his next international flight was from a different country.

He had a casual conversation with Grafton. Both men knew the impetus behind it. Grafton said Hamadi was being watched. He was still at a corporate address in Marseille. MacLachlan memorized it months ago. Once Grafton said it, MacLachlan went on to another topic.

Grafton ended the chat with, "Be safe and don't do anything I wouldn't do."

MacLachlan was pretty sure Grafton would do the same thing in his situation, so he boarded the plane with his new civilian US passport and flew to London.

He took a train from Gatwick to the city and got off near the Royal Bank of Scotland branch. He removed the Canadian passport, but left the gun, knife, and money.

Using cash he had brought, MacLachlan took a bus to the overnight ferry from Portsmouth to Le Havre, then a seven hour train to Marseille.

He arrived in the late afternoon. MacLachlan was not impressed with the dark and dangerous second largest city in France. It was a port city and known as the best place on earth to get a job as a mercenary. Some very tough men walked its streets and drank in its bars. He picked up a city map and identified where Abdullah Hamadi lived and worked. They were not far apart.

One thing the city did have was decent public transit. He changed dollars for francs at a local bank and picked up a bus schedule. Buses were not glamorous. But they were good for keeping a low profile. He saw a number of men wearing black berets. He bought one, as well as a leather jacket. He also bought a wooden handle Opinel folding knife. Every man in France probably had at least one. MacLachlan added heavy black reading glasses in the lowest power for a disguise. He saw his reflection in a store front as he did his surveillance detections. He thought he looked stupid, but he did seem to fit into to the crowd.

His bag was a small duffle with a shoulder strap. He could quickly shed the beret, glasses and jacket. If he put his own jacket back on, he would look like a totally different person. And, it was reversible from dark green to navy. Jeans and trainers were as popular in Europe as in Denver or Atlanta. So, he wore one pair of jeans and carried another in black. Trainers were the only shoes he brought.

MacLachlan took a bus to Hamadi's neighborhood. He walked past the townhouse. Upper middle class, probably. Going around the block, he found an alley. The back of the house may afford easier access, he thought. There was a Middle Eastern restaurant at the end of the long block. It was the demarcation between residential and commercial.

He walked the four blocks to the building where Hamadi worked. He was the chief executive officer. It was an exporting firm, ostensibly. Very unlikely, MacLachlan thought. A front. Not a legitimate company. A coffee shop was directly across the street.

MacLachlan went in and sat in a window seat facing the export company. He ordered a café au lait and chocolate croissant. It was not the Champs- Èlysées in Paris. But the coffee and pastry were good. He looked at the old Rolex. It was about time for French businesses to wind down. Whether that applied to ones run by terrorists, MacLachlan did not know.

After an hour, he saw a hard guy come out and look up and down the boulevard. Two others came out. One was another hard guy, a bodyguard like the first. The third man was Abdullah Hamadi. He looked a bit like the blurred photo in DC. He seemed younger though. But it was Hamadi.

They turned and walked towards home. MacLachlan took the last gulp of café au lait and walked out munching the chocolate croissant like a good Frenchman. He stayed on his side of the Boule-vard. A folded newspaper was on a bus stop bench. He picked it up for possible cover. MacLachlan stayed fifty yards behind the men across the street. He knew where they were going.

MacLachlan stopped at a bus stop bench in view of Hamadi's house, but closer to the restaurant. Nobody was around, so he walked into the alley and changed from the leather jacket to the reversible one he had flown in. He swapped the beret for a stocking cap and returned to the bench.

He pretended to read the newspaper while he watched Hamadi's house. An old man waited for the bus. When it came, he looked at MacLachlan. MacLachlan told him he was waiting there for friend in a car. He said it in French, pretty sure it was not the appropriate Provençal accent.

Three men. Two were tough-looking bodyguards. No shooting. MacLachlan pondered. He could have really used a hand grenade. But no such luck. A hit and run by a drunk driver would be his best option.

He took a chance and walked up the block to a small shop. It was like a convenience store in the US. He bought a six-pack of the cheapest beer they had and a pack of Gauloise cigarettes.

The Middle Eastern restaurant was a likely dinner spot. Maybe one guy and two thugs would cook at home. But probably not. MacLachlan noted the valet parking operation at the restaurant. One guy. Someone would come in and hand keys to the attendant. He would drive the car out of sight, probably curbside a block down and sprint back. Then, he would hang the keys on a board and repeat for the next customer.

It would be easy to walk past and take keys while he was parking the next car.

MacLachlan's guess was right. Hamadi and the two tough guys left the house and walked his way. It was too dark to hide behind the newspaper, so he got up and walked to the restaurant and around the corner where the valet took the cars. He saw the line of cars, parking stubs under wipers.

He returned in sufficient time to see the three targets come up to the restaurant and exchange friendly greetings with the valet. They went in.

It would be tough to gauge how long the three would be in and coordinate taking a car. The easiest way would be to go into the restaurant and eat, watching them.

He changed into the locally bought leather jacket, beret and glasses. That left room for the six pack of beer in his duffle. He went in and was seated. He could see the three across the room. Neither they nor anyone else paid any attention to him. He ordered green tea, baba ghanoush and toasted pita triangles.

He watched the men as covertly as he could. They were over half through the food on their plates. He could not predict whether they would order dessert. MacLachlan could not risk having two minutes to steal a car and get positioned.

He paid his bill and walked out. He stood near the valet stand and lit a Gauloise he had brought as part of his disguise.

A French kid pulled up in a Peugeot 205 GTI. It looked fast and the exhaust suggested modifications.

The valet gave him a stub and took the car around the corner. He came back and hung the key on the next empty hook before serving the next customer. As soon as the valet left, MacLachlan moved in, putting driving gloves on.

He took the Peugeot key and replaced it with the first key on the rack. Less likely to be noticed by the valet than a missing key just hung. He started to walk around the short block to reach the Peugeot from behind and not walk past the valet sprinting back.

MacLachlan started the car and circled two three blocks, allowing him to park halfway between Hamadi's house and the restaurant.

He opened all the beer bottles, pouring five out the window and one in the car. He dropped all six bottles in the car. It looked and smelled like a one-drunk party had been held in the Peugeot.

A few minutes later, he saw Hamadi and the two bodyguards come out of the restaurant. But they turned the wrong way.

MacLachlan cursed. The men entered the shop where he had gotten the beer. A few minutes later, they came out, one bodyguard carrying a small bag.

They walked his way.

When they were several hundred yards away, MacLachlan started the little rally car, revved and dumped the clutch.

Tires screamed and the staccato exhaust sounded as he went through first and speed-shifted into second at forty miles per hour. He moved the wheel sufficient to keep it in the lane but appear to be veering. It looked like a drunk driver. As he planned.

The three men watched the fast car, as men are wont to do the world over.

He was doing about fifty-five as he approached them. They had stopped on the sidewalk to watch his show.

At the last minute, he swerved to the left and hit all three dead on. They were thrown twenty feet and landed on the sidewalk and grass.

MacLachlan spun the car in a three hundred sixty degree "bootlegger turn." He identified Hamadi stirring, grievously wounded.

MacLachlan downshifted and ran over the man who had sent a kill team for him and destroyed his home. The car bumped over Hamadi and the curb.

Straightened on the street, he accelerated away as fast as he could with the damaged car.

As he flew through an intersection two blocks down, a taxi slammed into his passenger door, rolling the Peugeot several times.

The seatbelt worked its magic. MacLachlan was dazed and his leg sprained, but he was able to kick the windshield out, get his duffle and climb out.

He limped away from the still-quiet scene. Heading into a business area, he spotted a dumpster and put the leather jacket and beret in it and donned his own jacket and a watch cap.

He saw a bus approaching half a block away and waved as he limped for it as fast as he could. The driver saw him, and he waited.

For the next half hour, MacLachlan changed buses. He asked where the main bus depot was for buses to Paris. He transferred to the recommended bus and got off at the depot.

The first order was to visit the men's room and check his appearance. His jeans were ripped and a little bloody where he had struck his knee in the accident. He put on his fresh pair and discarded the damaged ones. He reversed his jacket to the green side. Nothing else appeared amiss. He had a ball cap in the duffle and discarded the stocking cap in favor of it. He looked both presentable and different.

Stopping at the small gift counter, he purchased a bottle of aspirin and a bottle of water. He took four aspirin.

An hour later, a bus to Le Havre pulled in and he got on, reversing his route from London.

It was late morning by the time the sequence of buses and ferry and more buses got him to Gatwick. He bought an Americano, as brewed plain coffee was called, at the gate and a square sausage sandwich. He took a couple more aspirin and boarded.

Though sore from the bouncing around he received when the taxi ran a stop sign, MacLachlan was largely all right.

It was late when he got back to Miami. He went to the parking lot and got in the Volvo Turbo. Lowering the passenger seat, he slept until daylight, then started home.

At home, he had a message to call Grafton. It was from early morning.

"Will, what's up?" he asked.

"Just a bit of news, if you don't already know. A drunk driver hit Hamadi a couple days ago. We just found out," Grafton said.

"I hope the bastard died," MacLachlan responded.

"We only know he and a couple of bodyguards were struck by a car at high speed. It was serious. All were taken to a hospital in Marseille. One bodyguard died and one survived, but he's a mess. Hamadi flat-lined on the way. Our guy cannot account for him now but thinks he's probably dead."

"No loss to society there," MacLachlan said. "Let me know when you get a confirmation. Sorry I missed you early this morning. I was fishing. You ought to come down. The snook bite is hot."

"Maybe later. I am working on something for your admiral. He seems to have adopted me," Grafton said.

"You could do worse."

"I know. I have done worse many times before. He's a good guy," Grafton said.

They disconnected and MacLachlan wondered if Grafton would check flights from Florida to Europe. He had used his real name, but paid cash. So, a credit card check would not yield anything. Now, he had the false-name Canadian passport. He would take Yaffa up on her offer and get a third set for home, then replace the current one in London. But now he had to get his life in order and make some money.

10

Casey Key, Florida, Washington, DC

Spring 1986

MacLachlan had moved into the new house and converted the garage apartment into his office. He installed the newly introduced Apple Macintosh Plus, a 128 KB desktop computer to keep track of his growing consulting and intelligence agency instructing business. The classes he taught in Northern Virginia already compensated for the loss of his military salary at the end of December.

He was scheduled for two weeks instructing on foreign travel safety and another week on threat assessment. He liked the work. Further, many of the students were senior enough to be potential contract hiring authorities later.

MacLachlan sat at the computer developing lecture

notes and exhibits to be used as overhead projector transparencies.

He and Yaffa were communicating less and less over time. It was inevitable, he knew, but still saddened him. Years ago, he told a friend in college that the most miserable being was a guy whose work was his life and had no girl friend or wife, not even a pet. And, here he was. But he didn't feel miserable. Maybe because he knew his work counted for something. And, the latest girlfriend was world class by anybody's standards.

MacLachlan had just returned from a ten-mile beach run and long swim. He showered at the new outside shower, put on shorts, flip-flops and a Hawaiian shirt and walked up the steps to his second story garage office.

As he disarmed the alarm, the phone rang. He answered and knew from the greeting it would be a good call.

"Hey, Slickmeister. What's up?"

"Not much, Will, how are you?" he said.

"Just dandy. Did your uniform get burnt up when the house blew?" Grafton asked.

"It did. The medal was in a bank safe deposit box with all my ribbons, thank God."

"Can you get another uniform?"

"Sure. Not sure why I'd need it," he said.

"'Cause you are coming up to dinner with the Prez and the Prime Minister of Israel, their wives, the Secretary of State and, of course, me," Grafton said.

"Wow. What's the event?"

"State dinner. Celebrate our support. Maybe off the record celebrate some of the kimchi you worked on with Israelis. By the way, the admiral says you are going to have some gold eagles on your shoulders, Colonel. Prez ordered it."

"I'm not back full-time, am I?" MacLachlan asked.

"No, same status, bigger insignia."

"When? Saturday. We will both be armed. I will be in civvies, so you need to get a dress uniform holster for the dress blues. Prez likes us to be armed, he says. Gotta love that old boy."

"Where do I meet you and what time?"

"Same old side entrance, about five. There will be three secret ceremonies before chow. Your pinning is one. The other two are need-to-know."

"I'll be there."

"See that you are. Watch out for Ford Tempo bumpers along the way, okay?"

"I hate those things. See you at 1600 Pennsylvania."

MacLachlan ordered his dress blues and belt and holster from Quantico. He thought an officer's Mameluke sword would be overkill, so he left that off the order. He bought shoes locally and began the spit shine a day before flying out. He went to the bank and got the medal and his ribbons.

He arrived at Washington National Friday morning and picked up the Jeep from its storage facility. The uniform fit perfectly. He had reservations in a downtown hotel and checked in early.

"Will, you got time for dinner? It's on me," he said into the phone.

"Thanks, Mack. But I have to pick up a new suit that's been altered, shine my brogues and be ready for five tomorrow. I'm not supposed to say, but one of those ceremonies is for me. I don't have a clue what it is though."

"Well, I'm sure it's well deserved, Will. You should have been decorated for that stuff you did in MACSOG in Vietnam," MacLachlan said.

"Not to worry. I was. Got everything? See you tomorrow at five."

"Roger to all," MacLachlan said as he hung up.

MacLachlan had a light dinner. The next morning, he ran around the reflecting pool. He went to the National Archives and viewed some of the nation's most precious documents. After lunch, he made some calls then got dressed. He loaded the .45 and holstered it. The uniform was perfect, and his shoes were, too. It was only a few blocks, but he wanted to keep his spit shine intact, so he took a taxi.

He presented his military ID at the gate and was on the list of expected visitors. There was an A for armed next to his name, as well as the one right behind him. William Grafton, DIA.

He was seated in a waiting room. Will came in and they did the famous cop hug.

Admiral Howard stepped out of a room down the corridor and motioned both to enter. Once there, MacLachlan snapped to attention and saluted crisply. Marines inside salute when wearing headcovers and are under arms. The admiral returned the salute.

"It's good to see both of you, together and in person. This is the President's, the Secretary's and my way of acknowledging your handling of the nuclear and power grid threats. You saved untold numbers of lives and I am proud you are on my team,

The President walked in, wearing a tuxedo. He smiled and shook hands after acknowledging MacLachlan's salute.

"Well, I've got a heavy schedule today, but we'll get to chat at dinner. First, Mr. Grafton, I want to present you with the Intelligence Medal." He hung it around Grafton's neck, not unlike the Congressional Medal of Honor MacLachlan was wearing.

Admiral Howard said, "Due to your clandestine work, Will, you cannot wear it during the picture portion of tonight's festivities."

"Roger that, sir," Grafton acknowledged.

"And, you, Colonel MacLachlan, let's make you a full-bird Colonel," the President said, pinning the gold eagles on with the Admiral's assistance.

"Thank you, Mr. President. And, Admiral Howard."

"Now men, we are all saved from speeches because I have to have Admiral Howard take you down the hall so I can have one other meeting before dinner. Thank you both for the American lives you saved, and" he winked at them," taking the foreign ones who are our enemies." He patted the .45 MacLachlan was wearing and asked, "Ever shot a Colt single action?"

"I'm from Texas, sir. I grew up with one."

"I knew it."

The President smiled and walked out, four Secret Service agents surrounding him even in this house.

Admiral Howard ushered them to another waiting room, where they discussed current terrorism topics.

A half hour later, a Secret Service agent stuck his

head in the door and said "It is time for dinner, gentlemen.

He walked them to a dining room and there was already a small crowd. They joined it to wait.

The President's Own, a Marine band, began playing a song MacLachlan did not recognize. It was Hatikvah, the Israeli National Anthem.

The Prime Minister of Israel and his wife were escorted in, with several Israeli dignitaries and, MacLachlan thought, the most beautiful woman alive.

She was wearing a turquoise form-fitting long gown, and he knew hidden by the hem, really high heels. She also wore the Presidential Medal of Freedom, the equivalent of his Congressional Medal of Honor, except for civilians.

She looked at MacLachlan and everyone there saw her give him the most dazzling smile imaginable. And, it was returned by a superhero grin equal to it. One tear streaked her makeup, but the smile stayed.

The Israeli party joined the crowd for the next arrival to be announced.

Yaffa stood next to the tall Marine, proud as he snapped to attention when the President was announced. The President's Own began *Hail to the Chief* and, the President and First Lady walked in.

As the music stopped, the President looked proudly at his awardees.

He moved his lips and MacLachlan read "At ease."

The most powerful man in the world stood for a second looking at the Marine and the beautiful spy. He knew there was something between them from the body language shown by how they stood touching.

"Damn," he thought, "they ought to be in the movies."

TAKE A LOOK AT: HONOR AND BLOOD: THE COMPLETE MACLACHLAN SERIES

BULLETS ARE FLYING AND SURE TO KEEP YOU ON THE EDGE OF YOUR SEAT IN THESE THREE ACTION-PACKED THRILLERS.

One of the deadliest men alive, Mack MacLachlan, is a security contractor for the intelligence community. Having spent the past twenty-five years as a conceivably deniable fixer for the US Intelligence Community, when they call on him to "fix" something else—quietly and permanently—MacLachlan is the man for the job.

From kidnappings to tearing down business empires, MacLachlan longs to fade away from the danger and into retirement...but that's not happening anytime soon.

Join Mack MacLachlan on three adrenaline-fueled missions as he navigates a world of danger and deception. Order your copy today and buckle up for a thrilling ride!

Honor and Blood includes *Honor Above All*, *Unsanctioned*, and *Highlands Blood*.

AVAILABLE NOW

ABOUT AUTHOR

G. Wayne Tilman is a full-time author. He retired from the FBI several years ago. Prior to that, he was a Marine, bank security director, deputy sheriff, investigator, and security contractor.

He holds baccalaureate and master's degrees from the University of Richmond and has been an adjunct faculty member there, as well as the University of Phoenix, St. Petersburg College and Florida Metropolitan University. Mr. Tilman holds the internationally-recognized Certified Protection Professional board certification, generally accepted as the highest in the security profession. He also earned a US Coast Guard 50 Ton Inspected Vessel Master Captain's license.

A direct ancestor was a sheriff in Virginia Colony in 1680. Another ancestor was the lawman who brought in outlaw Bill Doolin singlehandedly and helped to decimate the infamous Doolin-Dalton outlaw gang, sometimes known as the Oklahombres. Bill Doolin was the Desperado of song fame. Closer to home, his mother was a counterintelligence agent for what is now the Defense Intelligence Agency or DIA.

G. Wayne Tilman's primary interests are family and writing. His avocations are bushcraft (survival/primitive camping), hiking, boating, kayaking, shooting sports, and travel.